TEARS
OF
THE MOON

○-○-○-○-○-○-○-○-○-○-○

GARY ROSS

VIKING

VIKING
Published by the Penguin Group
Penguin Books Canada Ltd, 2801 John Street, Markham, Ontario, Canada
L3R 1B4
Penguin Books Ltd, 27 Wrights Lane, London W8 5TZ, England
Viking Penguin Inc., 40 West 23rd Street, New York, New York 10010, USA
Penguin Books Australia Ltd, Ringwood, Victoria, Australia
Penguin Books (NZ) Ltd, 182-190 Wairau Road, Auckland 10, New Zealand
Penguin Books Ltd, Registered Offices: Harmondsworth, Middlesex, England

First published 1988

10 9 8 7 6 5 4 3 2 1

Copyright © Gary Ross Consulting Inc., 1988

Printed and bound in Canada

Canadian Cataloguing in Publication Data

Ross, Gary, 1948-
        Tears of the moon

ISBN 0-670-81819-4

I. Title.

PS8585.0837T42 1988   C813'.54   C87-094872-5
PR9199.3.R68T42 1988

American Library of Congress Cataloguing in Publication Data Available
0-670-81819-4   TEARS OF THE MOON   88-50692

This story is dedicated to three people of rare wisdom and insight: Benoit Garneau, Kristi Magraw, and Sheila Willson

Acknowledgements

For their help with this book, I wish to thank Tecca Crosby, Charlene Eadie, Bob Fulford, George Galt, Cynthia Good, Lorraine Johnson, John Macfarlane, I.M. Owen, Dianna Symonds, Jan Walter, and Wanda Wilkinson. Thanks to the staff and inmates of Oakalla, Millhaven, Joyceville, and Attica. I also appreciate the support of the Ontario Arts Council.

TEARS
OF
THE MOON

○·○·○·○·○·○·○·○·○·○

A YOUNG intern with curly blond hair watches a distinguished surgeon step into a hospital elevator. The intern produces a pistol and fires, killing the surgeon, whose slumped body is transported up to the next floor. In the confusion the killer, ripping off his wig, ducks into a closet. He emerges a dark-haired man in glasses and a business suit. He walks out the lobby doors as police officers rush in—looks over his shoulder, breaks into a sprint. In the parking lot he finds a delivery van has blocked his car. He flags down a spotless Ford, pulls out a young woman, and climbs in. He burns rubber and knocks down the attendant in his haste to get away. Crossing a bridge, he flings the murder weapon into the river. He careers wildly along urban streets, sideswipes a parked police cruiser. Two cops, at a water fountain, put on their caps and hurry to their vehicle to give chase. Though they instantly get within closing distance of the Ford, they get no closer. They talk on the radio while chasing the killer through dangerous intersections and narrowly avoiding collisions, and the pursuit is suddenly climbing along a steep, winding mountain road. The killer watches the cruiser in the rearview mirror. Tires squeal at every bend in the switchback. A logging truck almost hits the Ford, then forces the cruiser out of control. The cruiser plunges into a slow-motion fall and explodes into flames on a rocky precipice. The killer grins in the rear-view mirror. The

Ford sputters, runs out of gas, and coasts to a stop. The killer pushes it off a cliff, watches its slow-motion plunge and explosion, and sets off on foot into the mountains.

So began tonight's episode. We vote on what we're going to watch and this program is always the overwhelming choice. The others provide running commentary, urging the killer to make the right choices and pointing out implausibilities along the way.

—What's he running for? Take it easy, goof.

—Think he'd dump the piece?

—Never get out of the city. They'd have blocks up in sixty seconds.

Tonio always has the last word:

—Road like that, cruiser'd take him. Heavy-duty suspension.

I look forward to the program—to the mood it creates. It brings us together and banishes for a time the sense of emptiness and isolation. I watch the show faithfully, deeply engaged, and I usually learn something from the others. Tonight I was surprised how quickly the episode went. Third time I'd seen it, maybe fourth.

VAL hurried down this morning, waving something. A letter, fountain pen, beige stationery. I didn't ask him to bring me his problems—he just does. Every day since his transfer he's found reason to come.

—Read it to me, Monkey.

It was from a woman urging him to keep up his spirits ... people were thinking of him. The hand was loopy and symmetrical. Signed (Mrs) K. Ransome. He isn't sure who she is. So far as he recalls he doesn't know a soul in her city. She doesn't say how she heard of him or what prompted her to write.

I handed back the letter, hoping he'd go away. But he rolled it into a tube and making different noises, blew through it, thinking of something.

—Like answering the phone—person on the other end hangs up? I hate that, Monkey, ever want to drive me crazy that's how. One time I got a call like that every night for a month. I was living with a word processor named Ann. I knew it was her old boyfriend, bothering her. I bricked that fucker.

He put the letter away and sucked in a breath ... his pectorals bulged like spinnakers, his tattoos shone. Isometrics, facing out. Between sets of exercises he watched the poker game on the tier. I watched the flag on his back.

—When Gary Gilmore was waiting to be executed ...

The toilets started—thirty seconds of Niagara Falls. I hate the roar, I dread it.

—When Gilmore was on death row, he got something like fifteen hundred letters from people he didn't know. I read about it in *Psychology Today*. Angela subscribed— the magazine kept arriving after her death.

He glanced at me over his shoulder. His voice has a deep timbre but everything comes out like an apology.

—Gilmore was on TV. Figure all the guys in all the joints—why does this lady pick me?

—The people who wrote him wanted to help him face the terrible end. No one mentioned the people he'd taken down. One guy wanted Gilmore's permission to witness the firing squad ... to clarify his feelings about death! Imagine! A high-school teacher had his students write to Gilmore as part of a project on capital punishment. Women wrote out of love, wanting to sleep with him. One pregnant girl asked for his views on child-rearing.

—Ten reps. You count.

He hyperventilated ten times and then pulled. He puts everything into it, as if will, added to muscle ...

—Thousand one, thousand two, three, thousand four, five, thousand six—he started to shake—thousand seven, thousand eight—his whole body was vibrating like a diving board—nine, thousand ten.

He gasped, slumped against the bars.

—Maybe you could write her for me? I'll tell you what to put. Tell her look, hey, I don't want to hear from you. Give me a cigarette, Monkey. Maybe I shouldn't. Should I? What's the point? Maybe shouldn't do nothing—make like I never even got the letter.

He turned in his sheepish way, face aflame, eyes brimming. He shrugged his heavy shoulders.

—Don't know, Monkey. I just don't know. What should I do?

PALUMBO is whistling again.

I don't like Mario Palumbo. A silver cross glitters on his bony chest. His hair is long and dirty—he wears it in a Psyche knot. The pulled-back hair, sleek features, and gleaming eyes give an impression of purpose, like a swimming rat. But what purpose? He cadges tobacco and choney and forgets to repay. Makes himself asthmatic to avoid work detail. We file in and out while he reads comic books. He whistles after lights out, never fails, like the sparrows under the eavestrough.

Angela didn't notice the sparrows—I found them impossible to ignore. At first they woke me with their chirping. Then I'd wake up before they started. I'd find myself lying in the dark, jaw clenched, waiting. I set out sunflower seeds treated with ant killer. Paid a hundred and fifty for an extension ladder, put wire mesh over the eavestrough, emptied a bomb of wasp killer into their nest. Nothing worked. Bought a pellet gun . . . they flew off when I poked it out the window. Angela was upset:

—Won't you please leave the birds alone.

—They drive me crazy. I can't sleep.

—It used to be the dog next door. Then it was the motorcycle. Now it's the birds. Why don't you ask yourself why they drive you crazy?

—I'd rather shut them up.

—They have as much right as you do. God, you infuriate me sometimes!

One night I got up, careful not to disturb her, and took a sleeping bag to the roof. Beneath the aerials and the stars and satellites I waited. (Patience and a single shot, as Dad would say.) Finally the sky lightened. When a sparrow appeared I squeezed off a shot. The bird dropped like a stone . . . heart racing, I hurried down. Up close the sparrow's drabness became a kind of beauty, each feather coloured and shaped to conform to the larger design. A drop of blood, vivid as nail polish, issued from its tiny beak. Guiltily, hoping I had not been seen, I put it in the trash-can.

The mate quit the nest but returned each morning
before six. Chirp, chirp. I shot it, too, put it in the trash.
But even after they were dead I kept waking before
dawn to listen. I missed them—Angela was right—I
needed them to be angry at. Here, there, Palumbo,
sparrows—nothing changes.

Why am I always angry or afraid?

If Vernon weren't here Palumbo's life would be worth
dick. Tonio'd get him transferred or else have him taken
down. Palumbo and Vernon meet by the wall near the
south tower and speak in whispers. Palumbo searches
his face shyly, like a schoolgirl. Vernon seems not to
enjoy the liaison but to be compelled to pursue it. Every
night after lights out he says quietly to himself, in a
sweet voice, 'Goodnight, Mario.' He moans in his sleep
—if he doesn't, I wake up, waiting . . .

I like Vernon. His nose is broad, his lips are thin and
mobile. His forehead conveys a sense of durable bone
within. His ears are fully joined to his head and the
veins in his temple light up in anger. He's as vital as a
stallion. He should be pitching hay, hoisting engines out
of tractors. After the show (he sang 'Heart of Gold' and
'Moonshadow') he asked if I thought he was any good.

—Terrible, but if you like I'll be your agent.

He grinned and lifted me by the elbows—felt like he
was going to bounce me off the ceiling. He set me down
gentle as a cat does a kitten.

—You're on, Monkey. You're my agent.

Vernon loves to play poker but he's no good. Bets
recklessly and gets this silly grin when he pairs up. At
seventeen he learned he had cancer. On his eighteenth
birthday he and his girl tried to rob a bank. I was
curious about his timing.

—Why'd you wait for your birthday? Could have got off as a juvenile.

—Wanted it to be the first thing I done as an adult.

His girl was shot by a cop who happened to be cashing his cheque. Vernon's gun was empty but he got his hands on the cop. His cancer is in remission. He opened his shirt and showed where they had cut out the malignancy, grinning the way he does when he catches a pair.

Last year Vernon broke his toe on a barbell. Loaded the bar with all the weight it would take and tried to clean it. Fierce strength, bad technique. Somebody tried to show him how to use his thighs but he continued in his faulty way. Over and over, not giving himself time to recuperate, he tried to muscle the weight. Finally he was too spent to get the bar off the ground. He kicked it so hard I expected the iron wheels to shatter. His toe shattered. He was in a cast for three months and still has a limp.

Maybe that's why I like him so much—we're different.

FOOTBALL game was blacked out tonight. Instead, on the big screen, we watched a wildlife program. Too much noise to hear. I love wildlife shows—baby orangutans clinging to their mothers' bellies, zebras necking, a pink lake of flamingos feeding on the marine life from which they take their colour. An elephant charged the cameraman ... remarkable footage ... one time at the zoo we watched elephants obliterating themselves in clouds of dust. I tossed peanuts. They came for them, like pairs of old men in elephant costumes. Not ten feet away they showed us the sinuous reticulation of their trunks, picking nuts out of the grass. Angela loved it.

—Let's do it again. I'll get more.

We saw Canada geese rout a rhino that had strayed close to their nest. A hippo lumber out of its algae-covered pool, plump down, and sweat blood. White egrets riding like warriors on black water-buffalo. Jousting wildebeests, their fur straggly and sparse as oriental beards. Giraffes running, slow motion, graceful as rocking-chairs. Lowland gorillas—three adults and three juveniles. The dominant male languished on an elevated platform, glaring at the spectators. Another adult slept curled up, covering its eyes. One of the juveniles played to the crowd, bouncing a plastic barrel. Another juvenile amused itself with the hose, splashing and manipulating the spray with its thumb. The other two groomed one another. The dominant male dropped from its perch—that startling lightness of apes. When it peed, the hyperactive juvenile came cautiously to sniff. The one with the hose confronted the hyperactive juvenile, sending the group into frenzy. Six animals screamed and jabbered. Bold, threatening gestures and noises ... terrible odour. The dominant male screamed at painful volume, exposing his canines—the hair on his headcrest stood erect.

The visitors thought it wonderful fun. People pointed and laughed, held children aloft, joked with their neighbours. When the gorillas subsided the people thumped the Plexiglas, to keep them agitated. I thumped the glass. More and more people picked it up, mimicking ape sounds, banging away—the whole compound vibrated, like the gym tonight, when hyenas showed up at the water-hole . . .

They wanted the baby rhino. The mother was helpless. Over and over she launched her bulk at one of the stunted, low-slung hyenas. The other hyenas tore at the baby's hide, trying to pull it off its feet. The mother ran in cumbersome ovals . . . the baby with great dignity stood its ground. Unlike the hyenas, the men in the gym were bright-eyed, aroused.

—Jump him! Take him down!

—Two packs says he hangs tough.

At the zoo Angela was appalled—told me she was embarrassed to be with me. The hyenas acted almost with detachment, answering a question they had not posed. Finally they gave up. The baby stood beside its mother, both of them heaving with exertion. The hyenas didn't slink away, they capered—no hard feelings. But the men in the gym were bitterly angry and disappointed.

Next came Thomson gazelles at the water-hole. Each had a black racing stripe, advertising speed. They drank timorously, lifting their heads. The camera picked up a pair of cheetahs in the long grass. The cats advanced a few quick steps . . . froze in odd postures like characters in a comedy. One split off, circling behind. The gazelles were in a state of suppressed panic. A cheetah broke . . . gazelles took off in all directions. One bounded in front of the cheetah but she had already singled out her prey.

At first the gazelle seemed as fast as the cheetah, even opening ground. Then the second cheetah cut in, forcing the gazelle to brake, skidding, and change direction. The cats worked a trigonometric partnership, back and forth, raising dust over the plain. Tonio and Billie. Finally a cheetah batted the gazelle off its feet. The gazelle was gone again in a blur, but didn't get so far this time . . .

The vaulted dome above the gym gathered the noise, redoubling it. The whole place shook. Everything seemed to shake: the floor, the stacking chairs, the vast machine-tooled facility, the planet itself. Four tiers of cells encircle the gym, a coliseum—inmates on the walkways pressed their faces against steel mesh and joined their voices to those rising from below. The men on the floor were out of their seats, raising fists, screaming. All of them.

All of us.

I was cheering death, yelling at the big screen and stamping in unison with the others.

IT'S splendid to hear your number called. The long walk is enjoyable since it includes passage through a part of the facility no longer in use. In a stone corridor between rusted iron gates the hacks usually allow me to linger, collect myself, gaze out to the east. The land drops off, making the wall appear lower than it is. The hill beyond rises graciously, dense green with conifers. Here and there a maple ignites in the fall. Clouds seem attracted to the hill ... the sky cannot be predicted. This is my richest apprehension of the world and it fills me with an odd sense of sovereignty.

The visiting room, partitioned into cubicles, is as barren as a liquor store. Shatterproof acrylic, bolted seats, oversized receivers that make us raise our voices ... three dozen raised voices. One receiver is especially bad and I always say a little prayer that Jay won't be assigned to it.

—How you doing, O?

Same thing every visit. Jay has gone first, led the way, as long as I remember. I tell him about the weight I've pumped. He tells me about the stock-market. We discuss the performance of our favourite teams. If I can think of anything lively I pass it on—I feel I owe him something for making the trip. It's a long way to come for an hour's visit but come he does, bless him, through snowstorms, heat waves, traffic jams. His dependability is typical and seems to me a striking proof of character.

The other men fascinate him. They're dangerous and exotic ... I'm just his brother. He enjoys hearing about the shows, which I make out to be excruciating. I listen to the animation in my voice and see delight on his face and marvel that we manage to carry on as if my incarceration had been cooked up for our mutual entertainment. Must be difficult for someone with his professional standing—he's not vain, but how easily we appropriate the successes and failures of those we hold dear. I recall my own fierce pride and jealousy—Jay accepting the history prize, the cross-country trophy. One of his high-school girlfriends gave him a key-ring that said 'Jay the Great.'

—How's the old fellow?

—Giles? Can't see how a flush beats a straight. Nice man, but lost something, you know?

Jay adjusts his glasses with a forefinger—Dad's gesture of gravity. It meant I was going to catch shit or else he was about to say something that didn't come easily. Jay meets my eye, holds it ... shifts in his chair, changing his mind.

—Still winning all the tobacco?

So it is now with Jay and me, something's coming that never quite comes. An hour every couple of weeks ... keep it simple.

—In general, union organizers are better poker players. I won six packs last night. I'm trying to quit smoking, ain't easy. Guess what I did this morning—wrote in my journal—I've started a journal.

—How come?

But not put so keenly that I cared to answer. An answer would have involved telling him I've signed for the T-group and I'm trying to get an appointment with the psycho. Jay doesn't have patience with such things. I suppose I didn't either while Angela was alive—because I was unsure what she did? Listened, I knew, her silence creating a gentle vacuum that troubled people were drawn to fill. But what people, and what made them seek her out? How did she know where to begin and end?

How am I to know?

I don't share Dad's belief that therapists are for people who hear the grass scream underfoot, but I guess I did share his assumption of weakness. More: the psycho scares me—more than Billie and Tonio and Val put together. But I have to do something, there's nothing to lose.

Jay's 'How come?'—Dad too had a way of poising every question between curiosity and scepticism. At least Jay gives the impression of wanting an answer, albeit one of which he'll need to be persuaded. Dad would have squinted over his glasses and, without setting aside his book or ceasing to scratch his foot rash, uttered the same 'How come?' with an interest as fleeting as the sweep of headlights. And been reading again before I could answer.

How can a man share a car with the thirteen-year-old son he's not seen for two months and, morose over contract negotiations going badly, speak not one word between the airport and the motel? How can a man jump up to cheer a touchdown and ask his sons, an hour after knocking their mother off her feet, 'Aren't you enjoying the game?'

Instead of answering Jay I inquired after the baby. Like throwing a switch: he lit up. He told me how much Jonathan eats, imitated sounds, gave me details of bowel movements. They'll stay with cloth, Jay said, though the diaper service costs a fortune. Not long ago he told me Jonathan had crawled across the living-room and today he had a Polaroid of the baby wobbling unsupported like a drunk. In the outstretched arms and glare of the flash there was something of the monster—in the radiance, the liberation of mobility, something quite angelic. A baby like any other, except this is my nephew. By the time I'm out Jay will have taught him to shake hands but I'll pick him up and hold him instead. These things reach so deep, go back so far.

He adjusted his glasses.

—Listen, decided what you want to do with that stuff?

Saved by the buzzer.

—Let me think about it. Thanks for coming.

It always seems to happen. My words, though deeply felt, seemed to travel a long way—came out sounding like 'Thanks for lunch.' Jay made a fist.

—Hang in there, O. See you in two weeks.

The room emptied, the receivers dangled on their cords like pencils in the liquor stores Dad used to take us into.

All those stores must be self-serve now.

I HAD to give Val two packs to get him to come with me. Told him I thought he might find it interesting. In truth, I simply wanted someone there I could depend on.

—First of all, gentlemen, each of you volunteered. I think that indicates a desire to get to know yourself better and maybe make changes. I don't know how many have experience in group situations ... don't worry, doesn't matter. Each group takes on its own dynamic. First thing is to get comfortable with each other ... sympathy and trust ... express yourselves freely. May take a while.

—No problem. We all got time.

The group leader waited for the laughter to subside.

—Great, it takes time ... sense of security. Maybe

start by introducing ourselves . . . Like to start off?

—Name's Kenny. I just wanted to come. I never been to one of these. Anything to get me off the fucken range.

—Fine, fine. People come for their own reasons—that gives a group its spark. How about you?

—Name's Alexander, I go by Rex. I been in these before . . . interesting the way they go. One guy, talking about his kids who he had to sign over, right? Very calm one minute, next minute he's pounding his head on the floor, right? Took four of us to restrain him.

—I can't promise any head-pounding, Rex, but I hope you find it interesting. You'll help make it interesting by your contribution.

Val's answer surprised me. I'm always underestimating him.

—Val Lundquist. I been in five years and I figure to get out next summer. Never served this long before and I wanted to hear from somebody who can tell me what it'll be like going back on the street.

—Owen Wesley. Mind if I ask what sort of training you've had?

—The fuck is this, twenty questions?

—No, that's all right. Fair question. I've had relevant academic training and a fair amount of practical experience. What brings you here, Owen?

—Well, I hope to get out next year, too. I wonder what it's going to be like.

—It's great, pal. Remember breasts? How soft they are, the taste . . . the way the nipple gets firm on your tongue. Remember sweet, full lips, going just where you want, remember running your hands down a woman's body, nice and slow, the way the waist goes in and the hips flare out, all soft and round, remember the way the panties slide off . . .

The leader waited for the noise to subside.

—You, sir? What's your name and what brings you here?

—Venell. Venell had it with hacks. Assholes, man.

—You find that's true of all correctional officers?

—Hacks. Assholes.

—I wonder if that perception is common to the rest of you?

A black with granny glasses and a long-suffering air:

—If I may, Mr Group Leader, sir. I'm not sure it matters who you put in the role. The role corrupts them —all of us are subject to their corruption. We are oppressed by definition, brothers and whitey alike. Let me tell you about an experiment... Harvard. They recruited subjects through newspaper advertisements. Told them the experiment had to do with learning—the effects of punishment on the learning process. Subjects were divided into 'students' and 'monitors.' The students were let in on the real experiment ... how long would the monitors continue to apply punishment to a protesting victim? Each student was physically re-strained and hooked up to an electrode. Supposedly memorizing pairs of words. Every time he made a mistake the monitor's duty was to apply electric shock. Each shock automatically stronger than the one before. The monitors included men and women of different ages, educational levels and occupations, whites and brothers. Most kept administering jolts even when they knew the shocks had reached the intensity you find in, say, the electric chair. Most never questioned the justifi-cation for these 'learning incentives.'

Freckled man, skin-tight pants, legs crossed so that he seemed to have no genitals:

—I know shocks. Put this meter on you, show you

pictures of one sort and another? The peter meter starts bouncing around if the pictures do it for you. You're wired to a box that gives you a shock if the meter jerks too far. It's a voluntary program—looks good on a parole application.

—Bullshit! I used to do everything—sodium-amytal interviews, capsule groups, I done electroshock a few times. Bullshit it looks good.

—Perhaps others have had experience with phallometric diagnosis of erotic preferences.

—Too much of that shit and they figure you for a kook. You're better off volunteering for research programs where they feed you shit that stops colds or fucks your brain. That's something they do like to see . . . you got a fifty-fifty chance of getting dummy pills anyways.

The leader glanced at his watch.

—Okay. Time's almost up. Anyone else have thoughts on that?

I'D WANTED to talk about the dream—told Val instead. He too has an excruciating dream, over and over— runaway car, he's in back, can't reach the wheel. By straining with all his might he grabs hold of it—it's disconnected. He turns it this way and that, but the car's out of control . . .

I hate my dream—over and over—we arrive to take possession of the house. With the realtor it had seemed wonderful—serene, spacious, artfully imagined. The vendor, a young architecture student, had done it himself and took pride in his design and fastidious work.

Angela hands me the key. I unlock the front door and —to her astonishment—carry her across. But something's wrong. Now that the house is ours we see imperfections everywhere. The vestibule has no light. One of the living-room windows doesn't close properly. The oak floor is marred . . . fireplace badly repointed . . . gobs of mortar in the hearth. We try the lights—no current. Kitchen tiles crack beneath our feet. The stove is caked and filthy. The oven emits a horrible stink. A sewer smell rises up the basement stairs.

Disheartened, we climb the stairs. I open the bathroom door—the knob comes off in my hand. The toilet, flushed, swirls leisurely, rising to the brim. The middle room is dark, gloomy. Our bedroom is a mess—oak floor splotched, white walls stained by urethane. The back bedroom hasn't been touched—ancient green paint on cracked walls, old linoleum on the floor, rusty screens on the windows.

Neither of us wants to admit that anything's amiss. So we pretend the house is as lovely as it had seemed. My mood turns to dread as we climb to the third floor, yet I'm feigning delight. Tar on the carpeted stairs. Water has found its way into one wall, staining it and warping the pine floor. The pine is badly fitted and pocked, as if someone in cleated shoes had walked on it.

Disturbed by our arrival, beetles march out of the cracks. Spiders have filled in the corners of the room, flies bat against the windows. The air is stifling—it's hard to speak:

—Isn't it wonderful?

—We're so lucky to have found this house.

When I open the deck door pigeons fly off, leaving a mess. The deck creaks . . . a board snaps . . . the railing is perilous. The chimney has eroded down to the roof, the eaves are broken and rusted. Wasps confer beneath the overhang as if planning a strategy for routing us.

—What a great buy.

—Jay and Sylvia are going to be green with envy. After what they spent on their place.

It's clear to us both the house is a disaster. I embrace her, to soothe her, but it has the opposite effect. She looks at me as if she doesn't know who I am—she's gone —reaching after her I almost follow. Her body twists in the air like a cat's, she's saying something, what? The roar of toilets, men hawking and muttering.

I hate the roar, I fear it. I listen for it, waiting. I reach for my pen and sit up, the dream perfectly real.

—As I write it's as if it had happened. Yet during the dream I'm aware of dreaming. Things fuse in my mind and I have no way of telling them apart—dreaming and waking, what happened and what didn't, my love and her death. I have the dream almost every night.

Val nods politely, lights one of my cigarettes. He cups the lighter in his hands, as if fighting a wind.

VAL had pruno last night. He raised the cup to his lips with both hands, sipping. I gulped and shuddered. He poured us both another and started talking:

—All the time growing up there was things I wanted but couldn't have. We lived in a project, my old lady, my old man before he fucked off, my kid sister and me, and I'd sneak rides downtown and look at the stuff I wanted and knew I'd never get. Wanted a nice pair of wellington boots and a turtleneck sweater and gold fountain pen. It was sitting there but it was behind glass, for other people. At Easter I used to drool at the chocolate bunnies they put in the department-store windows ... I'd see people come out the revolving doors with their packages and I wanted one of those giant bunnies, big as an armchair, wanted to eat the whole fucking thing, the ears, then the feet, then the rest of it.

—I wanted to lay my sixth-grade teacher but what did I know about that? I knew she'd never let me. Name was Miss Hernandez and one day she wore this sleeveless blouse and leaned over my desk, showing me something I was doing wrong. I saw all the way around the curve behind her bra and after that I wanted to lie with her and kiss that nipple. How I longed to kiss it meanwhile knowing I never could. I always hoped she'd wear that blouse, I hardly missed school that year, my last year, I couldn't read and I thought fuck it, and when she wore that blouse I'd sharpen my pencil in order to close the window and make her take her cardigan off, then I'd ask questions to get her to explain and finally come and lean over my desk . . . worked two or three times.

—I wanted to whip the dog from upstairs who snarled when he was chained to the stoop, I had to hop the railing to get in or out, but his owner'd beat shit out of me . . .

—Also there was this goof at school used to make me run the gauntlet every day and push my face in the snow. He was bigger than me but I was faster than him, I could run fast. I wanted to brick that sonofabitch but I knew I better do it right or else he would. I wanted to lay him out on my behalf and the behalf of all the guys he fucked over, several of us. Oh how I wanted to clobber that prick!

—And you know what? I found out you can have what you want. Just find the way. When my old man fucked off, he went west and said he'd be back but he took all his stuff, the one thing he left was his starter pistol. My old lady put it in the drawer with her bras and underpants, I used to pretend the bras belonged to Miss Hernandez, I must have seen that pistol a hundred times before I thought to take it, I wonder why I didn't think of it sooner. I stuck it in my belt and found out I could do what I wanted with it, all I had to do was flash it. Imagine—a piece that didn't do nothing except make noise! I robbed stores with that thing, got laid with it, I conked a motherfucker over the head and told him he was lucky I didn't kill him. I knocked off a variety store and didn't take nothing but chocolate bunnies, no shit, Monkey.

—I even got the dog to fuck off with it. Levelled it at him one day, I sighted down the barrel a good ten seconds and after that he was a different animal. I could shut him up through the ceiling with the sound of my voice. When he saw me coming up the walk, that was it —he'd fuck off until he ran out of chain and then curl up and whimper like he'd been whipped.

—Some people got ways of getting what they want, but I never had free money, I never had a silver tongue or that certain manner some guys got—you know?—I'm going to get it sooner or later so you may as well make it sooner. They're usually big fuckers and I'm only five-seven so I had to find my own way . . . a phony gun. How about that.

—Here, Monkey, have more juice. What are you in for? I don't believe you've told me. Angela, right?

BILLIE HOLIDAY showed up in the pit, pounded the heavy bag for half an hour, skulked off without a word to anyone. His size seems to vary according to circumstance. With Tonio, whom he idolizes, he appears big and forceful. But his laughter is as sudden as something being broken, and at night he conducts intense, incomprehensible monologues. When he's alone, fiddling with his hair—tight curls descending in terraced ridges—he seems frail, harmless, the cowardly kid brother of the other Billie. The other blacks hate him. At yard he came up behind me and tapped between my ribs—where the knife would go, if he'd wanted to kill me.

—Hear Val made more pruno.

—Something to ask him, ask him.

—I'm asking you.

—I've got nothing to do with anything. The guy came down to my cell, big deal.

—With pruno, right?

—Ask him.

—Tonio said ask you.

—Fine. You asked me.

—Not going to be happy . . .

Val used to share a highrise with Billie: 'Two thousand five hundred twelve days I slit the motherfucker's throat.' Next morning: 'Two thousand five hundred eleven days I slit that motherfucker's throat.' One morning Val gave him Percodan and Billie told his story. He and his brother got stopped in a stolen car and shot the cop. They fled to the coast, disguised themselves, began new lives. Two years later Billie's brother slipped back home for his parents' anniversary. Somebody spotted him and called police. The brother agreed to finger Billie in return for immunity. Billie was convicted on his brother's testimony. When he gets out, he told Val, he's going to hunt down his brother and kill him.

—I can't see it. Your own brother?

—Imagine being sold like that.

—Might hate him, but want his life?

Val, doing pushups—down, up, down, up—spoke to the floor:

—Going to get out of here, Monkey. Working on something.

—What do you mean?

He towelled himself with his shirt.

—Nothing, you don't want to know nothing.

—Billie asked about the pruno. Didn't you know?—
you have to get your sugar through Tonio.

—That little nigger.

He gripped the bars as if to pull them down, then sat
beside me, hands on my neck. Palumbo had started in—
his failed birdsong cut through the din of the range.

—That little wop.

—Somebody should maybe have a word with him.

Val massaged my shoulders.

—Why doesn't Vernon say something?

—He's not going to say anything. Why do you care?
Got cigarettes, Monkey?

—It bothers me. Palumbo's going to be executed by a
sort of democratic process. For whistling.

The duty hack used his billy, a kid with a stick on a
picket fence. His billy and his metronome voice.

—Lockup, let's go, lockup, let's go . . . .

Val gripped the back of my neck.

—Still going to see the psycho?

My eyes were closed—I nodded—he stopped massag-
ing. I opened my eyes on a face clouded with pain. The
pain he brings, the pain he wants to make me part of.

—Sleep well.

—Put your arms around me, Monkey.

—Thanks . . . the massage.

—What are you going to talk to him about?

Meaning, that you won't talk to me about.

—WHAT'S your full name?

　—Owen Stephen Wesley.

　—Residency number?

　—Six six two one three nine.

　—Where were you born?

　—Why you asking? You have it there, don't you?

　—Yes, but I like to get the information from you.

　—Why I'm here, frankly . . . get off the range for an hour.

　—Anything special in mind? Besides getting off the range?

　—Someone to talk to, I guess. There's a new guy, Val. We talk, he talks to me. Comes down to my cell and starts talking.

　—Why are you here?

　—I don't know anything about you—you have information about me.

　—I'm sorry that disturbs you.

　—Like fuck you are.

　—How do you feel about being here?

　—Most guys have friends or relatives inside, they've been in before, three meals a day. This was a place I'd seen on television and nowhere else. I had . . . problems of adjustment.

　—What sort of things?

　—It's not that bad. I get mail sometimes. Visitors. Jay comes every second week—my brother.

—Does he provide support?

—He comes, understand? Makes the effort. He's stood by me, but an hour isn't much . . .

—I see.

—'I see.' Angela was a psychologist.

—I'm here to learn about you.

—I'm in your calendar at one-thirty. Feel like a number, they play that song in the pit. I'm sick of it.

—I'd like to make one thing clear, Owen. You are a number, an entry in my calendar. To change that you have to talk to me. Perhaps you could tell me about Angela. I'm curious about her.

—She's gone. There is no Angela.

—She lives in your mind. Tell me about that.

—We met when we were eighteen, starting university.

—Did you have a lot in common?

—People took us for brother and sister.

—Do you still dream about her?

—Everything runs together—I don't know—maybe that's why I came to see you.

—Tell me about your dream. Perhaps it has something to tell you.

—Angela hated flying, used to drink before boarding. It was stormy, lightning struck the wing, felt like the plane was going to disintegrate . . . our flight to France. We went to France the summer before she died.

—What happened in the dream?

—I tried to comfort her, asked what I could do. She said, 'No, no, nothing!'—it was too late then.

—How did you feel at the end of the dream?

—I always wake up feeling awful.

—Is that a feeling you had with Angela?

—She was having an affair with her partner. When I

learned about it they'd been involved for five years.

—Did it make you angry?

—How could I be angry? I myself was having an affair with a woman at my office.

—When Angela told you about her lover, you told her you were having an affair too?

—She didn't tell me, I found out. We'd planned our holiday—I learned about Craig before we went. We decided we'd use the trip to sort things out. I'd broken up with Marnie by then. Actually, she broke off with me just before the trip.

—Did you feel guilty about having a lover?

—On our thirtieth birthday I bought Angela pearls. Had to borrow from Angela to buy them. I didn't tell her what the money was for—she never knew their real value.

—Tell me, how did you behave with your mother when you'd done something wrong? If she was mad at you, how did you win her back?

—Shit! What a stupid question! ... I said nothing ... the silent treatment.

—Did she love you?

—Sure, but Jay was the golden boy.

—Back to the dream. I'd like you to identify with each part of it. See what I mean? I am Angela, I'm afraid of flying. I'm the aircraft in the sky. I'm the lightning hitting the wing.

—Imagine myself as those things?

—See if anything comes of it. Maybe it will help you understand. Perhaps the dream has something to tell you.

—The plane was like this place. You can't get off— things threaten you. I have no one ... Val wants ... it's not the same.

—What do you think the lightning stands for?

—Does lightning have to stand for something?

—If it threatens to disintegrate your plane, your protection, perhaps it represents a threat. How did Angela die?

—Why are you sure dreams are so shit hot?

—I think perhaps we talk to ourselves in dreams, help ourselves understand. I find that in my own life.

—Why do you come here to see people?

—Well, the simplest answer is that it's my job.

—Surely there are more desirable patients. Rich, sedated housewives. Ulcerous executives.

—I suppose I'm drawn by the delinquent aspect because of my own delinquent leanings. Or, to put it another way, some things that interest me about people are sharply drawn among inmates. Also, perhaps, because my parents were sent to an internment camp during the war. But we're here to talk about you.

—Are you married?

—Yes.

—Do you have children?

—Three. Two girls and a boy. Did you have children with Angela?

—She didn't want children. I used to dream she was pregnant.

—Did you work out your dreams with Angela?

—That's something she got very interested in before her death—the extent to which you can direct your dreams, make them work for you. In a funny way I felt more involved with her clients, through her, than with people in my own life. Why did you become a psychiatrist?

—I'd prefer to talk about you, but I'll tell you a little about my motivation if it will help you. Perhaps make you less antagonistic?

—Please do.

—I'm eager to understand the forces that make us act. And how one goes about conscientizing those forces —if that's a word—to become more free.

—Are you good at your work?

—In my way I believe I am. Angela had her approach, I'm sure, and I have mine. What would you like to come from our conversations?

—I don't know. Val scares me a bit. Tonio scares me. This is basically a way of killing an hour. When my hearing comes up you'll be consulted? Maybe you'll help free me.

—Do you feel free now? In your mind?

—I'm on yard detail. Thank God ... I like to get outdoors.

—What goes through your mind while you're outside?

—It's so much calmer than the cellhouse. I can't believe people choose the shop. Val's happier in the shop!

—Do you carry your dreams through the day?

—Billie's on my case. I'm a point of weakness and others sense it. Look at someone the wrong way ... The only time I feel really safe is when I'm locked in.

—Before you came here, were you safe? Or did you have a feeling of fear and vulnerability among the people around you?

—I got fired—that made me feel vulnerable.

—Before you bought the pearls?

—After. Everything happened at once ... Angela made me feel safe. Until Craig.

—How did you feel safe after you found out? What door did you lock behind you?

—Actually, I did lock the house and smoke pot. If someone knocked, I ignored it. But I didn't feel safe.

—How about France? You must have been together constantly. Did you feel safe then?

—We'd agreed to talk things through, but it was too late. Things were intruding ... our effort went into coping with things.

—Just before she died—did you feel safe with her?

—Angry. Betrayed. Helpless. Sorry for her, for myself. I'd hoped we'd renew everything. But she couldn't leave him.

—And couldn't leave you.

—He'd just divorced, he wanted her to leave me. She wouldn't leave me ...

—How did you feel about Craig? Know him well?

—Angela was careful to keep us separated. I'd pick her up at her office and he'd be there. Say hello. We didn't have much in common.

—You felt angry in the last months of Angela's life. What did you do with the anger? Did you talk about it?

—I bet football, wanted to smash the set when I lost. The weekends she was at Craig's I watched two or three games a day. One night I slashed his tires. Drunk, used an ice pick. Never knew ...

—Do you feel angry now?

—Fucking right! This is a waste of time!

—That's why you came, isn't it? To waste time? Are you angry at being in this prison?

—My life brought me here.

—How much time do you have to yourself? Safe, locked in?

—Lockup is ten. Cells are sprung at six. You can put yourself in keep-lock any time after seven.

—When do you lock yourself in?

—Not too early—looks bad. Why would anyone lock in when he had the choice?

—What do you do in the evening?

—Television. Poker. Cigarettes. Read. I took Spanish for a while on Wednesday nights. I started a journal . . .

—Our time is nearly over. It's good you've started a journal. You could use it to focus on your anger—see what it's going into.

—Masturbating, pumping weight with Vernon and Val.

—I'd like you to feel it. The journal could help . . . a way of recreating your life with Angela. This may be something we could work on together—ways of releasing your anger.

—Want to know the truth? I think this is horseshit.

—Still, we managed to kill the hour, didn't we?

RECREATE your life together . . . ambulance attendants arguing over whether to try to revive her. The older one lost patience, kicked at a piece of shale, raised his voice against the roar of the falls.

—Listen, man, load her. This lady is through.

The ambulance could get no closer than the picnic area. Her body had to be hoisted by winch. The rescue basket wasn't properly secured—during the ascent it flipped upside down. Straining against the straps, as if eager to return to the river in which she had drowned.

—Hey now, you don't need to be looking at that.

The weather was extraordinary for late October. Storms had knocked branches off the trees, giving the park an awesome, plundered air. Refuse bins had been turned upside down, picnic tables upended against trees. The grass was stiff as canvas and covered with leaves but the air was charged with heat. False summer . . . we zipped our bags together, too exhausted to sleep. Rain pattered against the tent. When the sky lightened I sizzled bacon . . . boiled water . . . waiting like addicts as the coffee dripped through.

—Let's walk. Let's do something.

The park was draped with mist, hanging from the trees like Spanish moss. We fought our way down the tangled embankment and emerged beside the river—a thicker condensation hung over the water. Far downstream, the falls: faint, but with a steadiness that up close would be a roar.

—Listen to that.

—Let's go that way—want to?

She'd scheduled no clients for Monday. If the weather held, we'd drive into town so that she could phone Craig and have him reschedule her clients. We had resolved nothing, yet on Monday morning our moods were much improved. Angela seemed buoyant, almost giddy . . .

Maybe it was pure relief. Her workload had never been heavier—tranquillized housewives, overweight adolescents, husbands in affairs, a young woman who weighed sixty-eight pounds, couples locked in the most destructive patterns. Her practice had grown—she had to refer clients. Evidently she was superb at helping people. 'It's not what I do, it's what I am.'

After the interment I wondered how she would have helped me. Dreamed her answer: spend time with people, engage yourself in the present. Yoshino: 'Perhaps the dream has something to tell you.'

Still in my grey suit, I drove to the races. Chill winds, scudding cloud. I sat in the grandstand and bet each race. I chose longshots, kept occupied: there comes a moment when your horse seems poised to move. Finally, last race, my pick charged down the stretch and caught the favourite at the finish line. PHOTO went up. INQUIRY. For a moment I forgot. Would this be the process, then: moments of forgetting, longer moments?

When the photo was posted I studied it. My mare was behind but she had put her nose on the wire . . . $64.20. I funnelled out amid cigar-smoking men and wind-whipped piles of tickets and dust—every wound heals to a scar. But in the car, waiting for the lot to decongest, something shattered. I was thirty, unemployed, stricken. The bedroom closet still held her sweet smell. I had nothing left but a house full of her things, each endowed with the force of her absence.

TONIO'S thick hair, pocked skin, and perpetual smile make him seem adolescent. Yet his arms are rigged with the ropy muscles of old men and he told Val it was his anniversary: put the bits together, they add up to fifteen years. One of his shoulders is lower than the other . . . his neck juts to one side. He looks as if he was knocked into adulthood by a blow to the head.

The woman who surprised him burgling her apartment is in a coma. Tonio sends a card each Christmas. To blacks he tells jokes about Polacks and Jews, to whites he jokes about niggers. He smiles when he wins at poker, smiles the rare times he loses. He smiled when he learned his girlfriend was living with another man— hopped up on a table in the mess and read the letter as if reciting Shakespeare. Everyone applauded. He smiles when he drinks pruno, smiles when he throws up. Smiles in irritation, boredom, excitement, and once— when Vernon threatened to crush his ribs—in apprehension. A subtle range of smiles, like Eskimo words for snow. Val and I were playing chess when he flashed his apologetic smile through the bars.

—Hate to interrupt, Monkey.

Val was gone in two seconds flat.

Tonio wanted to know, was anybody on my case? Satisfied with the recreational opportunities? Complaints about food? He offered a cigarette, lit it for me.

—Most of the time I done was in upstate New York— Stormville, Comstock, Elmira, Dannemora, Attica, Auburn, plus more lockups than Warren Beatty's got girlfriends. Know where you find the best food? Right here.

He spat a piece of tobacco—I nodded encouragement.

—Three things make our food outstanding. First off, plenty of it. Been where you go short you'd understand what I'm saying. Don't have that prollem because your inmate committee fought a solid year to get unlimited seconds at evening meal.

—If you like potatoes. Good stuff always runs out.

—Second thing we got is excellent vegetables. Why? Grow them ourselves, same as we do our own baked goods which is why we have superior bread and doughnuts, the envy of every joint. Next year we'll be self-sufficient in vegetables. Think the hacks come up with that? Your inmate committee. My personal idea, which I passed along to Dimitrioff, who incidentally gets transferred in a couple of weeks. Shit, Monkey, I grew up on a farm. Said to myself first time I seen this place, 'This is prime land. Plant tits, prolly come up women.'

—Which brings me to the third thing we got. Choice. Most places have set menu. Salisbury steak, take it or leave it. Know how many places got choice like we got? Take last night—say you don't like meat loaf . . .

—I hate it. What's in it?

—So you have ham instead.

—I don't like ham either.

Tonio smiled, rubbing his tattoos.

—Joking aside, Monkey, done hard time you'd appreciate what I'm telling you. Whether ham, meat loaf, chicken, or what.

He extended three fingers and ticked them off:

—Choice, top vegetables, unlimited seconds. Makes our food better than any I ever ate. Thanks to your inmate committee.

—I don't like chicken, either.

—Fucking comedian. Fellows been telling me I should run for chairman now Dimitrioff's out of it. Incidentally, anything you need, let one of my people know. Treated wrong, detail you don't like . . . cell change? Might be surprised, things that can be arranged in here.

I had to admire the subtlety of the threat.

—You're obviously the man for the job.

He shrugged modestly.

—Somebody's got to represent the residents now Dimitrioff's out of it. Prolly as qualified as anybody else. Been turning it over, you know? Hey, why not?

Tonio ground out his cigarette on the floor of my cell. My attention was on the butt when I felt his fist. Before I could move—left left right—he'd boxed my jaw, pulling the punches, barely brushing the skin. Then he slapped my cheek, hard, and lifted my chin with his finger. I can't meet his eye, he'll see it spilling out . . .

—Just wanted to let you know what I been doing on your behalf as range rep.

—BITE on this. Prolly come in handy.

I hate Tonio and I've hated him since my first day . . .

I made it through processing in time for work detail. Hacks marshalled us down corridor C, across the inner yard, one by one through cage gates and into the bright morning. The sky was a shining blue dome. The air had a biting chill. Something in me started again. I felt lightheaded, glad to be moving with purpose and direction. Thrilled to be reunited with the world . . . utterly responsive to it.

Our detail moved to the farthest corner of the compound. Set in from the cyclone fence was a prefabricated aluminum toolshed. The shadow of an observation tower fell between the shed and a heap of cow manure fifteen feet high. We queued at the shed door, one man exiting before the next entered, to get a shovel or pitchfork. Our job was to move the manure past the shadow of the next observation tower.

Men stamped their feet to keep the blood moving. Their breath escaped in great white draughts. I was told to climb the mound and work on top. Tendrils of steam rose up as the interior manure was exposed—the last flies danced and preened as if drugged. Before long a couple of inmates ceased shovelling to smoke . . . more and more stopped . . . I paused, resting on my shovel, but a hack bawled at me through his megaphone. Soon everyone else had stopped. I worked steadily, trying to keep a rhythm — the hacks, at a distance, seemed to be waiting for something. The mood was intensely expectant. I dug.

—There's one!

Someone flung a shovel, cursed. The men tightened the circle, tools poised like spears . . . my life was over. I thought of Angela, Marnie, the nephew I'd never see . . . Buried in manure, erased from the face of the earth.

—There!

—Here!

Weapons were launched—men cursed, cried out. Another volley of tools, a high-pitched scream. On the side of the mound a plump dark rat was struggling, legs working, impaled through the gut, helpless as the groundhogs. A man with long sideburns clubbed it again again again with his shovel, like Dad with the rifle butt, clubbing. Metallic blows rang off the pitchfork, the rat screaming . . .

—Here! Tonio!

Another volley of pitchforks. Another rat had come out, a pale baby; then another, another, a tiny parade of them. They emerged at the same spot and froze a moment, blinded by the sun or else looking for the others. Men hollered in excitement beneath the brilliant blue sky. Some wore that look you see at ringside. One urinated steamily against the manure. Cheers rose up . . . rats emerged from all sides of the pile. I dug, forcing them out, I grew woozy—I started to climb down but a black with a shaved skull told me to get back up. I dug furiously, blindly, lost my balance. Got up and dug and slipped down again.

For twenty minutes rats kept coming. Dead rats everywhere, ten groundhogs in a single day. Some made it through the hail of weapons and disappeared beneath the aluminum shed. The men grew bored and distracted. Fewer rats could be made to appear, fewer weapons flew at each. My shoulders smouldered, the blisters on my palms had broken, the rest of my body lacked sensation. I half-climbed, half-slid down—no one said anything. Two men forked corpses into a wheelbarrow and buried them in the manure. One by one we returned our tools to the shed. On the way back to the cellhouse the hacks laughed at Tonio's jokes.

—One about the nigger ear nose and throat specialist?

The others filed down for chow . . . I tried to clean my boots in the toilet. Lay on my bunk with the pillow tight to my nose and ears, I couldn't stand my stinking clothes or the noise: boots on steel stairs, spoons on tin plates, men hollering over one another—the toilets roared. When the cells were sprung I went out and watched a poker game. Someone tapped my shoulder—I nearly cried out. Billie Holiday:

—Scuse me, man, come with me a moment? Friend of

mine wants to acks you something.

First time down the tier, each cell a tableau: a tattooed kid smoking, men taking medication, the shaved skull on his toilet, reading the *Wall Street Journal*. Billie led me to the last cell, stepped aside, then blocked the way behind me. My scalp turned to ice— nowhere to move—half a dozen men—no one made a sound. I sweated, smelling manure and all the other bodies that had sweated in my issue. Tonio handed me a bunched towel:

—Bite on this.

My scrotum shrank. I couldn't breathe.

—Stuff it in your mouth. Prolly come in handy.

—Do it, you fat fuck!

If I had been able to operate my body I would have. But the signals got crossed . . . I stared at the threadbare towel. Once it had been white, it bore a faint green back-sloping logo that took a long time to register—Holiday Inn.

—Bite on it.

Penis out of his trousers, rising, ardour making his smile grotesque.

—Grab the frame, get down . . . now!

Billie Holiday stood aside, freeing the bunk. Dreadlocks . . . instead of regulation issue, a military shirt in camouflage pattern. Sneakers. Rubbing himself.

—I'd rather do a monkey than this fat fuck.

—Do like the man say, fuck. Get down or we take you down, you going down, fuck—down, you new fuck!

—You heard him.

Tonio. But the pitch of his voice had changed, as if he now required my compliance.

Billie spoke to the others, for my benefit, of the purple erection in his fist:

—Check this out.

My towel fell to the floor ... I hadn't breathed. I
turned to Tonio to frame an apology. But he thought I
had deliberately dropped the towel—stepped aside to let
me out—I told myself go and this time my body re-
sponded. I thought it was a trick, waited to be throttled.
But all that came was Billie Holiday's fragile voice:

—Welcome to C-Range, Monkey!

RECREATE your life together ...

In first year I took calculus to satisfy the science
requirement of a humanities course. Lectures in a
cavernous firetrap, smaller tutorial groups in a windowless basement room. For my first tutorial I arrived late
—fifteen other teenagers were gathered at a round
table. I took the empty chair and studied the table's
grain a minute, in deference to the established mood of
the group. When I raised my eyes the eyes I met were
hers ...

Directly across from me, looking at me. I returned her
gaze ... she looked away. A shiny-faced, athletic-looking
student leaned so close to whisper he seemed to kiss her
hair—she smiled, nodded. Jock prick. For a week I
thought of the proprietorial way he had whispered. I

prayed he'd change courses, quit college, disappear.

At the next tutorial he didn't appear.

Again I sat across from Angela. I have no idea what went on in the tutorial. I managed to file out the door beside her, start talking. I felt foolish and frisky, had such an urge I feared I'd ruin everything.

—I'm going for chicken at that place up the street. Come with me?

—Well . . . I . . .

I took her arm. The sky was a parade of fleecy clouds, the air had the yellow rinsed sparkle of turning leaves— that fall weather timed to torment young people returned to the prison of schoolrooms. The racket in the restaurant, wooden booths scarred with initials, a lunch for which I had no appetite. Two detectives ate at the counter, the only non-students in the place. I wanted to say, 'I know we've just met, but . . .' I told her a fellow who used to help me with my papers had been arrested for trafficking.

—You have a paper route?

—Not any more. At his trial three pounds of smoke were submitted as evidence.

—Of smoke.

—Grass. Pot. Thing is, the police confiscated twice that.

She bit a French fry, waiting.

—What happened to the rest . . . the smoke?

I brandished a bone in the cops' direction. She glanced over: men in cheap suits, too big for their chairs, eating chicken. A wing of hair fell across her cheek—she had a way of pinning it behind her ear. I loved that, and her perplexed frown.

—Who?

—Cops. They stole it.

—Couldn't he do something? Your friend?

—Wait, your honour. That's three pounds. I had six, I swear.

It took a moment to register. With knife and fork she flaked meat off her drumstick, set down the knife and changed hands.

—When's your birthday?

Her answer made me laugh, but nothing about her suggested a joke.

—We were born the same day.

Studying each other ... it grew uncomfortable but neither of us looked away. Her eyes changed, the corners of her mouth ... in a moment we were grinning like idiots.

I sensed at once how deeply she reached in me but discovered why only gradually, as when I saw her turn pages in a magazine. When she closed a door it made almost no sound. When she put annuals in the earth she gave them extraordinary little pats. She sipped identically from champagne flutes and plastic tumblers, set them down the same way. She gave me an immediate sense of myself, as if she knew my worth without my having to prove it. She seemed utterly innocent and unharmed. My being so unlike her, clumsy and brusque in comparison, made it all the more incomprehensible that she seemed, when we met, a living part of me ...

—How will you tell them we're moving in together?

—They'll say, 'But honey, you're eighteen, you feel this way at your age. Please, a year or two—wait.' But I have been waiting ...

—You'll say that?

—Not those words—they wouldn't see—but it's true, so they'll understand.

I'd had no experience of people who meant no more or

less than they said . . . people who knew this about her surely had her at their mercy. When she took a bachelor flat in a renovated Victorian house near the campus, the landlord had her signature on a lease before she (or her mother) noticed the absence of sinks. Dishes, hair, socks, teeth, bras—everything had to be cleaned in the tiny tub. The man who installed the phone sold her the long cord even though there was nowhere to go: the sofa-bed filled the room. She seemed a child playing adult—signing cheques, ordering delivery of the paper, mouthing brand names as she made out a shopping list. I found in my adoration a protective urge.

—Don't give out information like that, you don't know who it is.

—What would you tell them?

—Hang up. A salesman has no right asking those questions.

She'd never seen the neon and chaos in which I felt most at ease. Men in tight jeans—three-hit cinemas— all-night burger stands. Cars cruised by, stoned boys in one, tapedeck blasting; girls in the next. Kids younger than ourselves studied Angela's legs from the alcoves of head shops. She lowered her eyes and gripped my arm. Waited patiently while I shot snooker with people I didn't know, fed quarter after quarter into raucous machines.

—See that bar? Fags go there on Hallowe'en. They dress up like women and arrive on motorcycles. Saw it last year.

—Was it sad?

—It was a riot. Everybody yelled at them.

Calculus was our only subject in common: differentials, integrals. I'd chosen courses so as not to get up in the morning, she always had eight-thirty lectures.

When the clock-radio clicked on I pretended to go back to sleep ... watched her pull a dress over her head. I waited outside her eleven-o'clock class, couldn't wait to see her, cared about nothing else. If the weather was nice, we'd buy sandwiches and eat on a bench in the park.

Traffic circled the park in waves, pulling away from one set of lights and stopping at the next. I pointed out a 1931 Packard, an Avanti, a 1,000-cc Triumph motorcycle. Amazing her with my knowledge, as she amazed me —she knew the name of every tree and flower, spotted delicately coloured birds, knew which was the male and the notes of its song. Joggers, derelicts, an elderly fellow who walked dogs for a living. Women with shopping bags, students hurrying to class, businessmen to meetings. A cop on horseback ... sparrows descended on the muffins. A wild-haired lady near the fountain, throwing handfuls of crusts in the air. Pigeons everywhere, males puffed and strutting, doing pirouettes and quicksteps ...

This suspension seemed to me a glimpse into the heart of things—the happiest moments in memory, the most abiding. It seemed to us both we'd been in the park before ...

My studies were aimless—I pursued no involvements beyond Angela. I loved to surprise her with cut flowers, albums, wineglasses. For some reason I pretended to have far more money than I had. One morning I spotted a likely ad, applied, got hired on the spot.

—Won't a job interfere with your studies?

—We could use the money.

—You spend all our money on me.

My employer was the newspaper I'd ceased delivering the previous summer, my job was taking death notices on the telephone. Evenings, while Angela studied—how faithfully!—I sat at a marble counter with a toad-like man who proudly showed me the ring given him by the company in honour of thirty-five years of death notices. Never happen to me. Funeral directors called, cracked jokes, dictated announcements. Now and then the caller was one of the bereaved. I'd soften my voice and help with the wording.

I discovered how to diddle the time clock and began skipping out early—couldn't wait to be with her. She would have prepared one of her mother's recipes, we'd curl up to watch the news on the tiny television I'd bought with my first pay. Rather I watched—the news upset her, haunted her, as her earlier life haunted me. One evening I had an awful, anxious sensation—raced home—found her sipping tea with her old boyfriend. His face was unclouded, expectant, he had a rash from his shirt collar, shook hands firmly, terribly embarrassed. He hoped I didn't mind, he'd heard about me and wanted to meet me. From the way Angela held her shoulders and neck I could see her distress. They had agreed it might be best to go their separate ways.

Angela kept a box of their memorabilia—napkins, pressed flowers, matchbooks. Many times, secretly, I'd gone through it. I asked if she planned to pitch it. She seemed surprised ... no, didn't intend to. I was telling Val about that box, combing through it ...

—I must have been frightened of her memories.

—Maybe you just didn't want her balling anybody else.

—Throwing out the box would erase the memories ... isn't it ridiculous? I wanted her to be as single-minded as I was.

JAY'S visits remind me of Granddad Wesley. Kind, ineffectual man—he gave us ginger ale when we went down to watch television. Mom gave Jay the money for the streetcar—he dropped in my fare as well as his own —chose our seat and pulled the cord for our stop. The hospital was shaded by elm trees. Granddad was in the room farthest from the elevator, at the end of a long hall ... motes of dust danced in the sun that filtered through the windows and the elm leaves. Each time we saw him he had shrunk a little more. He was happy to see us but his smile seemed to drain him. His head lay unpillowed on the bed—his elderly gullet seemed dangerously exposed. He sat up laboriously, felt for the wire glasses beside him, got to his feet as if invisible hands were restraining him. He began to struggle with his tartan dressing-gown—we watched before we thought to help. Where I touched his shoulder there was only bone.

Granddad sat on the edge of the bed and spoke so softly it was hard to know what he was thinking, especially when he started talking about hockey: it was summer. He smiled helplessly, sinking back across the bed. A nurse came in and lifted his legs to swivel him— something about it almost made me cry. Jay kissed him on the cheek ... I did, too, the way a grandson would on television. His skin had the texture of the newspaper Mom took out of dresser drawers she was relining. Jay said nothing until we were out in the sunshine.

—Granddad's going to die. Mom told me.

—He is not. Dad'd be here if he was.

For weeks he was precariously ill. Then he must have rallied because Mom told us to go again Sunday. He was desperately frail and frightened, curled on his side like a monkey. In places his hair was growing back. His eyes followed us across the room ... his lips moved in greeting. Lying motionless, he conveyed great effort. His smile seemed an apology that he had no words to spare—in the time we were there he spoke only once:

—Heard from your dad?

Next morning, after we got back from papers, Mom told us he was gone. Dad had got home in the middle of the night—too late, but at least Wilf had been with Granddad. Jay was old enough to go to the funeral but I wasn't—he had to stay with me and wait. It seemed they might not return home, might disappear into the ground with Granddad. Finally we heard the front door, again and again and again. It caught on the linoleum— Dad was always opening it to slam it, saying it needed to be fixed.

Mom was a mess, her dress wrinkled, her face splotched and puffy. Dad looked different in his dark suit—looked great. It restored his shoulders, drew attention from his sprung gut. He had a mickey in his pocket and splashed liquor in a glass. Jay sat on Dad's bed, I sat on Mom's while Dad chinned his pants and ran a wire hanger up the legs. He set his jacket on the hanger and returned the suit to the closet ... realized we were waiting. In socks and underwear, cradling his rye, he glanced in the mirror.

—That's the end of Granddad.

—What did he die of?

Dad swallowed—grimaced—set his glass on the bureau.

—Cancer of the pancreas. He was the weakest kind of

man. He did what was easy.

—What will happen to him now?

—What do you mean? People will rub his number out of their book.

—Didn't you like him?

—Your grandmother told him what to do. She made him what he was and he made your uncle what he is.

—What do you mean?

But Mom on some instinct had mounted the stairs and stood in alarm at the threshold:

—What are you telling them?

—The truth, dear. Their grandfather's gone and they won't find many people who think the world's worse off. What the hell did he ever do?

—Stop it! It's your father you're talking about!

—What did he do, dear? Tell me.

I was stunned. I was appalled that someone could hate his own father. Jay and I exchanged a look—what had Dad been going to say about Wilf? And how could anyone talk that way about Granddad?

Mom started to say something, but Dad shut her up with a look.

—Listen, and never forget. There are two kinds of people in the world—those who work to change it and those who keep it the way it is. Do you boys have any idea how fortunate we are? Do you? How lucky you are? A few people live off the sweat of all the other people who work in potash mines and lumber mills and steel plants, stand at checkout counters and assembly lines and blast furnaces, collect garbage and dig sewers and mop floors. The few people lie to them, cheat them, pay them a shameful wage to lose fingers and get silicosis and be deafened by the noise. Granddad was a nice man —he gave you cookies. But he worked in a goddamn bank!

—Don't leave your glass on the dresser! That was my mother's, damn you! Damn you to hell! You never think! You leave marks everywhere!

With a Kleenex Mom tried furiously to erase the ring.

Granddad must have died without having talked about dying—what was foremost went unsaid. Maybe his whole generation went that way, swallowing their terror. Jay and I discussed it once, years later, the guilt and frustration from those visits. Afterwards we had an aversion to hospitals—he mentioned it when Jonathan was born—I remember when Angela had blood poisoning.

Now she's gone ... Jay visits me ... same sense of impasse, of things left unsaid.

LAST night as I was watching TV it struck me: millions of people not under sentence were doing exactly the same thing, absorbing the same bright images and quick slogans. I marvelled that all of us, who can no more agree on whether to make seat belts mandatory than on whether to execute murderers, manage to agree on this. It was the latest instalment of what is apparently the most popular serial at the moment, a saga of rivalry and betrayal among members of a wealthy family, laced with commercial messages. Odd to think the mixture could be beamed indiscriminately to low-rent projects, penthouse apartments, hospitals, airports, recreational vehicles, hotels, appliance stores, limousines, cocktail bars, campgrounds, executive suites, and C-Range. What, exactly, is the difference between the prisoner and the free man? I mentioned this to Val, chalking my hands while he loaded the bar.

—I've had that sometimes, realize I'm doing what I'd do on the street. So what's tough about the grinder? Tell you what, Monkey, things fall into place, we're gone . . .

—I'm surprised they give us TV.

—Riots if they pulled the tube. They don't even do that in a joint that's blown.

—Wonder how many guys are in because of TV.

—One old-timer told me his good schemes used to come to him in dreams. Then, when TV came along, he got ideas from detective shows. When they came from dreams, he never got caught.

I squared my shoulders, aligned my spine on the bench.

—I used to smoke a lot of pot, made everything interesting or funny. The news was funny—game shows were interesting.

—Breathe, Monkey.

I hyperventilated ten times, eyes closed, moving the weight in my mind as he taught me. Then he talked:

—One time I saw a TV guy at a party, not ten feet away. They say people on TV look different in person but he looked the same—handsome, well dressed, friendly. Anchorman on the news, signed off with a funny story. When he said goodnight and straightened his papers, girl I lived with said, 'Night, Ben,' then shut off the set. Guy ended our day. She went up to him and said, 'Hello, Ben, wonderful to see you.' He looked at her like she was crazy ... fled. She thought there was something strange about him. Course, we were the ones who were strange.

—I used to watch anything, didn't matter, switching through the channels. Trying not to think where Angela was.

—Breathe, hold, work through the bar.

The bar seemed welded to the brackets. Then broke free—I got my arms extended—the bar felt oddly light. I banged off five with ease.

—Telling myself . . .

—Six.

—Have it out . . .

—Seven.

—Soon as she got home.

—Tuck your elbows. One more.

—Never did.

—Nine. One more.

—We never did.

—Up, up, up, ten!

Val helped me rack the bar, beat my shoulders like bongos.

—Beautiful, Monkey! Know what you did? Three hundred! Never gone over two-eighty before.

I'd have said I was incapable of bench-pressing three hundred pounds. Added the weight—sure enough. Val tells me I have strength I don't use—Angela used to say the same. I slid out from under the bar.

—What do I win? A brand new easy-to-maintain blender with digital programming and stick-free surface, chosen specially for me?

He imitated a game-show host and made me laugh with pleasure.

—A two-week dream vacation in fabulous *Hawaaiiiii*, where you'll enjoy sun, sand, sailing, surfing, mai tais by the jug, and dancing under the stars with Don Ho and the Hula Helpers—all yours as the guest of the fabulous Kauai Correctional Facility. Or you can stay here with your best friend. Dream vacation, or Val Lundquist? Five seconds.

—Dream vacation! . . . a passionate voice, as if I were part of the audience.

—Val! . . . different voice, another part.

I REMEMBER Giles, long ago, telling me:

—You're all right till you forget what it's like being with a woman. You're still a fish, you don't think it'll happen, Old Giles is loony. You'll remember sure as you remember the months in a year. Then comes the night you try to recall and what you recall is only that it was a good, sweet feeling. You inquire of your prick with your right hand—'What was the feeling again?'—you can't recall it. You can't get back to the feeling. You're not a fish any more . . .

I remember the letters for Gloria. Angela found one under the door one morning. It hadn't gone through the system, there were no marks on it. We opened it—a card bought at the variety store, two people in a meadow with a line of poetry by Rod McKuen. Small, careful handwriting covered the inside. 'Dear Gloria, I know you don't think I'm a person you could love . . .' It ended, 'You don't have to answer this and if you don't I'll take that as your answer, but I'm praying you will. Love, Don.'

Angela was saddened by the letter—I was intrigued. We didn't know who Gloria was. Had she lived in the house before the renovation? Asked the neighbours—they didn't recall any Gloria. Called the architecture student we'd bought from, the agent, nobody knew.

Few days later a second letter was there, slipped under the door in the middle of the night. In all there were six, over a month. The last, in which Don promised not to write again, came with carnations wrapped in green paper—the sort used at the local vegetable market. Angela made futile inquiries there. After a week we pitched the flowers. Threw the letters away, too, though it seemed a shame to waste communication of that sort . . .

A fat woman lived a few houses up the street. We'd be working in the garden and she'd come lumbering down the hill with her shopping cart or trudging back up with it full. When our poll was enumerated I found out who she was. Gloria Stennett, the only registered voter at number 58. We lived at 48.

—Could have been for her. She's the only Gloria on the list. Think we ought to ask if she knows anybody named Don?

—I'm not sure there's much point. That was months ago.

—What if it's her, though?

—We don't even have the letters any more.

But curiosity pricked me. I'd driven to the corner to pick up milk and the newspapers. When I parked, I saw her trudging up the hill, cart loaded with groceries. I fiddled in the car longer than necessary, stepped out as she approached.

—Excuse me, Gloria Stennett?

It was August and very humid. She was wearing a tight dark-blue sleeveless top and tight-fitting black slacks, an outfit that divided her into mountainous quarters. Her tiny head seemed stuck on, an afterthought. Her face was damp and pallid, her hair pasted to her forehead. She nodded warily.

—My name's Owen Wesley, this house here? A few months ago we got letters under the door for someone named Gloria. There was no address and we didn't know who they were meant for. Once there were flowers, too. I didn't know your name till I saw the voters' list. The cards—

—The bastard! How many times do you have to tell somebody to knock it off?

I remember Giles, long ago, telling me:

—You get like me ... or you start noticing the fish coming in. Look them over with an appreciative eye. Say to yourself, 'Now that's actually a fine-looking young man—blond, frail, fresh-faced, like a woman.' You think, 'What is that feeling again?' Put a blade to his throat—'Now I'm going to remember ...'

In the yard this morning there were oak leaves brought in on the wind. Heading back in I saw ducks. In the middle of the night I awoke just ahead of Vernon's moaning ... heard the distant howl of a train. Steady wind for two days now, spinnaker clouds sailing across the sky. Everything's moving about, going somewhere.

Day after tomorrow I see Yoshino.

Palumbo's whistling again. It's nice, really, the Largo from Dvořák's 'New World.'

Tonio got elected. In the yard I congratulated him. Billie snickered. Tonio smiled, a parody of perplexity.

—Some tiers I won unanimous. Not ours, though— two guys didn't vote for me. Don't matter, I guess.

He lit a hand-made, inhaled deeply, spat a fleck of tobacco. It stuck to my shirt.

—Still ... can't help wondering which two.

I WONDER if Yoshino is good at his work. What do I go by? Angela's work was inaccessible to me, especially after she went into partnership with Craig. My own brief experiences? They don't seem instructive.

Subject to moroseness (how I hated it in Dad), unable to keep my weight in check (like Dad), I asked Rudy Briggs to suggest someone I could talk to. He was in analysis and finding it tough but valuable. His analyst gave him the name of a psychiatrist at one of the old hospitals. I made an appointment, took the subway at lunch. The hospital was not unlike the cellhouse—the air of grinding boredom, the uniform of the elderly man who operated the elevator. I felt a pretender, a well person among the ill and infirm ...

The receptionist told me to be seated. I flipped through years-old issues of *Time* and *Newsweek* and wondered about the wisdom of consulting anyone who gave so little thought to reading material. Soon my depression was very real.

Campbell refused my hand, turning his back to lead me down a broad corridor to a stifling office with venetian blinds. He was a blocky, distracted Scot with greased black hair and bad teeth. Twice he told me he had trained in Austria. Closing our first meeting, he took out his bulging plastic appointment book—stamps, letters, receipts, phone messages, cheques, cash, newspaper clippings, laundry tickets—his life held together with an elastic band.

At the agency I mentioned that I'd joined a squash club, my weight having become material for office jokes. Campbell wore the same shiny suit each time, sat in the same stuffed chair, filled the same curved pipe without lighting it, began each meeting the same way—a weary sigh, a steeple of fingers: 'So then, Mr Wesley.' He charged more than was reimbursed by the plan. After six sessions I stopped.

Some months later I tried again. I'd begun to feel the pull to Marnie, though I'd not made overtures. At McEleney's daughter's wedding I overheard two women talking about a Dr Muller and the wonderful job he'd done with so-and-so. I looked him up in the book. He answered his own phone. His office wasn't far from mine. An hour later I was there. I liked Muller at once, his shapeless jackets and turtleneck sweaters. He did assessments for the prosecution, assessments for the defence. He listened to axe-murderers and speculated

about their fitness. He explored the thinking of child
molesters. Wrote long reports that were entered as
evidence. Though still in his thirties, he'd published
several books on criminal psychiatry.

—Everyone is or has been or will be quote crazy. I'm
interested in the legal distinctions.

His office was full of plants. Most of them had
mealybugs—I recommended a brand of insecticidal
soap. It did the trick, which made him so grateful he
started giving me tickets to the ball game—excellent
seats behind the visitors' dugout. I took Angela at first,
told her I'd got the seats from a client, but she didn't
like the noise. Usually I took Jay instead . . .

Muller said he was sure I'd get to the meat in my own
time. Angela and Marnie. Dad. Mom. My morose drinking, sudden jolts of panic and desperation—whatever
the meat was. We chatted, Muller giving a little shrug of
apology each time his phone rang, four or five times a
session. My recollection is of Muller telling me stories
frequently interrupted . . . of wondering, while he
talked, when the phone would ring again. He and his
son had sailed the Mediterranean on a chartered yacht
the previous summer. Angela and I had gone to Europe
each summer—Muller and I spent hours comparing
impressions of Spain, the south of France, Italy, Austria, Ibiza. In Greece he and his son anchored off a beach
that looked as if no one had ever set foot on it. His son
became ill from shellfish and nearly died. The experience changed him, he said, though he didn't say how.

—Enough about me. What's been happening?

Muller was twice divorced. He got his son every
Saturday and took him to the zoo, the museum, the
science centre. There were two doors to his office. His
name turned up in the papers. He lost money at the

track. I enjoyed him, but missed a couple of weeks and
never started again.

One afternoon I was drinking with a client. There
was a television above the bar, a program about a
psychiatrist. Like a soap opera—it took place entirely
indoors, the set consisting of potted plants, dark panel-
ling, stuffed furniture. An attractive woman lay on a
sofa talking, a man with an imperial nodded and offered
the occasional comment. Once or twice the woman
became hysterical. Organ music signalled commercial
breaks. I noticed Muller's name in the credits and called
him from the pay phone of the bar, asked how he was,
told him I wasn't coming any more. 'So I gathered.' I
inquired about his role on the program.

—I read the scripts and comment on their veracity. I
have someone with me. Phone again if you wish to
discuss it further.

With Yoshino it seems very different—I don't like
him but feel anticipation, apprehension. Fear. Yet I have
a clear sense of his desire to help. This anger business,
recreate my life. I need to figure out what I want from
him.

What did people want from Angela? After some new
clients she'd be drained and depressed, needing a glass
of wine.

—I've started seeing a very unhappy woman. God,
what a mess. She drains my energy, I have to be
careful . . .

With some people, though, she had emotional radar,
locating them instantly.

—Saw a very interesting new fellow, it's so exciting.
He really wants to go after it, you know? Ready to take
the responsibility. He's right on the verge.

I wonder what Yoshino said to his wife.

—Saw a new guy today. What an angry sonofabitch! What a hopeless case! I hope he terminates soon.

—HOW have you been?

—Up and down. Down.

—Anything specific bring on your mood?

—Val asked me what we'd talked about, I couldn't even remember. This is useless—maybe we should just forget it.

—Is Angela with you these days?

—I was remembering when we met.

—Good. Why don't you relax, close your eyes, spend a few moments recalling her. Especially toward the end. See where it leads us.

—I remember seeing a football coach on TV. Deeply lined face, peaked cap. It was in the papers that the opposing quarterback was seeing a psychiatrist, the coach was asked if any of his players were getting help. He said, 'I don't want that crap on my football team. I'd rather my players talk with a bartender.'

—I want to work on your body at the same time. You're very angry today. I can feel it, here in your neck and shoulders.

—Uh, it hurts, Uhhh . . .

—Did Angela work on you physically?

—Val gives me massages, he says my neck's always tight.

—Let's go back in time. When did you find out Angela had a lover?

—I was vacuuming the bedroom closet, a letter fell out of her brown tweed jacket. It didn't fall out, I used to go through her clothes. Felt pen, canary paper, the kind you use for your notes.

—What did the letter say?

—I don't remember. It's not important. Ah, that hurts.

—Recall the letter. Read it to me.

—It started, 'Darling,' it was signed 'C,' I forget exactly what it said because it stunned me, it . . . took so much for granted.

—What happened then?

—Angela was in the garden—May, the weekend we bought annuals. I was cleaning the house, I sat on the bed with the letter, disoriented. Beyond panic, just blank. The vacuum was shrieking—I looked up—she was there, wearing shorts, smudges on her knees.

—How did you feel at that instant?

—It wasn't anger, jealousy, sadness. It was nothing. God, that hurts. What are you doing to my shoulder?

—How do you feel now, remembering it?

—I look on it with detachment. Uh. A scene in a film I saw a long time ago. Uhhhh. What's wrong with my shoulders?

—Try to go back there. You're reading the letter as she . . .

—She said, 'Oh, Owen,' but I couldn't do anything. Even say anything. She looked in my eyes, gauging the hurt. Put her arms around me, I could hardly feel her body.

—Were you upset?

—One time, driving down from a friend's cottage? A woman had put her car upside down in the ditch. She was out, leaning against it. She looked fine except she was pale and her shinbone was poking through her pantyhose. She looked at her shin, couldn't figure out what it was. It wasn't bleeding, just looked strange. The bone was blue.

—Have you ever had a chance to feel the moment of reading the letter, liberate yourself from that feeling? In France, for example . . .

—By then there was simply too much to be said. Too much to be said simply.

—It might help if you were able to locate the anger.

—A guilty sense, because I myself was having an affair. Almost resentment, because I'd thought the deception was mine alone.

—The anger is still here—your shoulders and neck. I can feel it. It might help if you were able to move it.

—That's why people are here. Got angry, lashed out.

—This office is safe.

—I was angry at myself. For not . . .

—Why couldn't you be angry with Angela? Afraid she'd leave you?

—My father used to put his fist through the wall. My mother was very good with Polyfilla. Jay and I would hear them. Dad kicked dents in his car when it wouldn't start. He got six phones installed in the house so there would always be one within reach. But something screwed up, you couldn't call out so he ripped them out. He slapped Mom around. That's why I hated him.

—Have you ever got angry? Really let fly? Given

yourself permission to say, 'OK, goddamn it, this is *it!*'

—When Angela started spending weekends with him I'd play music so loud it hurt my ears. Put on dance programs and fantasize about the pretty girls. Marnie had broken off with me—Angela and I didn't sleep together. Is that what you mean?

—If you were to get mad at Angela now, what would you tell her?

—Look, there were reasons . . .

—Were you angry at Craig?

—Maybe, when I found out. I imagined blowing up his car, pushing him out his office window. One night I ripped the wipers off his car. They never knew I did it.

—Tell me about Craig.

—I never understood why Angela was attracted to him. I sensed something fraudulent in him, and he let her down. Just like I did.

—Why didn't she leave you to be with him?

—If I asked about him, it sounded as if I was trying to get information I could use. It was hard to raise the subject.

—Why didn't you talk in France?

—Things happened—fires in the hills. A kid died before our eyes. We met a guy in Marseilles . . .

—You never expressed yourself to Angela. Nothing was resolved.

—Craig had told her he wanted to end it because she wouldn't leave me. She hoped to work out a way . . .

—How was she before her death?

—She couldn't concentrate, eat, sleep. Trying to keep up her practice, trying to be there for Craig and for me. Like a battery, everything draining, nothing recharging. I felt powerless to help.

—Do you still feel powerless?

—I *am* powerless, for Christ's sake. You smug

asshole—you drive out of here every night.

—Growing up, did you feel powerless in your relation with your father or your brother? With Angela? Locked into certain aspects of your personality?

—Jay was great, the person I loved when I was little. With Angela I had a sense of . . . connection. You make it something negative.

—Pretend Angela is here. She's here in your memory, and I think it's important to come to terms with her. What would you ask her?

—To choose, she couldn't choose.

—Fine, but we're talking about what you want. You're two people, not halves of a whole.

—Stop seeing Craig. Make up your mind.

—Breathe deeply, Owen. Let your voice go.

—What will I do if you leave me?

—I can't hear you. Again.

—What's going to happen to me? Stay with me! Me!

—Owen, look at me now. Show me the power in your eyes.

—My eyes don't open wide. In photographs I'm always squinting.

—Anything else you want to say while Angela's here?

—She's not here, you bastard! What stupid game is this?

—She lives in you, doesn't she? What else would you say?

—I'm sorry . . .

—Do you feel it's your fault?

—Both our faults—all our faults.

—Our time is almost over. This week I'd like you to think about what you did right through all of this.

—'You gave her a wonderful present, very generous.' She's dead!

—You're alive, Owen, and you tend to see only where

you went wrong. Let's break that pattern. I'd like you to recall things you did right. Is there some way of doing that?

—Use my journal? Find memories that are pleasing—does that sound like a good idea?

—Does it sound like a good idea to you?

IN foul-smelling basement rooms Angela spent long hours among monkeys, rabbits, pink-eyed mice. She volunteered for studies in sensory deprivation, short-term memory, depth perception. Eager to share her excitement, I volunteered for the same experiments, skipping my own classes. I stuck my face in a stifling box and pressed a button each time a red light came on. Sometimes I got a puff of cool air, sometimes not. I didn't know if unpredictability was built in or if the equipment was malfunctioning. In one experiment I had to rate the attractiveness of six women, then revise my ranking, if I wished, after each of them had read a paragraph of nonsense syllables. In another study I was given all but the final chapter of a novel to read. I had to recount the story to a second student and speculate about the ending. Paid an hourly rate, I described the story in painstaking detail. The second student went off to relate it to a third, and so on. As well as first in the chain, I was eleventh. The tenth student confidently related to me a story that bore no resemblance—none— to the manuscript I had read a month earlier.

I was an English major and attended the theatre faithfully—seeing *Waiting for Godot* or *Romeo and Juliet* meant I didn't have to read it. Angela enjoyed the plays far more than I. At Christmas, finding myself with several papers due, I headed to the library, pored over the card index, and looked up articles in scholarly publications. I toned them down so that plagiarism would be impossible to prove. This worked fine and I spread the word that I'd do papers on any topic for twenty-five dollars. Using back issues of *PMLA* and *Victorian Studies, Chaucer Quarterly* and *Journal of Romantic Poetry*, I mastered the knack of turning out a B essay in hours. Behind the marble counter, between calls from morticians, I typed papers that bore others' names and helped pay the rent. The toad-like man thought me the world's most diligent student.

By now we had a lovely apartment. The rent seemed exorbitant but it was a rare place, high-ceilinged, tranquil, commodious. The other tenants were mostly elderly. We painted our bedroom the colour of brown eggs and bought a queen-size bed, for which Angela made a bedspread and matching drapes. Her parents contributed a fine bureau and a dining-room table. The dining-room overlooked a ravine in which cardinals cavorted all winter—in summer humming-birds were drawn to the fuchsias we set out on the balcony. A creek ran through the ravine . . . at dusk the seagulls circled high in the sky, calling their distinctive pleas.

Were we happy? In memory, at least, never happier.

Eating at the cherrywood table, watching the ravine gather the last pink light. Classical music—how she enriched me—listening to Beethoven and Vivaldi with contentment and attention. Simple moments and yet so harmonious I imagined at the time I would remember them all my life; and I will. Breezing through university, earning a bit of money, growing into a life quite unlike the one I'd known. Things were new and intense . . . our connection seemed immutable.

—How was your day?

—Great. My adviser wants to talk about my thesis topic, so I'll see him after class tomorrow. I don't know how late I'll be. There's chicken in the freezer. Did you go to your seminar?

—Wasn't much point. Hadn't done the reading . . .

My aimlessness was made clear by her diligence. When I spotted an ad for a junior copywriter I applied on impulse. The interviewer was a striking woman—blonde hair, black eyebrows. She showed me a photo of a bikini-clad girl straddling the tide line. If this were an ad for a Caribbean resort, what would I suggest as a catch line? My ideas were terse and suggestive. She excused herself, returned with a fellow in a bushy moustache and silk bow tie. We chatted . . . the lung association was considering a new campaign urging people to stop smoking. Any ideas for a theme, an approach? From television I knew the distortions and syncopations of advertising—my answers won me the job. I thought Angela would be pleased, not concerned.

—Shouldn't you at least get your degree?

—Now you can study as much as you want, not worry about grants and bursaries. And if we decide to have a kid . . .

—We can't think about children. Not yet, anyway.

I'd intended to graduate, but once I started at K & K there seemed no point. I never officially withdrew, just stopped going. Jay had a job with a management-consulting company and rode an elevator forty floors to his office. Suddenly I had work that paid equally well. We celebrated with Jay and his girlfriend of the time—met them at a student hangout also popular with the dispossessed.

The huge room was jammed. Men argued over shuffleboard ... muscular waitresses elbowed their way between tables, sticky trays aloft, bills folded between fingers. On stage a woman in a pink party dress played the organ for a succession of amateurs who clung to her repetitious chords as to lifebuoys. People yelled above the entertainment. The harsh lighting and bare walls drained artifice from faces—you saw people for what they were. It ought to have been depressing but was made gay by the sheer determination of the drinkers. I loved it. Angela was sensitive to the noise and smoke but did her best to enjoy herself. We drank glasses of beer and watched the tuxedoed emcee, a dwarf, introduce the vocalists, each worse than the last. Angela had angled her chair to the stage and I rested my chin on her shoulder. After one number she seemed to be wearing an expression of the most wrenching sadness.

—What is it, sweetie? Want to go?

—I was thinking the last time I sang was at Christmas. I used to sing all the time. When it was my turn to do the dishes I used to shut the kitchen door and sing my heart out.

—Don't blame me, it's not my fault you don't sing any more.

—I wasn't blaming you.

—Now that you're with me you don't sing, right?

That's the message I got. That what you did when you parked with your old boyfriend, sang? Waitress!—another round, and a shot of vodka.

The first summer we went to Europe—my first vacation from K & K—we found a bargain to Yugoslavia and caught the train to Trieste. When we crossed the border Angela stood a long time in the aisle. I stretched out and watched her silhouette against the falling dusk. The day had been intensely hot and we had the windows open. Trains passing the other way caused a deafening racket—a shower of sparks lit up woods, tilled fields, a highway beside the tracks. I woke when Angela returned to the compartment. She seemed lonely, wistful—I took her hands.

—What is it, sweetie? Homesick?

She shook her head sadly.

—Some of the little trucks in Italy only have three wheels.

—You've got to be kidding! Is that any reason to get depressed? This is supposed to be a holiday, come on.

Florence. Setting off from the station we happened on the vaulted elegance of the cathedral. It seemed to glow and change tone in the hazy afternoon. We sat mesmerized, studying it and drinking cappuccino.

—It's the colour that makes it so lovely, isn't it. Those shades of salmon and turquoise.

Angela's eyes were closed . . . her private world.

—I'm imagining how it would look if they cleaned it. I wish they would.

—Not everybody's as spick and span as you are. Can't you just appreciate it the way it is?

I remember one time we had Sylvia and Jay to dinner. Telling a long, potted story, I mentioned that Rudy at lunch had knocked over his wine. This was unimportant to my story but Angela peeked past the candles to catch my eye, apologized for interrupting, and asked:

—Red or white?

Why would that make me angry? Why would I embarrass her, and Syl and Jay, by shouting, in exactly the tone Dad used on Mom:

—Jesus, Angela! What the hell difference does it make?

Cellhouse, yard, gym, mess, the procession of days. Memories are an invitation to pain. I have pain enough as it is. Such effort ... what's the point? What's changed by remembering?

WHEN Yoshino asked about Jay, my answer was inadequate—didn't reflect the complexity and richness of my feeling for him. Great ... how many times have I said and thought and heard that? But growing up in his shadow, how could I not have longed to throw as prodigious a shadow? There was a time when, if I had been granted a wish, I would have asked to be exactly like him. He was too assured, too accomplished, to be entirely likeable, except that he knew it. His air of apology was his greatest charm. He knew he had a disproportionate share of Dad's affection and it made him kind to me. When Dad arrived home Jay usually found reason to come down the hall to my room, bringing with him something of the aura that made his bedroom warmer and safer than mine. And so Dad, when he came up, had to enter my room and greet us equally.

My feeling was made of admiration, love, and envy that was at times visceral. Besides his standing in Dad's eyes I envied him his girlfriend, his marks, his prowess at sports. His paper route and the money it gave him. He bought himself a Raleigh bicycle, a magnetic chess set and a baseball glove that bore the signature of Luis Aparicio. When a sign went up saying the *Star* was looking for carriers, I told Jay I was going to get a route too.

—The *Star* pays more than the *Globe*, but remember it weighs maybe twice as much. And you have to come home after school to do your route. The *Globe*'s better. You can whip through it because nobody's around in the mornings and the paper's light, except Saturday. You have afternoons free. You also find stuff in the morning.

—But there aren't any *Globe* routes open.

—Start helping me if you want. I'll give you a third of what I make. Wait a sec—think first. If you say yes, you've got to do it. It's hard getting up.

Jay began tapping my shoulder at five-thirty as he stumbled to the bathroom, penis half risen. Together we set off into mornings that in winter were so cold they made us laugh with shock and exhilaration. Some days we'd discover the city muffled by an eiderdown of snow, or every twig and wire glazed with icy incandescence. The streetlights would still be on when we got home. In summer when he woke me it was already light, and my sneakers got soaked on the first lawn I crossed. On spring mornings the trees were draped with green lace. Partway through the route we'd have to take off our windbreakers. Autumn mornings were pageants of crisp leaves—the air was filled with the powdery smell of their rattling. Jay showed me how to use the cutter, setting the bound papers on their side for purchase, working the wire until it heated and snapped and the bundle burst with an inky exhalation. I didn't have strength in my wrist. He showed me how to free the middle paper, then the next, until they all slid out.

—Some guys carry wirecutters, but you don't want any extra weight. You organize your route to get rid of as many papers as quick as possible. Leave your bag when you have to retrace your steps. Never carry more weight than you need to.

He opened his orange envelope of stops and starts, amended the list he carried but never had to consult, counted his papers.

—If you're short, take them from the box. Bring a pen. Write how many and your route number and put it in the slot. That way the guy who operates the box gets his money back. You can also make four papers out of three. A customer won't complain if he's only missing one of the four sections, but he will if he doesn't get anything. Four people missing one section each is better than one person getting nothing. Just remember not to screw the same customer twice.

He taught me how to fold papers in three, or, if thin enough, four, and how to throw them—crisply underhand, like a pitchout, or lobbed with a stiff arm, like a grenade. He seemed to me masterly and extraordinarily unselfish for cutting me in. When we saw the milkman

Jay bought a quart of chocolate milk and introduced me. He and the milkman talked about sports while we passed the sweating bottle back and forth, finishing it so we didn't have to pay the deposit.

Morning was a bounteous principality, my brother the prince. On the way home he took me to a greasy spoon, bought jelly doughnuts so fresh they compacted to nothing and squirted jam. Stuffed, we'd go home and fall asleep on the living-room floor until Mom came downstairs and told us it was time for school. She tried to feed us French toast or cereal and worried that we skipped breakfast.

Jay was right about finding things. Garbage days yielded treasure—a run-over wagon with good wheels, a raft of 78-r.p.m. jazz records Mom still has, a weight shaped like a power drill that Jay said was a sewing-machine motor. But the real finds were made in the milk boxes of apartment buildings. Marketing strategies of the day relied on getting consumers to test the product—the era of the free sample. Jay's route included an old four-storey building. The halls had such a smell you wondered how anyone could live in the place. We were supposed to use the tradesmen's entrance, but that meant going through the dingy basement. Jay used a penknife to pick the front door, which caused a running feud with the Hungarian superintendent.

—How many time I tell boys, back door!

One morning there was a sample bar of chocolate-covered coconut in each milk box. We swept through the building, floor by floor, relieving customers and non-customers alike. The sample was bite-sized, but thirty made a banquet. Poor Mom: 'Sure you don't want scrambled eggs this morning?' Then ballpoint pens, which we handed out at school. Another day it was sanitary napkins. These were a hit, though Jay had to

answer questions in the headmaster's office. One morning we discovered miniature containers of dishwashing
liquid—left the building with paper bags bulging.

Detergent seemed like good booty, but we weren't
sure what to do with it. On the way home Jay began
experimenting. He fired one at a billboard, but it
ricocheted harmlessly. Dropped one off the railway
overpass, but it bounced. A bus rumbled past and he
had a brainwave. He waited for the next bus and
skidded a bottle under its rear wheels. Head-turning
concussion ... bubbles everywhere. A cement truck
rumbled past and we both tried it. Kaboom again. Rush
hour was starting and the buses appeared at shorter
intervals. We held a competition to see who could get
more detonations. A bus headed the other way was
worth triple. We waited nonchalantly on the corner, two
kids with paper bags, until a bus approached. Then
fished out bottles and launched them with the concentration of curlers, trying to appear as surprised as
everyone else by the concussions and the bubbles raining down. We laughed and laughed and didn't take note
of the blue Plymouth until it made a quick U-turn. A
hulk in a suit and fedora flashed his badge, made us get
in back and slammed the door. There was no handle
inside. He and his partner argued about whether to take
us straight to Bowmanville or home first.

I was sick with fear. The evidence was overwhelming
—an intersection slick with detergent and pink plastic.
Jay, though outwardly deferential, seemed to grasp that
we weren't destined for the electric chair. To the cops he
gave straight answers and to me, under his breath,
alternative versions.

—What do you think your father's going to do when
he hears about this?

—He's out of town. (Probably laugh.)

—What was that?

—Out of town on business, sir.

—What about your mother? Going to be happy?

Jay hung his head, for shame, for shame:

—No, sir ...

—You boys know what's at Bowmanville, don't you?

—Yes, sir. (Mosport.)

—What was that?

—Reform school, sir.

The cops drove us home and woke Mom. The hulk attempted to explain ... Mom, foul-breathed, still not awake, shook her head: 'Detergent under the bus?' Once she came to she arranged her features in an expression of shock and alarm. 'A *stupid* thing to do,' she told us, aiming for more snap than came across. She asked the cop in for coffee, which got rid of him.

—Really, you two. Did you bring a paper home for your mother?

—Sorry, Mom. I've got three routes and you're not on any of them.

But he always had one for her.

—Go get ready. Go on.

We went up and put on ties and jackets. While I was studying myself in the bathroom mirror Jay came up behind me and let his wallet fall open, as the cop had done. He scowled, Joe Friday.

—You know what's at Bowmanville, don't you?

Secure in the sanctuary of his presence, I laughed and laughed and laughed.

FIRST I thought I was dreaming it. Then I thought it was happening here. Reek of smoke, everybody frantic, hacks nowhere to be seen. Billie scurried from cell to cell, eyes lit.

—The brothers took it—drugs, weapons, hostages. Show time!

I told Val one of the other ranges was rioting—petrified, shocked by my own deep emotion. He reassured me—the riot was actually happening at another facility, not far away. Val—many of the men—knew the place. The news galvanized everyone ...

—If it blows, don't fight it. Be part of what's going down.

Marshalled for work as usual. Among the hacks this decision—routine instead of keep-lock—was unpopular. They kept their distance, weapons at hand, walkie-talkies crackling with static. The air was freezing ... a cutting wind rose in gusts. We swept out an empty storage shed, stamped our feet to stay warm, conferred in low voices. The brothers had voted to sacrifice hostages. The authorities had guaranteed no reprisals and safe passage to Cuba, Algeria, South America. The dispensary had been smashed ... the brothers had drugs enough for an army. A glorious, fearful time, a bright, bone-chilling November morning ...

We were marshalled in early. No tier time before chow—the mood was suddenly disrupted. Good for

them, burn it down, except our lives were constricting
in proportion to their fragile liberty. More hacks than
usual, more shotguns in evidence. When we filed down
for chow there was a head count at every landing—
surveillance cameras were activated—the no-talking
rule was enforced. Val slipped in behind me.

—What about it, Monkey?

I actually considered it. It's not loss of liberty—it's
the lesser indignities. Blades so dull they hack the skin.
Issue that binds one week, slides off your hips the next.
Socks you keep pulling on no matter how soiled. Timed
showers, as if thirty seconds made a difference. The
noise, the Muzak in the mess hall—the first reform by
our progressive warden. Work that is make-work, useless and demeaning, keeping in equilibrium the resignation and the longing not to resign. The hacks who will
not hear unless you address them as sir. Knowing your
deprivation is a livelihood for men whose mouths work
as they count to six. The frisks, blunt and thorough,
reminders that our bodies are subject. The counts,
reminders that our existence is numerical. What they
gain is hard to fathom. Security—the favourite word—
is a mask on the true motivation. I don't like to think
people torment other people by instinct. 'Not me,' I
whispered, and saw the question in Val's eyes—good
sense or cowardice?

Meat loaf, beans, potato cooked to be eaten by spoon.
Instead of mess hall, keep-lock. Stories were passed and
embellished. The brothers had penetrated administration, gained access to the files. Every rat and diddler
was known. Men were trying to lock themselves in, but
central was smashed and cells once impossible to open
were now impossible to close. Death squad moving cell
by cell—diddlers castrated with blow torches—rats'
tongues pulled with pliers.

Now silence envelops the range like fog. Whose eyes are gaining lustre, whose turning inward? Me—death squad or marked man? On an upper tier someone rattles a tin plate on the bars—an empty, urgent racket picked up by all. Squawk box: any inmate making unnecessary noise is subject to thirty days' dissociation. Obscenities and bold threats. Shotguns at the duty stations ... hacks in gas masks move down the tiers.

No Palumbo. No Dvořák.

The word, just after lights out. The authorities have gone in—inmates slaughtered, hostages sacrificed, the prison reduced to debris. Nobody's asleep—a terrible darkness punctured by urgent whisperings—the reckless trying to incite the others. I wish Val were with me.

Please God—don't let it happen here. Don't let me die locked in. The toilets roar.

Angela.

AT RISE bell the hacks rang the bars as usual, bored and blank, another day. Men don't make much noise at that hour, only hawk and piss and mutter. The tension had evaporated like a dream. We filed down for chow. Up-tempo Muzak ... avoiding one another's eyes. Our detail was marshalled into the drizzle, a warmer morning that seemed colder. Cowering in a field, smoking, envying the hacks their ponchos, waiting to file in, the mood balanced between relief and lost hope. In the gym an oldtimer talked to me, a man with a glass eye to which my attention was drawn. The eye has a milky, opal quality and gives him an air of deliberation.

—Monkey, the niggers had the principle. It was Spina, I believe, who wrote, 'Liberty is something you take for yourself. No good begging it from others.' Where the niggers fucked up, you don't spring a whole facility at once. Show me the precedent! Has it been done in all the years men have been putting other men in penitentiaries?

Tonight Val came down.

—We're lucky, Monkey. I was in a joint that blew in 1979. You go with it, you have to.

—It's all over, isn't it?

—Right now. But the hacks' contract expires end of next month. We don't want to be here if they walk off the job.

SPRINKLING of snow ... the sun found glittering pin-points, our boots made delicate shapes. Toward noon the sky tightened. Flurries, then it began snowing steadily, then the clouds became pillows torn open and shaken. Lying in the snow, not moving a muscle ... Jay's cabin. We took a week and drove up. Pulled off at the top of a long rise, parked against the snowbank, tied a cloth to the car aerial. Hauled provisions by toboggan two miles to the cabin. Already, in mid-afternoon, the scent of night.

Once we'd dug out, got the current running and a blaze roaring in the wood stove, we poked around and found snowshoes, board games, paperback mysteries, back issues of *Consumer Reports* (Sylvia) and *Forbes* (Jay). Sylvia's boots fitted Angela and Jay's were only a size too large for me. In the morning, we decided, we'd teach ourselves to ski. Early dinner—asleep by ten-thirty—then we were jolted by a dreadful cacophony. Snowmobiles had stopped out on the lake. Drunken yells as the machines came closer. The noise was shattering ... headlights swept across the bedroom wall.

—What are they doing? Should we call the police?

—What police? We don't even know where we are.

Two snowmobiles had approached to within fifty yards of the cabin. Three men, or boys, I couldn't tell— thermal suits and balaclavas turned them into bulky silhouettes in the odd illumination of snowlight. Over the idling engines I heard voices. Passing a bottle and arguing, two against one. The one capitulated ... they revved the engines, headlights waxing and waning, and roared off. Even if we'd screamed no one would have heard us, yet we spoke in whispers:

—What do you think they were doing?

—Probably drunk.

—Why would they come here? To break in?

—Why do you always think the worst? Probably just kids out for a good time.

Alarmed, I tried to sound offhand. I wanted to get up and see if Jay had the Cooney but was afraid of frightening her. I spent the night on the edge of sleep, waiting . . .

In the morning we waxed the skis and set out—awkwardly, but soon we were striding around the lake. The snowmobiles had packed trails. We so enjoyed ourselves we agreed on a day's outing. Again that night I had trouble sleeping. I'd searched the cabin: no rifle. Sure enough, after midnight combustive noise tore the darkness, heading our way. I got up to make sure the cabin was locked.

—Are you worried?

—Why would I be worried?

But I was, about the faces behind the balaclavas, about my job, which I hated, about my life, which seemed unaccountably vacant, about Angela, who'd gone into partnership with Craig. I worried that her work was directed beyond me, excluded me. Her eagerness to make her own way seemed a refutation—made me want to know what was lacking in me, to shake her until the answer spilled out. Which was crazy, of course, her growing independence was to be applauded.

At breakfast neither of us thought of a map or compass or emergency kit. The air was still, the sky azure, the light dazzling in reflection. We crossed the lake, and before long were bathed in perspiration, moving in an easy, rhythmic shuffle. The stiffness left my legs—I lost track of time. When the snow began we must have been six or eight miles from the cabin. Cirrus cloud thinned the sun, filtered it completely . . . the sky lowered itself like a white awning. One minute it was clear; the next minute snow was falling in a dull, steady rhythm, silencing all that it touched. Huge swirling flakes caught on our clothes, turned the pines to blurry triangles. Wonderment keened Angela's senses: she loved it. I grew fearful, and irritated that she failed to see our plight. We followed our tracks toward home but soon they were covered. We stopped to rest. The snow became a kind of gentle entombment—the majesty of forces no power can alter. When we resumed, the hiss of skis seemed louder. She had a more fluid technique and broke trail. Her rhythm took on a sense of purpose. I couldn't keep up—I called after her—a few strides ahead she became a ghost. The air was losing warmth ... light was seeping out of the sky. In an hour it would be dark, but we had only to hit the lake. Besides, there were people in the area—I tried to picture faces behind the balaclavas.

Wind set the snow on a slant ... I lost confidence in her direction. We speculated about which way the lake was. Awkwardly, feet rooted, we reassured one another. Now she was growing concerned, which angered me—I pretended there wasn't the least cause for concern and insisted on leading the way. Keep moving and we'd surely cross a hydro line or a road. The soreness was back in my thighs—my sweat was absorbing the cold—I pushed on, feigning nonchalance. The wind had strengthened, blowing snow in our faces. The flakes were no longer soft and moist: they stung. The idea of freezing to death—of such incompetence—filled me with determination. I would get back no matter what. I struggled to keep my form, trying to go so fast that she'd ask me to wait.

I suddenly knew my efforts would be futile. I'd plod along until I'd exhausted myself, my legs would stiffen ... she'd carry on, I'd die beneath an eiderdown of snow. Fear sent a surge of energy (strength you don't use), I

blundered on, convinced I'd die in Jay's boots, probably
—once the snow stopped—within sight of the cabin. Not
for lack of resources ... for not knowing how to use
them.

Half an hour later Mozart swelled from the speakers
and a fire took hold in the stove. Outside the window
was a blessed scene, pine boughs laden, half moon risen,
the world cleansed and renewed. I apologized for having
lost my temper.

—You seem so upset these days ...

—What do you mean?

—Everything gets on your nerves.

—I don't think that's true. I'm happy to be here, just
the two of us—we never seem to spend time together.
Want to know the thing that pisses me off? It's that you
keep telling me how pissed off I am.

BILLIE HOLIDAY sat in tonight and tried to cheat Vernon.
Five-card double draw. Vernon opened, Billie raised,
Vernon raised back. Giles stayed, Tonio and I folded.
Raises back and forth, which drove out Giles. Billie and
Vernon drew again, Billie collecting discards and deal-
ing off the deck, smooth as can be—he used to deal in

Reno. Raise after raise until Billie called. Vernon beamed:

—Three tens.

—Kings, baby—read 'em and get the Kleenex tissues.

He showed his hand and reached for the pot. Vernon grabbed his wrist:

—Lemme see.

Billie jerked his arm free and, indignant, showed his hand again: three kings, six, ace.

—I dumped that king hearts!

Tonio smiled:

—Sure about that?

—Sure I'm sure.

Billie chuckled, narrowing his eyes:

—Sure as shit.

Vernon's face went dark with blood.

—Hold her there, nigger. I kept three and drew two. I got three tens right off, that's how come I was bumping. I dump queen king hearts, that's how come I remember, three toward a straight flush. Didn't get nothing so I drew two again, didn't get nothing. Lookit here. Here's the queen hearts in the discards. Where's king hearts? In the dealer's hand! Break your scrawny neck.

—Oh, help. Save me.

—Prolly better give Vernon the pot.

—Shit! Three kings, fair and square!

—Better give Vernon the pot.

—Come on, man, I don't like losing neither but you don't really 'speck us to buy that shit, do you?

Tonio's voice was as level as an airline captain's announcing engine trouble:

—Give Vernon the pot.

Billie raised his eyes to meet Tonio's—the animal's apprehension of danger—no emotion, only perfect attention. Billie started to shake. The shaking became uncontrollable. He jerked his head at each of us in turn, working his mouth as if unable to get air. He pushed the pot toward Vernon ... fled in a rage and put himself in keep-lock.

Vernon shuffled clumsily, the cards too small for his hands:

—Goddamn rights.

Vernon could take Billie apart like a barbecued chicken, yet he presents his grievance to Tonio. Tonio mediates and gives his judgment—his judgment is adhered to. The fulcrum of the cellhouse: the slightest movement means upheaval elsewhere. Someone whispers, Tonio nods, somebody who owes somebody fails to return from the showers. One morning Tonio refuses to say a word, the hacks exchange a glance, the warden invites him for coffee. Bribes and offerings are brought to him, nothing is done without his approval— how does he command such power?

Total relaxation—his body is so loose it seems puppet-like, not subject to laws of mass and gravity. His wowed neck reinforces the impression. Willingness to confront anything—not the summoned courage of a man in a fix, but thoughtlessness toward danger. Like Audie Murphy, braving fire again and again, baffled by the medals —the courage of insanity, but Tonio is not insane. Crafty, calculating, the one better poker player than me. An element missing?—he's unmoved by the smell of blood, the percussion of a beating, the sight of viscera. When he told me about the redhead in the coma there was remorse, but not at what he'd done. Sad these things happen ... as if she'd been a child darting out between cars. Devoid of feeling, then? Told Val he once went to knife a rival and, finding him peeing, turned away—didn't seem right to shiv a man with his cock in his hand.

Most frightening is that he's so at home here. (Am I at home here?) He's been hurt—his hearing is bad, there's a pucker in his side, Lord knows about his neck. He's been in solitary, which he seems not to like or dislike. Given the chance to walk out of here he might choose to stay. He communicates that fearlessness is the centre of his calm. A freak in whom fear has never arisen, or does he transcend it? I wish I were like him—beyond fear. I told Val.

—Course he's got it over you, Monkey. Natural life— the government'll pay for his funeral. You're going to get out ... maybe sooner than you think.

To think that Val's right. To think that getting out could be more frightening than staying.

JAY'S Cooney ... I remember when we got it. Mom was making hamburgers, packing them, lining them up like snowballs. She squinted out the window.

—Here's your father.

She scooped the balls back in the bowl—six would have to become eight, the story of Mom's life. We could tell by the way the car bounced up the hill that Dad had been drinking. We hadn't seen him in weeks, months. He had presents—beaded moccasins for her and a .22 for Jay and me, a gleaming, single-shot Cooney.

—You must have flown down, did you?

Her questions were minefields and he knew better than to tiptoe through them.

—Hi, Jay. I'm starved, dear. How you doing, Owen?

Next morning, eager to use the weapon, we woke him. He made us endure a safety lecture and a detailed explanation of how the mechanism worked. He broke the rifle down and demonstrated how to clean it. How to handle it in woods, in open country, in the presence of others. Made us climb back and forth through the rail fence with the empty weapon. He selected a site past the outhouse, where the property dropped off and a scrub hill rose beyond—tacked paper targets to the walnut tree—counted his steps. We took turns, five rounds each, sighting it in.

—Make a soft fist. Tighten your hand smoothly, don't jerk your finger.

Some of Jay's shots missed altogether. Mine drifted into the outer rings, but made a tight group. Dad put up new targets and we fired again. He adjusted the windage screw, and I put four of five rounds in the centre ring. Dad hit it twice, Jay once. At lunch Dad poured Scotch in his coffee.

—Got a marksman in the family.

Mom raised her eyebrows . . . Dad nodded at me.

I couldn't wait to use the rifle again, but he wouldn't be rushed—drank cup after cup of spiked coffee. Finally he slapped the table and told us to change out of our trunks.

—Why? It's hot.

—Put on pants and long sleeves. Your arms and legs will get scratched to hell. Wear a shirt with pockets—it's easiest getting ammo out of a shirt pocket.

Dad gave me the rifle. I handed it to Jay before I squeezed through the fence and he passed it back before he climbed over. Dad unscrewed his mickey, took a long pull, wiped his mouth with the back of his hand. We'd head for the road, he said, cross to the far corner of the section, come back along the property line.

—You don't wander when you hunt. You cover ground.

The hay reached my waist, swishing as we moved through it. We saw dozens of groundhog holes but no groundhogs. The air was stifling—Jay and I quickly became dispirited. We stopped so Dad could sit on a log, take another pull, and smoke a cigarette. The back of his shirt was soaked through.

—Christ, only fools come out in this heat.

As we set off we flushed a rabbit. Jay got off a hopeless shot—the report caused a flapping in the trees behind us. Once out of range three crows called to one another. Jay put a shell in the breech, swung the rifle vaguely in the crows' direction.

—How you supposed to get anything with one shot?

—That's how you hunt. Patience and a single shot.

—Can you get crows with a .22?

—Only if you're really good. They're smart—sometimes you'd swear they know when the rifle's loaded. Let's go see if Uncle Don's here.

Dejectedly we headed back. At the summit of the last rise Dad put a finger to his lips and sank down. My heart changed gears.

—There's a groundhog straight ahead of us. Big fat bastard. Fifty yards straight ahead.

He took the Cooney from Jay and passed it to me. I put a shell in the breech while he told me, whispering, to get as close as possible—one shot. The rifle was sighted for twenty-five yards. Further away, he said, aim over its head. Feels wrong, but do it. And think where the bullet will end up if you miss—you don't want to surprise your mother in the kitchen.

—Is a .22 big enough to kill it?

—Goddamn right.

—Even in the stomach?

—Be like you getting hit with an elephant gun. Now go on. Don't poke the barrel and plug it. Don't rush the shot.

I set off on elbows and knees. The grass pricked, sweat trickled into my eyes, my heart raced—the chance I must not bungle. My progress felt unbearably slow, but when I looked back I'd left them behind. The ground wasn't flat as I'd imagined. I passed over a rise, raised my head, saw nothing. Had it gone under? I got into a crouch to cross the dip, crawled as I approached the crest. At the top I came on a mound so fresh the earth was damp.

I didn't see it until it moved. I was on top of it—how could it be unaware of me? It was feeding by a path in the grass, raising its head, nibbling again. I drew the butt to my shoulder and aimed . . . the barrel swayed. I squirmed to one side, flattened myself so it rested on the mound. The groundhog continued to feed and look up in rhythm. Surely it could hear my ragged breathing, drumming heart . . . I got the bead in the V and the V on its shining body. How could one creature be so intent on another without alerting it? Go! Sweat found my squinting eye and blinded me. I made a fist—nothing happened—the safety was on. I clicked it off and the groundhog froze.

—Go!

It rose on its haunches like an arcade bear.

—Run!

I made a fist—gasped, as if I'd been under water, a backward scream. I got to my feet, soaked and cramped. I could have wept with relief ... at least I'd tried. I brushed myself off—Jay came running—Dad walked up disgusted, shaking his head.

—You meathead, you weren't close enough.

—There was another one. There. I missed it.

He went down on one knee and conjured an animal.

—The hell you did. Atta boy!

Jay looked at me in a way he never had before. The groundhog shivered and twisted in Dad's hand. He took the Cooney and, with the butt, thumped the creature again and again. The butt seemed to shake the earth itself. He held it out for me, a furry sack dripping urine and blood.

We found Mom and Uncle Don on lawn chairs. Jay set the dead animal by the cistern. Mom studied it, neither squeamish nor callous, simply curious. Uncle Don whistled.

—Look at the teeth on that fucker.

—Owen got it.

Dad rubbed my head. He never rubbed my head, never touched me. I leaned against his leg and he rubbed my head again.

—Born hunter, aren't you?

—Good for you, dear!

I put my arm around his leg. He cuffed the back of my head. I leaned against him. He cuffed me so sharply my eyes watered. I tried to hold onto his leg but he started for the picnic table where Don had set a bottle.

—Hog dog! Shall we christen this? Make you guys a deal. If either of you gets ten this week I'll buy a deer rifle for your birthday. A Winchester .30-.30.

Mom clucked her disapproval, spoke as if to herself:

—Money coming out his ears.

Dad and Uncle Don moved the picnic table into the shade—bottle between them. Mom sat beside Dad. She wouldn't take a drink until Uncle Don moved her hand, which was covering her cup. Jay sat beside Uncle Don, eager for the bullshit—he loved union stories. I sat beside Mom as long as I could, watching the chestnut tree . . . it started swaying a moment before the breeze arrived. I grabbed the rifle and filled my shirt pocket.

—He's all right by himself?

—For Christ's sake, dear.

It was cooler now . . . groundhogs were feeding. From the toboggan run I could see a dozen brown spots in the grass. I waited for each spot to move, distinguishing groundhogs from cowflaps. I stalked the nearest groundhog and got off a shot, but I was trembling—it scurried off. I felt a kind of stupid relief—I was glad it had got away, but I'd just have to shoot another. I kicked dirt in its hole, then peed down it.

I lay on my back in the grass. Faintly, on the breeze, I heard Uncle Don's laughter. Surely, somewhere in the world, frightened and lonely, was someone like me . . .

The moment I sat up I spotted another. I stalked it carefully. After a few minutes I thought maybe I'd worked my way by it. I crawled another body length— there it was, not twenty yards away. My excitement could only be calmed by grief . . . I trembled with the certainty I would kill it. The animal sensed me and ran, plump and graceful. But instead of diving it posed on its mound, showing its profile as though in assent. Its nose worked like a cat's. I didn't think of it as lovable or unique, I simply had no wish to do it harm.

I made a soft fist, the rifle sounded, the groundhog twisted spasmodically in the dirt. Like you getting it with an elephant gun. I fed in another round and shot it again and waited before I went to it. Flies were busy. I pulled a piece of straw. Surely even a dead creature would flinch if I touched its open eye. I knelt and gingerly wielded the straw—it wasn't the groundhog who flinched. I used one of my socks as a mitt but still recoiled at the warmth. I got my mind on something else ... jerked it off the grass. Half-ran to the farm, holding it like dirty diapers. Dad jumped up to meet me.

—Hot dog! Got one already!

I hoisted the corpse over the fence, handed him the Cooney before climbing through.

—Puts the old man to shame. Look at that belly, Helen. Must be full of young.

—The hell it is, that's grass.

—Ten bucks.

—Let's not get carried away.

—Where's my hunting knife?

Mom went and fetched it. Dad knelt and gripped the groundhog's hind legs.

—At least it's a female, you're not out ten bucks yet.

He slit the animal open—he had to jerk and saw.

—I'll be goddamned. Look, Helen. Boys.

Uncle Don put his arms around Jay's shoulders and mine, some people did it easily, drawing us closer. I held onto his leg and he let me. The groundhog's belly spilled a bolus of half-digested grass ... bitter and eternal as tears.

—Ten bucks, coming up.

Dad cleaned his knife in the lawn, then poured drinks. Mom, beginning to show through the rye, looked from Dad to the corpse.

—Don't leave the bloody thing there! Am I supposed to clean it up? That it?

—Does it have to be done this second, dear?

—You watch.

I stepped through the fence, went off and killed another. It got part way down and I had to work it out with a stick. I carried it with my other sock. I hated the warmth it gave off, the crumbs of earth stuck to its bloodied fur. I hated its slack, buck-toothed grin and its bulk, the weight of loss.

Dad leapt up and came to the fence again. Uncle Don whistled.

—One Winchester, coming up.

—Christ, another? What a hunter! Aren't you?

I was telling Val about it before keep-lock.

—Funny the way the first ones made him proud. So, especially, did the crow. The first ones affected me, too, made me feel bad. Then it didn't matter so much. I shot ten that same day, but Dad never got around to the deer rifle.

—Least you got a nice Cooney out of the deal. One day you'll pass it on to your own boys.

—Jay ended up with the Cooney.

THIS morning someone set fire to the trash drum. The air was sharp with cold and the men huddled round. I found myself next to the Hound. His rash had spread, pants were falling down, he wasn't wearing socks. When he held out his hands to the fire he looked like something out of the Depression.

—Winter seems to come sooner every year.

The Hound rubbed his hands in the flames.

—Give me Florida. One time in Miami they had this convention of shoe retailers and I knocked over a hotel room. I struck it rich—there were half a dozen quality stones on the dresser. I don't know what they were worth but I moved one ring for three thousand. I read in the paper where the cops said a quarter-million, so somewhere in between.

—When I got lucky I used to like a fix and a woman. Go to the Holiday Inn, something along those lines. Not plush, but comfortable. I liked to cook up and be attended to by the lady. When it all came together I was not part of this world. They say you can't get off the stuff but I never found that. I only used it on special occasions, as I say, between times I never touched it.

—So I rent a car in Miami, Ford product I recall, not a Thunderbird, nothing flashy, just a means of transportation. I buy a woman and we take a room in a motor inn in Coral Gables. I have four or five fixes and I figure I'll lay low a couple days and enjoy myself. You don't want to stay longer in those places in case they start noticing you never go out, phone in your plate number. I order up ice and so forth only like an idiot I've left my piece on the night table. Bellhop spots it—I can see he isn't too happy. I give him a good tip but you never know.

—Me and the lady have ourselves a time except the air-conditioning is on the fritz. August, maybe September. Gets hot and humid down there and we can't get fresh air. The windows are the kind that don't open and I don't want to call the desk because I'm in no condition. I tape the glass and remove it, intending to report it as an accident and pay damages when I'm straight.

—Next thing there's troopers in riot gear surrounding the motel. Everybody else has been evacuated, there's me and the lady in the whole place! They're calling up with bullhorns, 'Throw out your weapons, arms raised, you're surrounded, we got gas.' I flush the dope. I go out, I may be crazy but I'm not stupid, vice versa, whichever way it goes. They take me and the lady in. She tells them I kidnapped her. They've got a sheet on her and don't buy that shit. Me, I swear up and down I'm an addict.

—They check me out on a number of counts, including, ironically, the grand larceny, but I've got no stones and I've stashed the money. They can't make me but they're dying to. I'm worried they're going to press the unregistered weapon, which sounds Mickey Mouse but some judges will sting you. Fortunately I get the shakes which leads them to buy the junkie business and put me in a treatment centre instead of the grinder even though, as I say, I can take the shit or leave it.

—Well, at the centre I go through the methadone program. A dash each morning with my apple juice— strange, I thought, we're in the heart of orange-juice country, one of the guys said he laid Anita Bryant when she was starting out, but apparently they'd had a cold winter and lost a lot of the crop and they'd already contracted to sell tons of the shit to Saudi Arabia, place like that.

—After a while I come to like my morning cocktail a great deal. I don't enjoy getting less of it, I want more. By the time they let me out I'm craving the shit but I know better than go after it on the street. I only cook up on special occasions, as I say.

—You're wondering what I'm doing here? Well, I come up a few years ago because I didn't like what was happening down there. Development, condominiums spoiling the view, plus the crime rate. Terrible. Parts of Miami keep out of if you're white, believe me, get down that way remember what I told you.

—Also the motor inn had launched a suit against me for loss of revenue suffered during the siege—that's what they called it, a siege, like Leningrad or something. Plus damages for harm to the reputation of the place. You'd think I was talking about the Ritz when it was a dime-a-dozen motor inn, a glorified motel. Comfortable enough, you know, but nothing out of the ordinary.

The Hound put his hands in his pockets and hunched his bony shoulders.

—While I'm here I use the shit from time to time. Getting it isn't the problem you might think although like everything else the cost of blindfolds goes up. I find this institution a very dull place despite the work, recreation, rehabilitation, and P.D. programs, so I hit myself up to pass the time of day, though I'm not an addict in the conventional sense and I don't believe the shit is addictive like they say, least not if you don't already have psychological problems ... which you, judging by appearances, don't have.

He extended a closed fist.

—Cook it if you want—I'll show you if you don't know, no obligation. I find things go easier, that's all, if you decide you'd like it on a regular basis we can maybe work something out.

The Hound held out his hands, washing them in fire.

—I want to stress I'm not a dope-pusher, a drug-dealer, seducer of the innocent. I don't fit the stereotype. I'm not after more than I need, I don't rip nobody off. A matter of pulling together, all of us, helping one another out. I don't mean to sound like a Communist but we're equals here, got the same problems, face the same obstacles. Long as we're here, all we've got is each other. Take this if you want, don't if you don't. You're free to make the choice.

Free to make the choice.

HONEYMOON bridge. Val's not good at trick games and hates to lose but—given the tobacco he wins at chess—he can hardly refuse. I hate his smoking and yet I've cut back on cigarettes so he can have mine. He got me lifting weights because he thought it unhealthy to be fat. Now he needs prodding and I can't wait. He doesn't understand why I object to his medication but broke his habit in deference to the strength of my feeling. It bothers him that I see Yoshino but he's reluctant to say so. It bothers me that it bothers him but I'm reluctant to say so. We badger and humour and finesse one another —everything by indirection—Mom and Dad.

Today holiday tinsel was strung in the mess. How about lights on the guard towers, a giant Santa on the roof of administration? And spineless arrangements of carols Angela and I used to sing with her family. The carols bring home in a piercing way that another year is coming. Anger swells at each turn of season, but Christmas is the keenest reminder—the life that has harmed us is proceeding oblivious. The world seems no less criminal than the inhabitants of its prisons, yet the world rings in change . . . we're locked in static lives.

—Next month is January. The year you and me get out.

—Just because you're eligible doesn't mean you get out. Hearts.

He led a diamond when he should have led trump.

—Hell kind of outlook is that?

—Why get your hopes up when you might be disappointed?

I took the trick . . . he slapped down a card.

—Damn! Everybody turns corners. Some people take them on four wheels, some two, some hit the wall—we all hit the wall, you aren't the only one. Wish to hell you'd snap out of it. Moping around.

It stings when he dresses me down . . . I took another trick.

—Being eligible doesn't mean you automatically make it.

—Open your eyes! Wake up!

—I wish I knew how I'll deal with people who knew me and Angela. See?—thinking ahead to being out, otherwise known as optimism.

—Oh no, don't start that shit, talking figure eights. Me, I don't know where I'll go, what I'll do . . . debt up to my ass. Insurance company'll be all over me the minute

I step out, tax people, everybody.

—And you give me hell. I've got the rest, I've got spades—you're void.

He was glad the game was over—returned a pack of my cigarettes—stepped out to look quickly up and down the tier.

—Who you looking for?

—Tonio. I owe him again. Funny, huh? Funny how it turns around? First you can't wait. Then you start thinking . . .

—Dear, I'd like you to meet my parole officer . . .

—Maybe that's not what I'm talking about . . .

—What are you talking about?

Val broke into a slow grin.

—I got great news for you, Monkey. Guys on A—I talked them into letting you in.

—In what?

—Been putting it together a year now—since before my transfer. It's no Boomerang stunt.

—I don't know that I want in.

Panic touched his face, leaving about the eyes a wounded look I pretended not to see. He fumbled with a cigarette.

—Think of it—nice charred steak, pink inside. Bottle of wine. Baked potato, sour cream, chives, bacon bits. You like those bacon bits? Salad with blue cheese. Dessert—what's your favourite dessert?

—A thousand things can go wrong, Val. Christ, you tell me to wake up. You'll be out this summer.

—Being eligible doesn't mean you make it, said so yourself. Everything you done for me, writing parole letters, teaching me to read—I wanted to do something for you. If the hacks walk out this place'll be a zoo. Listen, think it was easy, getting you in?

—I told you, I'm not sure I want in.

He turned away, grasped the bars. The flag on his back was inflamed, his voice barely audible in the din of the cellhouse:

—You are in.

—How have you been?

—Somebody offered me heroin.

—Did you accept?

—I shared a highrise with an addict once. Nausea, constrictions, pacing, puking, insomnia, kneebends, retching, back and forth, back and forth. No thanks.

—What else has been happening?

—A dilemma. But I'm not sure if I can discuss it.

—Tell me and we'll see if we can discuss it.

—It has to do with security.

—Will talking it through help you understand your own situation?

—I think so.

—Well, this is what I'm interested in and what I'm paid for. What is said here remains here. Period.

—Someone has architectural drawings of the cellhouse and the administration building. He's found a

route as far as the south wall. There's a duty guard who
can be bought, another inmate with money. These guys,
in concert, have the means of getting out. Soon, while
there's snow. They'd wear bedsheets and use them to
do the wall while the guard's picking his nose. Val's got
me in on it, figured I'd want to go with them.

—Do you?

—This place is deadly.

—We might discuss what you'll need to feel at ease
outside—to feel you aren't in another type of prison.
You might consider that question as you consider the
possibility of escape.

—If I were to escape, I'd spend every hour worrying.
But to get out now ...

—What about the pressure of being pursued?

—There's pressure here, too. Besides, people have
succeeded in taking on new identities.

—That's a fascinating notion, changing identity. In a
sense it's what we're working on. I think you'll have to
change your interior identity before you'll feel comfortable, whether now or on your release.

—The other thing escape would do is remove the need
of facing certain things ...

—Would that solve your conflict with your old life?

—Most guys who talk about escaping are impractical.
They're not only criminals, they're unsuccessful ones.
If they were successful they'd be stockbrokers and
lawyers and politicians. But this has been planned in a
methodical way. I think they have a chance.

—Let's talk about the identity you'd take on if you
escaped. You'd have a degree of choice. What man
would you choose to be?

—The opposite of what I am now. I'd stop being
middle-class, brown-haired, overweight.

—Overweight? You seem very fit to me. Anyway, let your imagination move. What would you change in your appearance, your personality, your way of being? Tell me in detail the person you'd become.

—Well, my body type and gait would change. I'd become strong and fit, instead of soft and weak. My features would change—the colour of my eyes, the shape of my nose, the scar on my forehead.

—Your personality—how would that change? Describe the character of the freed Owen, the one you envision ...

—Someone who drew vitality from life. I'd live in the present.

—Relations with women?

—It's hopeless to think of the sort of thing I had with Angela.

—Would the new Owen want to get into such a relationship again?

—This is stupid. I'm not approaching this as a fantasy—I'm considering it.

—I know. But I'm asking you to play with me—a game. I want to know about the Owen who escapes. The new Owen. Who is he?

—Someone free of iron bars, concrete, steel mesh, electric locks, closed-circuit cameras, uniformed men. The slow grind of days. Free of all the things that imprison him.

—Are there other constraints he'd be freed of?

—I know I'll never really be free of Angela, but why can't ... But that's not what I wanted to talk about. I need advice.

—I don't think it's for me to offer advice. You'll be out eventually, one way or other, and I'm concerned about who will be out there and what needs to happen first.

That's why I want you to picture how you'd like the new Owen to be.

—For Christ's sake, don't you get it? I have to think right now whether I want to be part of this. That's more important than what kind of person I'll be.

—You think it's off the point, but I think this will prove more important. We're only talking for an hour— humour me, why don't you? You'll make the decision, I can't advise you. That's not what I'm here for and I don't think it's what you come for.

—I'm sure the Owen who escapes would be very different from the one who waits to be paroled, who's told good luck by the warden.

—If you decide what your world is going to be, the way to get out may follow from that.

—You make it sound as if escape would be cowardice.

—There will be things to face either way. But different things.

—I've never understood why someone would walk into the police station and say, 'I did it. Two years ago.' A guy here did that—Palumbo—vehicular manslaughter. Why escape if you find yourself tortured by a need to confess?

—I'd like to help you achieve the changes that will let you be happy with who you are. I don't see how else you'll ever be at peace.

—I can picture going . . . then what? A little money, a weapon, warm clothing, the names of a few people. What next?

—This place is temporary. Why not think of it as something that both constrains and, in a funny way, shelters and protects? A cocoon—a safe place in which you can evolve and prepare to emerge.

—Val's put us both in an awkward spot. When you

know about something like this, you're in. Backing out
would take explaining.

—Once you're out you'll have pleasures and freedoms
denied you. But ask whether that's what you need most
right now.

—I wouldn't mind sitting in Rome, eating pasta with
smoked salmon, ogling the women and drinking wine.
Then asking whether I really needed all this.

—Wonderful, Owen. That's funny.

—I worry that one thing that makes me want to go is
Val. That's also one of the things that makes me want
to stay—I don't want to be tied to anybody. And
cowardice . . . I'm afraid of going. I'm afraid not going
would put me in jeopardy . . . Val, too. God, I'm afraid of
Tonio—he knows Val and I didn't vote for him, knows I
hate him. I'm afraid of so many things I can't even say
what they all are.

—You might use your journal to try and say what
they are.

—It takes courage to say, 'To hell with this hole.'

—Staying, committing yourself, takes courage of a
different kind.

—Very inspiring, Ron. I see you every two weeks.
This plus my journal is all I'm able to do for myself.

—I believe you can do much more, by watching
carefully. Seeing how you create your world.

—Such a deadening place. So brutally predictable.

—Could you have predicted Val would offer you a
chance to escape? Or that someone would say, 'Shoot
this, Owen. Escape the pain.' Are there people here who
have escaped, and then come back?

—Boomerang has escaped custody twenty times . . . I
suppose you could say he's never actually escaped. So
they say.

—What happens when he's outside?

—Breaks into a house, robs a gas station, goes on a bender. He's spent so much of his life inside he can't handle anything else ... But we're going off on tangents. I came here for direction. Stop being a blank wall. Tell me what you think.

—Let's do this, Owen—let's switch. Be me. I'm Owen and you're Ron. Something's brewing, the day is drawing close. Should I go?

—'Only you can answer that. You must do as you decide.' How's that for a psychiatrist's answer?

—Come on, Ron, take it seriously. Stop being a blank wall.

—All right. Personally, I don't think it's a good idea, if only because the chance of success is slim.

—It's a good plan, believe me. People have spent a long time putting it together.

—Even if it does work, they're going to spend time and manpower hunting you. They take these things very, very seriously.

—What do you think I should do then, Ron?

—Forget it. If your long-term goal is to reconcile yourself with the world you'll be returning to, I don't think escaping is the way.

—Val—what do I say to him?

—Maybe he'll also decide it's a bad idea.

—You seem to have answered your own question. Let's go back to the Owen who walks out, perhaps this summer. Breathe deeply to relax, then tell me anything that comes to mind. I'll work on your shoulders.

—I don't want him to be one of those dismal people who bear helpless witness to their own lives.

—That's good. That's wonderful. What else?

—I want him to say what he thinks—the opposite of the way he was with Angela—like Dad, unable to talk about what was important. I want him to be able to convey things directly, instead of turning them inside out so they show in a negative way.

—Does the new Owen have spiritual values? What is his purpose on this planet?

—I could always justify not opening up to other people. To more things. Possibilities.

—Do you really believe the new Owen will be capable of all this?

—Christ, Ron, if I can survive this ... You know something? I feel I'm moving in that direction. If nothing else, time is removing me from the old Owen toward the new.

—I'm beginning to have a clear sense of that progression. How else do you imagine Owen? What else can you tell me about him?

—See that plane crash on the news? The man on the ice who kept passing the life ring to someone else? Five times he passed it on. I dreamt I was the man, I awoke thinking, 'I'm capable of things I thought were beyond me. How marvellous!'

—That might be a good place to start next time. Before you go, I'd like to repeat what I said. Whatever passes between us remains here. Whatever you decide, think it through carefully.

—I'm not going. My problem is what to say to Val, how he'll explain.

—Remember the other side, too, the strength required to stay and work things through. Val may see that yours too is an act of courage. They all may.

—Great. Picture it, Ron. Val explaining to a rapist, an illiterate kidnapper and a bank robber that we're not going after all—his friend has things to work through with his psychiatrist.

I'M AFRAID because this life, which once seemed dread-fully circumscribed, has come to seem normal.

I'm afraid because I'm among men who inflict on themselves blue wounds: Lucy, Maude, Claire, Raise Hell, White is Right, Born to Die, LOVE on one set of knuckles, HATE on the other. Who view transgression of the law as liberation of the spirit. Who have little on which to base their self-respect except their capacity for doing harm. Afraid I've become one of them.

I'm afraid because it seems the possibilities of my life will never match my aspirations, though I can't say what my aspirations are, and I'm afraid that finding out will be a disillusionment—using sex to serve a yearning and discovering the yearning wasn't for sex.

I'm afraid because Val gives me complete access to himself. Because I sometimes have a longing for his company so sudden and violent it resembles a seizure.

I'm afraid that any effort to overcome this stupefac-tion will prove futile, like starting backwards from a hundred as the anaesthetist pricks his needle.

I'm afraid because I hate Tonio and he knows it.

I'm afraid the world is changing and I'm not.

I'm afraid because in this place what you claim to be will sooner or later be tested.

I'm afraid of what Ron's going to find out about me. What I'm going to find out about myself.

SAD news from Mom: *Phoned Jay, tried to phone you but they wouldn't put it through. I said it's his uncle and they said uncles aren't immediate family. He was in San Diego on vacation, he and his friend Len both killed. Terrible terrible shock. At least he went quickly. Poor Wilf.*

And poor Mom—her best friend. Dad made fun of Wilf's vanities in the same disparaging tone he used on Mom. She was not physically attractive and her body lost definition earlier than most women. He hastened her transformation into a middle-aged, asexual thing.

—Notice anything? . . . A new dress, you clod.

—Where's the party, dear?

Wilf made an effort for her—concerts and films—she wore the silk scarf or the brooch he'd given her. Gin and tonic in crystal glasses . . . his birthday present. Articles and recipes, annotated and stapled. They talked hours about drapes for the living-room, what china would go with Mom's grandmother's silver. Dad had no opinion on trivial matters, contempt for those who did.

Wilf took his avuncular duties with good humour and was unfailingly kind to Jay and me. His birthday gifts were thoughtful and witty—a paper punch inscribed with my name and the words PAY UP!, a tie patterned in diamonds during Jay's passion for baseball. He invited us to his apartment—tiny, meticulous, decorated with huge posters of Montgomery Clift, Kim Novak, James

Dean. His bedroom was filled with books on film, his coffee table covered with glass paperweights, his kitchen wall hung with teaspoons from all over the world.

Wilf's phone had a long cord ... he took the phone while he got me a refill of ginger ale. Held the receiver with his shoulder—cut cheese into little cubes and stuck toothpicks in each. When he hung up he apologized for having been so long—the phone rang again— he gave a long-suffering look, but the calls didn't really irritate him.

—I do not want to see her again ... I know you did, Carston—I was with you ... long in the tooth then ... I realize she's a living legend. I must go, my nephew's visiting.

Five minutes later he warned the next caller that Carston was trying to enlist people for the opera.

—What have you seen lately? ... Oh, that's wonderful! Did you hear Bobby on Sandy Dennis's latest? 'A rabbit getting over chemotherapy.' Isn't that Bobby?

I asked Dad why he didn't like Wilf. Dad gave a sneering laugh—'Wilf's a flake.' To me he seemed mysterious and fascinating. I began skipping school, forging Mom's signature. I headed for the area where Wilf lived. There was a pool hall—my excuse. Really I was drawn by the strangely narcotic ambience of his world.

With Mom's help Wilf had bought a black convertible —one day I spotted it on Yonge Street. A huge, brassy blonde sat beside him, eyes heavily outlined in mascara, thick arms protruding from a black evening dress. Rush hour! Another time I saw him with two other men, all in the front seat, all wearing short-sleeved shirts rolled to the shoulder. I began playing hooky every day, eager for my next glimpse. He turned the tables on me. One day I crossed at a light—there was the black convertible, polished to a glittering sheen, waiting for me. There was a twinkle in Wilf's eye, but I didn't know if I could trust him.

—I don't suppose you need a ride to school.

—I wasn't feeling too well. I feel better now.

—Hop in—we'll go for a ride.

He reached to open the passenger door.

—What you wish to tell Mom and Dad about this happy coincidence I'll leave to your discretion, shall I?

It was his way of giving me his blessing—thereafter we shared a bond. I had the sense that Wilf, unlike Dad, felt closer to me than to Jay. I was always urging Mom to invite him over. She was fond of him—a different person when he was there—I wondered why she'd married Dad instead. I imagined how wonderful it would be to have Wilf as a father, then wondered if, in fact, he was my father. I became convinced—it explained everything. It explained why, when Dad was around, Wilf stayed away. Coming home during an organizing campaign was for Dad an undisguised disappointment, and the presence of his brother only deepened his gloom. Two men in love (in their own ways) with the same woman. We saw Wilf in bursts— almost daily for several weeks, then hardly at all.

Only once did Mom betray anything but affection for him ... the year Jay got his licence. Dad was away, trying to organize potash workers, and at every opportunity Mom took Jay and me to the farm. Gazebo, really— three rooms, a pump in the kitchen, outhouse in the trees—but it stood on a hill and had raspberries, black walnuts, surprises in the cistern—we loved it. Mom bought it with the small inheritance from her mother.

Between our papers and her volunteer work—stuffing envelopes for Save the Children, knocking on doors for March of Dimes—we never had long. Came and left at odd hours, a day or two when we could. One evening when we reached the dirt road Mom let Jay take the wheel—he had his learner's permit. I had to open the gate, which was heavy and gouged a rut. Jay started off without me, kicking up pebbles and dust; then stopped and backed up, practising reverse. We were surprised to find two cars under the chestnut tree—one the black convertible. When we got out, Wilf appeared suddenly to greet us.

—What a pleasant surprise . . . I thought you weren't coming until the weekend.

—The boys found someone to do their routes.

—We've had a lovely picnic dinner—just about to leave.

—No rush.

Behind their words was an intense exchange I couldn't understand . . . Mom was pleasant enough, but cool. Wilf's eyes hung on hers, asking something. Jay and I unloaded the trunk . . . rounded the house and saw seven or eight men at the picnic table. Candles and bottles of wine. Wilf introduced each friend in turn.

—Lynn works in the land-registry office with me. And this is Pat, an old friend from New York.

They said how delighted they were to meet Wilf's family . . . gathering things, not wasting time. They piled into the cars and set off. We stood by the cistern and watched their headlights cut the darkness as the cars bounced down the hill. They waved—Jay and I waved back—Mom did too, but her jaw was set, her eyes seemed to glisten, she might have been hypnotized. Her lip quivered—anger, frustration, what?

—You know about men like that, don't you?

She tried to say it evenly—her voice had a gaping hole it in.

—They're a bunch of queers, and your uncle's one of them.

THIS morning a cell came vacant ... an hour later someone was through processing, a tall, sour albino. He hadn't been detailed and remained on the tier for afternoon shift. At yard he kept to himself, walking round and round, shoulders hunched, hands in his pockets. Going for chow Tonio gave him the smile.

—What's your name there, Whitey?

—My name's Fuck You.

Tonio chuckled and strolled away. Tonight he didn't sit in—neither did Billie Holiday. Vernon played, the Hound, Giles, others drifted in and out. The albino wanted to sit in but hadn't earned the right to ask. He stood behind me, smoking, shifting his weight from foot to foot. Made me nervous, I was about to say something when Billie, bright-eyed, all politeness, tapped his shoulder.

—Come with me a minute, man? Just take a minute, friend of mine wants to acks you something.

The albino, suspicious, looked to us for a clue. I kept

my attention on the game. Billie led him to the end cell
and, when the albino balked, shoved him in.

Bite on this, prolly come in handy ... the lopsided
smile, penis jacking itself up in little knocks. Holiday
Inn, screaming rats. Drop the towel! Throw it at him,
spit in his face, anything! Silence, worse than the
silence of a mute ... then Billie's laughter, like breaking
glass—the whole tier had gone quiet. Gradually other
voices arose, festive sounds that merged with the noise
of the cellhouse. The albino finally emerged, his face
smeared with blood and humiliation.

—Welcome to C-Range, Fuck You!

I tried not to watch him return to his cell, hunched
over, holding himself and sobbing.

I can't go against Tonio, challenge the order. He'd
break me in pieces or have someone do it. I can't say
anything, reveal my feeling in any way. At best I'd get a
careless smile. What if I moved across his ledger from
all right to not?

Later, in the pit, I mentioned it to Val.

—Nothing you can do about it, Monkey. Nothing I can
do or anybody else—if it wasn't him be the next one like
him.

The reassurance I wanted, yet it failed to reassure
me. Val racked the dumbbells—cinched his belt,
chalked his hands, adjusted his footing as he bent to
test the weight. He straightened up again.

—Some advice. Worry about yourself. Plenty to handle on your own.

—Know something, Val? I hate it when you start.

—I'm telling you what I know about being in the
joint. Lesson number one. Be self-contained.

—Shut your eyes. Plug your ears.

—People get fucked over on the street, Monkey,

you're not going to change that. All you can do is stay clear of it.

—Confucius say.

—I'm going to do standing press ... not sets, reps. Many reps as I can without breaking form. I'm going to go forty below maximum and see how many I can do without breaking form. I'm going to concentrate on form and put reps out of my mind. Count the reps.

—Count your own fucking reps.

Val sat on the bench beside me, draped an arm over my shoulder ... squeezed, waiting for me to meet his eye. I studied the tattoo and scars on his forearm, layer on layer of scar tissue ...

—What's wrong with you, Monkey? You don't look so good.

His brow was deeply furrowed, his eyes bright with longing to understand my distress—intensity that, focused on me, makes me cringe, and yet wonder how I managed without it. I jumped up, all business, and stood at the rack, deciding how much weight to use— chalked my hands—spoke as if dictating a letter.

—I've decided I'm not going with them, Val. I've thought this through. I don't think you should go, either.

WONDERFUL surprise! Card from Miriam—I assumed she'd shut me out of her life. She wished me a joyous holiday and told me she had won a symphony job. She must have been selected over hundreds of very talented musicians. It's easy to believe in retrospect but I did glimpse talent and determination where her own family saw only irresponsibility—even Angela was short with her. I was like an older brother, but with a better perspective. Her success seems a vindication of us both.

The first time I saw her she had returned from the pool, a shivering child wrapped in a beach towel. Her lips were purple, her teeth chattered ... she wouldn't go change because she idolized Angela, didn't want to miss a moment. Angela and Sandy were solicitous and worrisome. Growing up, Miriam happily fulfilled their expectations—left the stove burning, forgot to close the refrigerator, ran the bath to overflowing. Forgoing the usual modes of rebellion for a more subtle approach? The Berrys were a deliberately close family ... Miriam set herself apart. I liked her very much.

—Mother, these should go into albums. That's something Miriam could get for your birthday—albums. Listening, Hammy?

At Sandy's house the photos were in albums, humorously captioned. The pad by the phone was divided into quarter-hours, recipes were typed and filled on index cards, the water in the toilet bowl was bright blue. Angela had something of the same fastidiousness, urged that we keep the house spotless. Toward the end this became the focus for all our discontent—the closet door left open, shaving cream not put away.

—Who's this tall girl?

—What's that?

—Who's the tall girl?

—Please, Hammy, don't get fingerprints all over.

Miriam was exasperating to Angela, a puzzle to their

parents. Mr Berry didn't understand why smacks between the shoulder blades failed to correct her posture
... why she went jogging at midnight.

—Why, the tall one is Aunt Caroline, you know that.

—The one who played the violin?

—What's that, dear?

—She was the violinist?

—Don't yell, Hammy. Aunt Caroline played the cello.

Mr and Mrs Berry, Sandy, and Angela were all
sensible, Miriam the opposite. It is not sensible for a
striking young woman to hitchhike alone, or to agree—
first year—to rent a house sight unseen with five other
students, four of them strangers. She specialized in
running out of gas, got a ticket every time she parked.
The family held its collective breath ... the full-fledged
calamity never came. When she lost her wallet it was
returned. She drove home through snowstorms that put
other people in the ditch.

Once music became her focus she needed little else ...
never seemed to have to wrestle with questions of who
she was or wanted to be. The flute gave complete
answers. She discovered it in high school and became
devoted. For hours on end she shut herself in her
bedroom and played scales, the notes struggling free
like stunned bees—one of those sounds you simply had
to tune out. (Why couldn't I tune out the sparrows?
Why can't I tune out Vernon's moaning?) For months
we paid no attention ... one day Angela and I set aside
magazines at the same instant. Rising through the floor
was not discordant effort but the burbling tremolo of a
hatched bird demanding to be fed. It was music—raw
and beautiful and bespeaking the life to come. Over the
years Miriam's music contributed inestimably to my
sense—the sense I had in the warmth of Mr Berry's

well-made fire—of being home at last. In a strange way, contributed even more than Angela did. Someone else's home, perhaps, but it seemed better than the one I came from, or than Angela and I could ever hope to make.

And now, out of the blue, a Christmas card. A portent?

TALKING with Jay today about the role of television ... got remembering our first set, a tiny, black-and-white portable with rabbit ears he bought with money from his paper routes.

—Mom drove me out to a furniture warehouse in the suburbs to pick it out. Did you come with us? I forget.

—Sure I did.

—That's right. You said to Mom, 'Since Jay's buying it, we get to watch what *we* want.'

—And you said, 'We, white man?' Prick. The next year you'd saved enough to buy the Healey. Great little car.

—I needed it for my papers. I had the three best routes in the city—almost three hundred papers every morning. By then you had your own route, didn't you.

—Most days I'd get up with you—you'd drop me at

my bundle. When I'd finish I'd wait in the schoolyard and help you finish. I loved the last street on your last route—huge old trees, deep lots, big houses with nice porches . . . garages in back. We'd stop at the top of the street, remember? You'd turn off the engine and we'd fold the papers and jam them between the seats. Then we'd give the Healey a push . . . it would start down the grade, picking up speed.

—That street has speed bumps now. The trees are gone—Dutch elm disease. Those houses are worth a fortune! Most have been renovated and divided up. The garages have been turned into fancy coach houses. The front lawns have been bricked over and turned into parking space—Audis and BMWs.

—Progress.

—We'd sit up on the back of the seats and fire off papers. You'd backhand them out the passenger side and I'd loop hook shots over my head. We got good at it.

—Every morning you'd say, 'I'll get the doughnuts if you hit every one.' I'd usually make it as far as the bottom. By then the Healey was sifting along. The house I had trouble with was the last one on the north side—what was her name?

—Miss Cronk. Office pay.

—I usually put it in the honeysuckle.

—Tough shot. Her house was set back and the porch was enclosed, remember? Your aim had to be perfect— just miss the jamb and just clear the top step.

—Sometimes we'd stop and I'd go put it on her porch. Usually we didn't bother. Didn't tip at Christmas—all she could do was phone in.

—There'd be a complaint in the bundle next morning. I got as many complaints from her as everybody else put together. She started waiting for us, remember? She'd peek out from behind the curtains. If we missed she'd come out and give us shit.

—We'd be careful for a few days, then I'd land it in the bushes, and before she could get out the door to shake her fist you'd slide down into the seat and pop the clutch. The engine caught with a boom . . . we roared off like bank robbers.

—You took that route over, didn't you. After I started university.

—I kept it till Mom and Dad moved west and I started university. I used to take Angela out on the money I'd saved. And in all the time I had that route the customers never stopped asking about you, know that?

—No kidding.

—I'd go collect and they'd rummage in their purse or their pocket—funny how many people in big houses couldn't come up with two bucks—and they'd say, 'How's Jay? Tell him the Hardacres were asking after him, will you?'

—I didn't know that.

—'He's fine,' I used to say. 'Blind, of course, and he lost his arm in the accident, but otherwise just fine.' I got some looks. I was trying to get a laugh but they never thought it was as funny as I did.

—Too bad about Wilf.

—Did you go out for the funeral?

—Couldn't take time . . . I was never that close to him, not like you.

—He really liked Angela, too—only one in the family who did.

—By the way, O, what do you want me to do with the pearls? Maybe sell them?

—No.

—How come? I know it's none of my business . . .

—But.

—Well, you have this recollection of her, and if you ask me—

—Fuck you. You never liked her.

—I liked her OK . . . just didn't think of her like you do.

—Dad didn't like her, Mom, you. Fuck all of you.

—I didn't like the effect she had on *you*. I hate it that three years later you're still . . . Look, you changed in the time you were with her—moody, stoned half the time. If that's a special relationship, you can have it. Christ, in some ways she's the reason you're here.

—Bullshit! You hated her, Dad hated her, Mom—

—You became part of her family—did she make an effort to get to know me and Sylvia, or Mom and Dad? She was caught up in her own world. Her 'energy.' 'Nurturing' her clients. Helping them 'actualize' their lives. What about your life?

—She was busy, taking courses, reading, she didn't have time. And you think she couldn't sense your disapproval?

—All I'm saying is that you have this idea of her that doesn't fit with what I saw. You thought you had this incredibly free, open, special relationship. She's the one who wanted it, not you. And maybe it looked fine from the outside—young couple, good jobs, nice house—but what was at the core? She didn't want your children, didn't care about your work, wasn't interested in your family . . . she ran around behind your back! I bumped into her once with him. She fucked you around!

—I don't need this shit! Fuck you!

I threw my receiver at the Plexiglas—stormed out— left him sitting there. What's the matter with me? How could I lose it like that? Jay's a rock . . . where would I be without him?

Meanwhile my outburst goes into my file.

CHRISTMAS letter from Marnie. She's been seeing 'a very nice fellow' for almost a year. 'He has a little girl he's been raising on his own for two years. I'm close to her, too.' Marnie doesn't say her communication will now cease altogether but that's the feeling I get. In her gentle disclosure and closing sentence—'I hope in the weeks and months that lie ahead of you'—I read an implicit request that I stop writing her.

I remember Giles telling me, 'It's a slow death in here. You die so little every day that after a while you don't even notice . . .'

Marnie was not the sort of woman to whom I was ordinarily attracted. She was tiny, wore the highest heels I'd ever seen, half-ran everywhere in them. For years she whizzed past my office as if nothing could stop her short of an open-field tackle. She popped in half a dozen times a day. I welcomed her appearances— everyone did. She was lively and straightforward and knew how to exit—popped out as abruptly as she popped in. If she'd been a waitress she'd have told you the soup was lousy and the quiche made yesterday. Then, if you hadn't made up your mind, scooted off. There were things to do and Marnie was eager to do them. Once in a while, at her desk, when she'd finished one thing but not yet started the next, a wave of melancholy swept across her face—this was a great part of her charm. I'm sure she made a wonderful assistant ... efficient, loyal, competent but not threatening. She kept McEleney organized, covered for him beautifully. He'd come in late and find her gaily chatting with his appointment, who'd be unaware of the time.

Marnie's appearance as remarkable. Her clothes were expensive and well chosen, if not made on her own machine. Her silk blouse always had two buttons undone. Solid, striking colours set off black hair so carefully shaped it looked as if it could be removed like a helmet. Her face made me wonder why she wasn't prettier. Her lipstick matched the polish on her almond-shaped nails. Her eyes swam with life—dark and large, balanced by shadow and mascara and enlarged by the bulging sheen of contact lenses, gathering in all they registered. Later, in bed, her eyes sometimes seemed so voracious that looking in them almost gave me a physical sensation of falling, being drawn in.

I began to feel attracted to her soon after McEleney took over. I wonder if my feeling had its roots in his manner—innuendo, little gifts, the way his hand touched the small of her back as they went through a door. It was probably his way of acknowledging his attraction and dissipating it, but it bothered me. Her playing along so readily, so happily, made me want her. What began as resentment of him turned into longing for her.

Other people seemed to do it so casually ... I needed a strategy. I decided I'd ask Marnie to have a drink after work one day. In the course of chatting I'd discover if she was seriously involved. If not, as I suspected, I'd confess my desire and see what happened. It seemed crude and awkward in the contemplation but at least, I told myself, it had the virtue of directness.

Late one afternoon Marnie, McEleney, and I were the last in the office. I'd popped down to the Xerox room. Returning, I heard her cheerily assuring someone she didn't mind, she understood, she had lots to do. Her bearing, usually pert and erect, seemed slumped and defeated. She set down the phone, paralysed a moment, her vitality turning to utter desolation.

—I couldn't help overhearing.

—Oh! You scared me.

—If you're not busy, why don't we have dinner? Angela's having dinner with her partner. We'll have fun.

—Aren't you sweet! Coming to the rescue like that! I'd love to.

Such gratitude, such desperate relief ... in that instant I saw the reason she wasn't prettier and the way to her bed. She could not bear to be alone.

We went to a Greek place, traded gossip, waved to people we knew, laughed at the gyrations of a belly-dancer who by North American standards could have stood to lose fifty pounds. Ate grilled scampi and left potted. I drove her up the Parkway to a compound of buildings like upended egg cartons. She gave me a peck ... we agreed to do it again.

Over a couple of months we had dinner five or six times and the question was no longer whether we'd sleep together but what we needed to get clear first. We began talking at length on the phone, choosing restaurants where we were unlikely to run into acquaintances. She insisted we split the bill. Laughter and drunkenness—the goodnight kiss became many kisses. She was a listener as well as a talker and we exchanged confidences. She told me about her upbringing on a farm in Nova Scotia, to which she returned at Christ-

mas. Her cats, her astrologer, her men. Her last lover
had been an older fellow on the verge of divorce ...
finally, after two years, he told her he couldn't do it to
his children, though they were in their twenties. A
rueful, self-mocking smile:

—That's one mistake I won't make again. I've often
wondered what makes a couple marry ... or decide not
to marry.

Angela hovered over these dinners—one of us was
careful to pronounce her name early on. I told Marnie
we'd not married because we were eager to retain a
sense of choice and individuality. I told her I loved
Angela, hoped always to be close to her. But we were, I
said, more like brother and sister. It seemed misleading
then but not in retrospect.

—Does she know you see me for dinner?

I had told Angela about the belly-dancing dinner, and
this one, but not the many in between.

—It's not a traditional relationship. We live our own
lives.

Marnie considered a moment—popped the last bit of
lamb in her mouth—nodded. We wasted no time on
coffee or dessert. I came to a stop at her building.

—Would you like to come up?

The taste and expense with which her apartment had
been done surprised me. Wool broadloom ... Italian-
looking sofas at right angles behind a table inlaid with
ivory and mother of pearl ... Tiffany lamps ... Japanese
prints. A lacquered screen separated the dining area
from a kitchen with every gadget. Rows of silver
candlesticks, all shapes and sizes, filled the win-
dowsills. I wondered how much was the legacy of the
older lover. Marnie read my mind.

—Being someone's secretary isn't all I do.

—You're a courtesan, too? You won the lottery. Your grandfather invented Pampers.

It turned out she had given evenings and weekends to a cosmetics sales scheme. She had her own territory of field agents, each of whom had a string of field reps, each of whom had sales reps who pushed the cosmetics at get-togethers and tried to recruit sufficient innocents that they themselves moved up the line. Marnie related it all in good humour ... well she might. She took South American vacations and kept emeralds in a safe-deposit box. On her bedroom walls were Miró lithographs.

This secret life was not the last of her surprises. Unclothed she seemed frail, more modest of bust and ample of bottom than she made herself appear. Her embrace was wonderfully firm—she was immediately passionate—generous in ways that shocked me. Fastening on me with all her senses, she unlocked something. When I was on top, pinning her to the bed, her legs worked feverishly, as if she were struggling out of a hole. Once she had found her pitch she seemed to hold it indefinitely. Loving Marnie was like trying to embrace a lion cub at the moment it gets its first scent of the kill.

She put on a kimono ... kissed me rather primly. I left glowing, astonished, guilty. Her depths had frightened me, like shining a flashlight down a well. I stepped in the elevator—this had to stop—the first, exhilarating as it had been, was the last. Fervour was something Angela and I had never had and if not with Angela I didn't want it at all. It was late but not too late. I studied myself by the dome light in the rear-view mirror.

I know you as I know my soul ...

I resolved to confess the moment I got home—and began a split life, knowing what I ought to do, wanting to do it, incapable of doing it. I, who always heeded the rational, nodded agreement at its demands but was unable to carry them out.

CHRISTMAS, dry turkey, another year of my life. Val intends to sign up for conversational French ... gave him my French-English dictionary. He worries about athlete's foot and someone stole his shower sandals ... gave him mine. He gave me a cigarette lighter he won from the Hound and a metal contraption he made in the shop. I turned it in my hands.

—Impressive, whatever it is.

He held his cigarette in his teeth:

—Pull a wet sock over here, squeeze this till it clicks. It's a dryer. Rinse out a sock and this'll stretch it enough it'll dry overnight.

Angela's father in his workshop ... sign on the door: NO SPYING. For her waiting-room one year he stripped and repaired captain's chairs. He cut open a barbecue, screened the hole, welded on a vent, and attached a manual pump so the charcoal could be fanned. He made bird-feeders and cheeseboards of hickory and a hinged gizmo for pulling off boots. Most of the presents under

the Berrys' tree were made. Miriam spent weeks turning out candles, macramé plant holders, hot pads made
of clothes-pegs. Mrs Berry ducked into her sewing-room
at odd moments and made outfits for the girls, dressing-
gowns for Mr Berry and me, a jogging-suit for Miriam.
Christmas morning was ceremonious. The recipient
and giver of each gift had to be divined from a riddle.
Wrapping paper was recycled—shrieks at the picture of
chicken legs crossed like a fat woman's. Mr Berry sat in
his stuffed chair, jumping up to snap Polaroids, putting
on his spectacles to watch them fill in.

All the girls played the piano uncommonly well.
Evenings ended with tea and carols. Sandy's husband
Henry was a computer salesman with a confident tenor.
He sang 'Good King Wenceslas' and 'Joy to the World' as
if being recorded ... the girls wove clever harmonies.
The voices of Mr and Mrs Berry fitted together especi-
ally well. Mr Berry—a man who put his arms around
his daughters and raised his voice in song. I heard Dad
sing twice—both times drunk, both times 'Solidarity
Forever.'

I hadn't tested my voice since childhood but this was
something I wanted in on. I knew the first verses of
most carols. Self-conscious at the start, but no one
noticed ... I was able after a while to let go. My voice
was true and mingled sweetly with the others as we
stood round the piano. By then my parents had moved
west—I never again spent Christmas with them.

When Jay and I were young Christmas had an aura of
painful suspense. Would Dad appear? On Christmas
Eve we decorated the tree. Shoeboxes of glass balls and
paper bells and strings of coloured lights. Jay tested
bulbs—stood back to direct Mom and me.

—Do it from the top, O. If you start at the bottom and

it doesn't go all the way you'll have to unwind the whole thing.

We looped a long, fuzzy silver caterpillar, draped laces of tinsel. Mom set out presents—'From Santa' or 'Love Mom and Dad'—always in her writing. Jay and I retrieved our hidden gifts.

On Christmas morning there would be more presents beneath the tree, uniformly gift-wrapped—Dad had made it. Who cared if the turtleneck was too small, if Jay had quit hockey the year he got skates, if I already had a watch? It was Dad, dependable as Santa Claus. When we woke him he seemed happy to see us ... smelled of sour booze, took forever to get rolling. One year he gave Jay and me fountain-pens and a set of *Britannica*. He gave Mom perfume she never opened and the aluminum tree that we set up each year thereafter.

Val asked which Christmas I remembered best. The year Jay and I got up for our papers and found no new shapes in the dimness beneath the aluminum tree. I hurried through my route, reaping tips from doors and milkboxes, then I helped Jay. We knew Dad wasn't going to show but we buried the knowledge, hurried home to see him. Mom was already up. She wore an expression on her puffy face I'd not seen before.

—Merry Christmas! Go empty your stockings.

Dad's heavy grey socks with red toes and heels— bulging with oranges, peanuts, chewing gum, a puck, jawbreakers, and little puzzles. The cornucopia distracted us only for a minute. Jay stopped in the middle of loading his Pez gun.

—Isn't he coming?

Mom held herself like her mug, careful not to let anything spill.

—He fell asleep on the way down. He wrecked the car

. . . lucky he didn't kill himself. I'll drive up and bail him out after we open our presents.

—Tell you the one I remember best, Monkey. One time I was running a car out west and I happened to hit Salt Lake City on Christmas morning. People were filing into Temple Square. It was snowing and the square was lit with tiny lights. Everybody was in their Sunday best but no one batted an eye. I had three days' growth and hadn't changed my clothes. The Mormon Tabernacle Choir was giving a recital with the Salt Lake Children's Choir but what you noticed in the temple was the shit that goes along with a television broadcast. It was going out live and they'd turned the altar into a set—cameramen on hydraulic lifts, banks of lights, guys with walkie-talkies. The announcer hid his stopwatch behind the binder he was supposedly reading from. He read from a prompter, then the choir sang, then everything stopped for a commercial.

—At first it had a bad air—you don't like to think the Mormon Tabernacle Choir is made up of men who sell Hondas and women who talk about floor wax. Many of them were fat and they all seemed to have spent hours on their hair. But when they lifted their voices it was something, Monkey, beyond the lights and prompters and shit there was music . . . I told myself there was a lesson in that.

—The program ended with a little sermon. The guy told us that in spite of war and selfishness there was still the spirit of goodness in the world. He said each of us could choose to be a part of that spirit by helping the sick and the widowed and the poor. I nodded at what he was saying . . . at the same time felt it slipping away. I was onto something while the choir was singing but then I lost it. The announcer said you could choose the path of righteousness and I knew what he was saying was true. Right then I could have made a choice, been a different man. But I had a car full of stolen suits I had to get to Las Vegas—the sick and the widowed and the poor were going to have to find someone else to help them. I chose my path then and there ... I think of it every Christmas.

YESTERDAY when I got back from the library Val asked about her. Usually I steer the conversation elsewhere. I've never talked about her with anyone but Ron. Not even Jay—when he and I get on the subject it's disaster. It seemed impossible ... I had a craving for dope or pruno.

—What was she like?

—I don't know what to tell you. She was ... aware of things I was blind to.

—What do you mean?

—On the beach, for example. She'd spot bits of shell, drops of jelly, living things I walked by. She noticed a tiny patch of moss, the little universe of a puddle. She taught me to see these things, some of them, and I taught her things in return—more practical things. We were so compatible . . . never fought.

His lip curled in incredulity. He lit one of my cigarettes.

—Never had arguments that turned into fights?

—Too many nights I'd heard my parents yelling. Seen my old man, drunk, slap my mother off her feet. I hated my father.

—How do you live with somebody and not fight? Sounds like let's pretend.

—That's just the way we were. She couldn't stand arguments, fights, torture, violence—on TV, a movie, anything. She was incredibly sensitive to these things. She believed she'd been tortured in a past life.

—Sounds like a whacko to me.

—Fuck you.

—She does. Sounds like a complete fucking—

His mouth kept working—nothing came. He struggled—couldn't shake me off—stared at me in horror. His face flushed pink, crimson, purple . . . he stopped resisting. He lay there, unmoving, eyes wide, as if gazing at something a long way off while concentrating on something else. I felt his life in my hands. His eyes seemed about to pop . . . I realized what I was doing and let go—he grabbed his throat with both hands, gagging violently.

—Get out of here!

He coughed and coughed, clutching his throat.

—Stop coming to my cell!

He tried to sit up . . . lost his balance, doubled over, gasping raggedly. I began peeling his fingers off the bars, pushing him onto the tier. He gripped the bars mightily, a drowning man clutching the buoy. Winged snakes entwine his forearms, like the snakes on Mercury's caduceus—when he closes his fists, the snakes jump. I pried, I yelled:

—Keep away, you fucker! Don't you ever come back here. I wish you'd never been transferred.

—Don't say that, don't ...

—Stay away from my cell.

—No, no—tell me about her, I want to know.

—So you can tell me she's whacko? Fuck you!

His voice was hoarse, face white as paper. He was looking at me in a new way, like Jay when I shot the groundhog ... searching my face with wounded eyes, bright and shocked, brimming with tears. I let go—he pulled himself up on the cot, sat hunched.

—I won't say nothing ... never heard a story like this, that's all. She didn't like arguing, she couldn't stand fighting ...

—I'm sorry, Val. I don't know what's happening to me. Christ, I didn't mean to do that, what am I doing? Forgive me ...

—I'm all right, Monkey, tell me the story. She had these nightmares ...

—She remembered everything, she couldn't forget. Recalled conversations in detail. If she told me I'd said something I couldn't deny it. She recalled the restaurant we'd been in when I said it ... She was able to keep in mind the sum total of what people had said and done, which must have been invaluable in her work. She was a psychologist in private practice.

—Remembered everything.

—But she forgot we had ballet tickets the evening she invited people to dinner. Forgot her class had been cancelled ... raced all the way out to the university. She forgot to file income tax, send invoices to her clients. I did those things for her. I knew when her Visa was due and her car needed servicing. I reminded her she had to book her ticket by Friday to get the cheap fare. She reminded me, when I couldn't get an answer at my

brother's place, that they were spending the long weekend at a friend's cottage. In some ways we might have
been from different planets—but somehow we seemed
to fit together.

—She believed paper boys who told her they were one
subscription short of a trip to Florida. I told her
Howard's End, a book I had to read, was about a guy
named Howard who died of gangrene of the ass—she
believed it! She figured winos bought coffee with the
change she gave them. Our house was always full of
girl-guide cookies, pens, light bulbs, chocolate, raffle
tickets. I got us out of magazine subscriptions, vacuum
cleaners, encyclopaedias. She never said no to people
who knocked on the door. At first it charmed and
fascinated me. How incredible that a person could be as
innocent as a lamb. Then it pissed me off—I felt I had to
watch out for her, like a child who was always trying to
drink the Drano or dash into the street. I tried to change
her . . . never occurred to me you can't change anyone
but yourself. She fell in love with someone else, but
something I want you to understand. Everybody says
this, I know, but I didn't do it. I loved her . . . it's hard . . .
I don't think I know what love is.

He rubbed his throat.

—Monkey, something I want you to understand, too.
Don't matter to me if you killed her.

—Val, listen.

—Sometimes in the shop I'll stop what I'm doing and
wonder where you are. I like it when you talk like this, I
hate it when you lock in with your journal. You know
what I'm driving at—stop looking at me like that.

—Sure, I know. Listen, Val, I care for you, too. It's
just—

He put his hand on the back of my neck, pressing my
forehead to his—he groaned.

—Come with me, Monkey. This thing is a go. Imagine how good it will be to have a beer, just walk the streets. We're going with them, we'll be out—be together. Monkey, please—there's nobody else I can talk to. We got to go, can't back out now. But if you're not going, if you really won't go . . . I'm not either. I'm staying with you.

My heart leapt against my ribs—Tuffy slamming against the gate, happy to see me or acting as a guard dog? I pulled back—pity, longing, disgust? Kept my breathing rhythmic with great effort. Told Val to leave. Soon as we were in keep-lock I sought my penis, fumbling it free of my pants. It felt more durable than any other part of me, than bone. All night I thought of Marnie's embrace, I listened to Vernon toss and moan, I heard Billie Holiday censuring himself, men stirring in dreams . . . I couldn't sleep and then I was searching through the first noise of the cellhouse. I picked out his footfall among the others. When I heard him I busied myself in my cell. When he spoke to me he was still hoarse. I greeted him lightly, a morning like any other. I went for chow but couldn't eat.

Circumstance has brought it on, pressure, one time Dad and Jay and I hauled up red snappers from so far down their eyes popped and their guts filled their mouths. It's not me—is it? Is it why Angela and I never had proper sex? Why Dad never accepted me? Because he detected something of Wilf and despised me in advance? This edge of panic—I can't find answers, gain access to myself, why have I never had access? Why can't I acknowledge here, now, my depth of feeling for Val is profound?

This is what I want these words to do—testify to my feeling for Val. Perhaps I love him.

There. Love.

—WE SPOKE last time about the possibility of escaping.

—Haven't really had to confront that yet. What I want to talk about is sexuality.

—What's happening in your life right now?

—Val. I'm going to have to turn him down explicitly. I'd like to be able to explain.

—I need background. What was your sexual life like before you got here?

—Angela and I were more brother and sister. We did make love, at first anyway, but it wasn't the animating force, as it was with Marnie. Not even at the start.

—Were you ever aware of your parents as lovers?

—Only once. I came home late from a baseball game, must have been twelve or thirteen. I opened their door to say good night—my father was on top—I closed the door.

—What do you recall of that discovery?

—The V of her legs, the wedged moon of his ass.

—What emotions did you feel?

—He was a big man and I imagined her being suffocated. It upset me for months.

—What about when you were younger? Three or four, perhaps. Have you sexual memories of that time?

I told him about private school, ties and blazers, being youngest in the class, the others talking about things I could only pretend to understand. The time I stayed over with a childhood friend, and we got erections and poked at each other. Six years old, maybe? Ron asked if, at the time, I felt the encounter was shameful. I talked about Dad's attitude to Wilf, and to homosexuals in general—or, rather, faggots, gearboxes, cocksuckers, ass bandits, queers, buggers, queens, fairies. I said I couldn't recall Dad ever having used the word 'homosexuals.' Then Ron asked an astonishing question:

—Do you think your father ever had a homosexual experience?

—No way ... maybe ... I have no idea.

—Did you know his parents well?

—His father was a bank manager. Very kind, and I think weak. My grandmother was bright, extremely strong-willed and spoke several languages. Dad, if he'd been speaking about anyone other than his parents, would have said: 'We know who screws who in that family.' Granddad ate the same lunch for thirty years— peanut-butter sandwich and chocolate ice cream. She made it for him.

We talked about the first emergence of sexual instinct. I asked Ron when he thought the awareness begins:

—My feeling is that the instinct manifests itself early but gets canned, put away for later. Perhaps the way it's dealt with at the start establishes the way it's handled later on. In early adolescence, you're finally given permission to acknowledge those forces. I think we react profoundly, unconsciously, when we allow our sexuality to resurface.

—In here, if you desire other men, you're perceived as having a weakness. The weakness is exploited, and the way it's exploited, ironically, is sexually.

—Have you had sex since you've been here?

—I restrict my sexual activity to myself.

He questioned me about childhood fantasies toward Mom, and my sex life with Angela, which I guess was dismal. When I described our mutual indifference, he asked another question that caught me off guard:

—Do you think Angela castrated you in some sense?

—How do you mean?

—Well, did you feel Angela was placing a burden on you with her implicit demand for emotional contact through sex? That your own self-esteem was insufficient to create the emotional energy she wanted?

I said I'd always had a vague sense of inadequacy with Angela, yet with Marnie I'd felt quite secure and at ease. I asked Ron how I might understand this difference.

—My own idea is that feelings of sexual adequacy are closely related to larger feelings of self-esteem. That confidence and potency—or the opposite—are clearly distilled in sexual expression. Or, to put it another way, one's sexuality says a great deal about how one's whole self relates to the partner's self.

—Angela and I began with traditional ideas: I'd be the clever one—strong, successful, the breadwinner. She'd be there supporting me, applauding me. But I found myself in an unfulfilling job—my grandfather eating the same lunch every day—and tried to tell myself it didn't matter, we had each other.

—Angela, meanwhile, was moving in the opposite direction.

—She began to thrive. Stood at the top of her graduating class . . . she'd been only average in high school. She started her own practice while working on her master's —thought she'd never get clients, and soon had as many as she could handle.

—The balance shifted soon after you met.

I found myself posing a question that made me feel very uncomfortable:

—Do you think my sexual relation with Marnie was satisfying only because she was in one sense my inferior?

—I don't think one can have a satisfying relation only with one's inferior. How did Marnie make you feel?

—She couldn't get enough—it was wonderful. She tapped something in me I hardly knew was there.

—How long did the affair continue?

—It started going wrong when she realized I saw no future in her. I'd told her at the start ... I suppose my actions contradicted my words. Once it became clear to her how entwined my life was with Angela's, things began to sour ...

—What about Craig and Angela? What stage were they at?

—I suspect they had a strong relationship that went wrong once he'd left his wife. I'm sure he expected Angela to leave me for him.

—What kept her from leaving you?

—Something ... kept us together.

Again he asked a question for which I was totally unprepared:

—Do you think that's why she jumped? She had no other way of leaving you?

—Oh, no, God ... I think despair. She began with two people. One renounced her ... the other felt betrayed.

—What kept you together? Was it simply your manipulation of her?

—Mutual need, recognition, attraction, weakness— mutual something.

Ron brought the conversation back to Val. He asked

me to do some free thinking, engage in an imaginary
conversation:

—I'm Val . . . I want to be close to you.

—It makes me cringe. It frightens me . . . I'd rather
keep to myself. I don't know how to tell him—you—
without alienating you. I want to be friends, that's all.

—Wouldn't you like me to make love to you, Owen?

—This makes me squirm.

—What is it? Tell me why.

—I value our friendship . . .

—Owen, please. Give it a chance.

—Can't you understand? I don't want this. I'm not
gay.

—What does that mean? I feel an incredible
attraction.

—It would cause me more grief than happiness.

—How do you know? Are you afraid?

—It's more disdain, self-contempt, confusion.

—You don't want me . . . that's it, isn't it. I couldn't
even read before you taught me—I'm not of your
standing. I'm inferior.

—Val, listen. I like you, admire you. I think you're a
strong, sweet person. That's got nothing to do with it.

—Doesn't your body want to be close to mine?

—I want a woman's body. Marnie's, someone I know.

—Treat my body like a woman's.

—Stop it! Can't you understand? I don't want what
you want. I don't . . . I don't!

—Our time is up, Owen. I think you'll have to be very
clear and confident in your own mind to transmit that
message.

MARNIE . . . ripeness that verged on decay. She unzipped her boots and I knelt to feel the imprint of the roulettes with my tongue. She accommodated me in an elevator at the office. Her breathe, the powdered scent of her breasts . . . the odour of her period intoxicated me. Gluttons. There was never awkwardness and this might have been my definition of love if not for Angela. I didn't share with Marnie any inkling of past and future, but I didn't share with any of Angela this sensual immersion . . .

Funny, Angela and I underwent a revival. Angela had suggested we needed to talk—that phrase, for some reason, sent a chill through me—and we began making time for things sacrificed to schedules: the zoo and the museum, camping trips, lunches during the week. One Friday it occurred to us to do something we had not done in years—jump in the car and drive, mapless and aimless. For a time we set aside a weekend each month. Warm eggs and dirty potatoes. Small-town fairs, stock-car races, fields of rain-shined pumpkins. One morning we went up in a small plane, and I felt the extraordinary certainty that I'd flown before, could almost will myself aloft. We stopped to picnic by a marsh . . . the slamming of car doors raised so many red-winged blackbirds the sky went dark. We slept soundly in ramshackle motels, spent a night as guests of an elderly couple we had met at a driving range. The world seemed a banquet of possibilities—we never did talk, about ourselves at least. But we were doing things together, the need seemed less urgent—we returned from our low-key adventures exhilarated.

Marnie kept busy with her friends and her cosmetics. She did not enjoy these weekends. She seemed to accept Angela's place, but grew more easily hurt and dismayed. When I tried to explain we always ended up in each other's arms ... all would be well for a time. Gradually Angela's name dropped out of our conversations. She became an unspoken presence behind everything we did together. One night after Marnie had worked herself into tears I told her Angela and I had stopped sleeping together, used different rooms. I thought this was my trump—it didn't soothe Marnie. If we weren't making love, my attention fully on her, she simmered with pain and resentment.

It simply wasn't fair to Marnie. If only to salvage my self-respect, I had to break it off. Angela and I had always agreed we needed latitude and independence. Why, then, did I feel deceitful sleeping with Marnie? So deceitful I was unable to utter her name to Angela and vice versa? I asked Marnie out for dinner after the tenth-anniversary party, intending to ask her if it might not be best to end it.

In the afternoon everyone gathered in the art department ... downed much wine before McEleney cleared his throat. He told us history was measured in decades, singled out those who had been in from the start. Of thirty people I was one of three originals—the applause brought home in the most unpleasant way that I had spent a third of my life in the same office. The others drank a toast—I drained my glass, looked about for a refill. Marnie came, bless her, bottle in hand, while

McEleney gave a little talk full of baseless optimism.
Despite tough times K & K's future had never looked
better. Breaking new ground . . . the upturn around the
corner . . . cliché after cliché, on and bloody on. Some of
us exchanged glances. Why so ardent a rebuttal to an
attack no one had made?

McEleney concluded to a burst of applause . . . slipped
out. Soon the art department was thick with cigarette
smoke and the din of people competing with the robotic
funk that the art director generally fed directly to his
brain. People donned their party selves. Available
women became available, randy men randy. Secretaries
off to meet girlfriends became teases, disengaging themselves from account executives who, minus alcohol, saw
them as extensions of the Xerox machine. Kevin and
Maxine danced . . . Bob Rix hid two litres for the hard
core. Marnie pretended to sip from the same half-filled
glass. She answered the phone, made sure no one was
alone for long, found clean glasses for anyone who
happened by. Marnie's kind heart—how valuable is
simple kindness.

She stayed late—I helped clean up—returned from
the men's to find her in a heart-to-heart talk with
Maxine, an alarmingly thin woman who smoked and
talked compulsively and ended every celebration in
tears. I was afraid Marnie was going to ask her to join
us for dinner. I went to my office to return calls I was
sure would be fielded by an answering service, checked
my cubbyhole at reception, put on my coat. Marnie was
returning empty bottles to the case. I watched her like a
spy . . . felt the void that parties always put in me.

—Almost ready?

She made a noise—the most easily startled person
I've known.

—Sorry, baby. I need to pick up some things across the street. They close at nine.

—Maxine's in the powder room. I better wait.

—Anything the matter?

—Men.

Maxine echoed the word gaily—'Men!'—and I knew she'd divined our affair. Her mascara was a blur . . . her wool dress caught on the bones of her hips.

—I've been crying. I get this way when I drink . . . shouldn't drink, but what are parties for? Let's find a bottle and talk.

—I'd love to, but I have to run.

The story of my life—with Angela, Marnie, Val . . .

I pushed a cart up and down chilly aisles. The Muzak, the fluorescence, the dented cans marked 'Super Saver,' the rows of encased produce . . . by the time I reached the checkout I had a sense of unnatural clarity. The doors had been locked and a uniformed woman with keys was letting out each shopper. She would not allow Marnie to enter and Marnie was not merely frustrated but panicked. She tried each door in turn . . . beat the glass with her fists. How deeply I needed what she gave me, how little I understood her. She too wanted children, my children, and for a moment . . .

I know you as I know my soul . . .

Marnie returned to the one door by which shoppers could exit—forced her way in. The woman with the keys made a fuss which Marnie imperially ignored. She stood by the posts erected to thwart cart stealers and searched for me. I waved from the express line—she took my arm with such relief I might have survived an earthquake. I remembered what I planned to say . . . the thought of losing her stirred me . . . I wanted to go back to the office before dinner. She was nervous but game—

splendid lover, always game. In the boardroom we kissed gently and sank to the sofa ...

When the cleaning woman knocked I covered Marnie's mouth with my hand. Those bright eyes, aroused and frightened. The idea of saying what I had intended to say, ending our sweetness, seemed a cruelty I could not inflict on her.

On her? Or on myself? Have I ever, in my entire life, truly put anyone's welfare ahead of my own?

I TOLD Jay his glasses had become too small for his face.

—I haven't put on that much weight. Just because you're turning into Mr Universe.

He was not being facetious—his remark astonished me. When I arrived I took a thirty-eight and the trusty had a hard time finding issue that fitted. Only one other man in four hundred took a thirty-eight. Now I take a thirty-two and bench-press three hundred pounds. Yet I don't see myself as he does ... I still think of myself as overweight and of him as fit and athletic.

The roles are reversing in another way. He asked as he usually does if I'd had word from Mom. It was always Jay to whom they gave joint praise or reprimand

... after they moved it was Jay they phoned with news. He called regularly, I almost never. Now he drives all the way down here and asks if there has been word.

—Got a letter after your last visit. Sounds fine, same as ever—keeping busy, helping at the hospice four days a week ... Jay, listen, I'm sorry I got so upset last time ...

—I can't imagine what it's like.

—It's funny, Mom mentioned the pearls, too, after you did. Wondered if I'd had them 'disposed of.' Made me feel guilty as hell for borrowing from her—lying about what the money was for. I still haven't paid her back.

—If you decide to keep them I might put them in a safety-deposit box. I don't like something that valuable lying around the house.

—I don't know ... wouldn't feel right to sell them.

—Did Mom say anything about coming east?

—She plans to come in early summer. See the baby. Visit me. I'll be eligible by then, so there's a chance I'll be able to talk to her without these things. It was awkward ... poor Mom.

—I've got a feeling it won't be so awkward next time.

He asked what I was going to do when I got out—I said I hadn't thought much about it.

—Sylvia and I would like you to come live with us. Plenty of space in the new house ... chance to get to know Jonathan.

I felt my good fortune in having him for a brother. I started to tell him how important it is that he comes without fail—how I value his fidelity—but he turned the moment around, as Dad would have:

—Figured you'd be cheaper than a sitter.

Our father's sons—we cannot bear closeness. He also

has Dad's habit of taking refuge in questions.

—What's the worst thing about being here?

At the start the worst was knowing I couldn't leave—not today, next week, a year from now. Not the constraints but the knowing. That merged with my own inner climate of fear. For a time I was troubled that people leave here aware that no matter whose bones they crack they will only end up back here ... not so different from their lives. Lately I've had the frightening sense that what I once called my needs are not mine at all but shadowy creatures with unpredictable wills of their own, animals moving in moonlight. I react out of deep wells of personality and my reactions are often incomprehensible to me—like Tuffy after defecating, an atavistic parody of covering his trail. I conjure visions of love and tenderness—they arise at odd moments—but I don't know whether they will have correspondence in the world. I've lost part of myself and I don't know what's going to take its place.

—The worst thing is that I know what's coming on every television program and every commercial. Life holds no surprises.

—Think of the movies you've missed. The big thing now is home videocassette recorders. You can rent any movie you want—play it on your television screen.

—I love you for coming down here, but there's so much we can't get to. Guess it was the same with Angela. It was like that with Dad. I don't think I ever had a real conversation with him, know that? You could talk to him, he was proud as hell and you didn't seem to have trouble communicating ... with me it was a different story.

—Think it was his fault?

—I never understood what made him tick. Guy with

maybe the best-equipped workshop in the country, all the tools with their own little silhouettes on the wall and the sonofabitch hardly knew which end of the hammer you hold. He could only afford the tools because somebody was stupid enough to send him a credit card. They hung unused on the wall till he died.

—He was always going to learn. First you find out what tools you need for the perfect workshop, then you get the best even if it means importing them from Sweden—then you're ready to learn. Except by then he'd lost interest. He was a funny guy. I liked him.

—How can you not like a bald guy who reads *Consumer Reports* to find out the best blow-dryer? I asked what the hell he'd bought a blow-dryer for. 'Four reasons,' he said. 'To thaw the car locks. To fan the fire. To inflate the air mattresses. And to clean the bathroom mirror so I can see to shave.'

—He was nothing if not original.

—I could never figure him out. He functioned at extremes and there was nothing between. The way he worked—twenty hours a day if there was an election or an organizing campaign. Otherwise he might not get out of his pyjamas until dinner. Remember the afternoon Mom gave him shit? 'What if people drop by?'

—Dad drained his glass and said, 'A man wearing pyjamas in his own house on a Monday afternoon. Big deal. Don't buy it, Helen. Don't buy the bullshit.'

—He said it as if Mom were a fuck-up for even thinking of it. He figured you were wonderful and I was a fuck-up. But he was the one fucked up, wasn't he?

—To me he had a lot of good qualities. He was idealistic, which I admired. In many ways he was a perfectionist and we both maybe learned something from that. Maybe he was eccentric ... what the hell. I never thought of him as fucked up. Just a guy doing the best he could. Doing what he thought was right.

—I think of us all as fucked up—mostly him and me. Mom's a decent person. You are, too.

—Mom does her numbers ... used to get on our nerves. The only person you've got a really good fix on is me. You're quite right about me—I am a marvellous human being.

—Prick. At least Mom could talk like a normal person. With Dad it was either silence or sarcasm. He made praise and disparagement sound alike. He thought he had this great cynical wit. It wasn't wit, it was bitterness without tears.

—He was bitter because the world wasn't a better place. Idealists end up disillusioned.

—I've been trying to think when I stopped thinking he was wonderful, when he started reaching me in a negative way. I got so that everything I did, I asked myself, 'Is this like Dad?' If it was I'd do the opposite. No way I wanted to be like him.

—You quit to work at K & K and one of Dad's regrets was that he quit before he graduated. How many times did he tell us that?

—No point getting a degree when I wasn't interested in teaching and a nice job came along. I made that decision because it seemed wiser to take the job rather than *not* dropping out simply to avoid following in Dad's footsteps.

—Same result—neither of you finished university. What about money? Remember the phone calls and registered letters and debt collectors after Dad? Caps it off by buying the Chrysler when interest rates are way up and gas costs a fortune and he doesn't have a cent to begin with. Well, you bought Angela a ridiculously expensive present when you could least afford it. Ended up following his pattern of being reckless with money.

—Bad time for us . . . I thought the pearls might help. I thought they were worth it.

—Dad thought it was worth it to drive around with a huge V-8 in the middle of the energy crunch. You used to drive like him, too, racing around, yelling at everybody who didn't drive the same way. You got into the vodka, you drank the same way—doubles with a beer chaser. You even shot sparrows when you got pissed off, just like Dad.

—Yeah, I guess. Thanks for coming.

—Hang in there, O—see you in two weeks. Hey, O.

—What.

—I love you, too.

LAST night I dreamed of Katrine. She lived alone in a tiny apartment with money from her parents who sent a monthly cheque but never spoke to her. Angela saw her for six months before Katrine confided that her father had sexually abused her. When she told her mother, the mother sided with the father.

For weeks afterward she would say nothing more. Sometimes she wouldn't respond to Angela at all although she always arrived early for the appointment. One day she began suddenly beating a pillow, and the next trauma was revealed. She used to cut through the schoolyard coming home from piano ... she was attacked ... four boys took turns raping her. She composed herself and made her way home—never told anyone. Katrine began to talk more readily, go blank less often. Then she arrived for a session with both wrists bandaged. She had slashed herself with a kitchen knife. In describing what had happened she spoke as if she had witnessed a stranger. Angela told her to call whenever she felt the need.

Katrine began phoning every night, late, after we'd gone to sleep. I developed insomnia, lay awake, waiting ... Angela too found her sleep disturbed. She began to lose her appetite. Her cheekbones became prominent, her chin developed a point. The musculature of her body became apparent—her breastbone seemed to expand, her skin tightened over her ribs, her clothes hung loosely from her shoulders and hips. Angela felt she was making gradual progress with Katrine. It seemed to me it was not progress at all but a perilous kind of balance. As Katrine gained strength, Angela was commensurately weakened.

—Tell her to stop phoning. This is wrecking our lives.

—I can't, Owen. I'm worried about her, I can't back off now. I've got to see this through.

—I'd like to support this whole business, but it's your work, intruding on our lives. I don't have clients phoning me at all hours. What about us?

—I don't think our work is quite the same. This isn't just what I do ... it's what I am.

—Public relations isn't just what I do, either. It's what I am.

—You're impossible. It seems so hopeless ...

Angela consulted friends she trusted, therapists of one sort or another. Some suggested institutionalizing Katrine. Angela did not want to see her committed ... medicated out of her mind. But she also feared her own growing responsibility and involvement. The more Katrine's fate depended on her, the more it seemed out of her control. Angela began to have nightmares as I lay awake, waiting ...

In her dreams Angela was being cross-examined—Crown-appointed psychiatrists testified that her treatment had been unorthodox and negligent and had contributed to Katrine's suicide. At my urging she took out liability insurance. The insurance made her feel guilty ... did little to ease her anxiety. Her life had become entwined with Katrine's, far more intricately, I believed, than with mine.

Another breakthrough—Katrine told Angela she had had a boyfriend by whom she had got pregnant. The boy wanted to marry but Katrine found the idea loathsome. She undertook to arrange an abortion ... the boy refused to help. She found a doctor and checked into hospital telling her parents she was spending the weekend at a girlfriend's. She expected to be out in two days but the procedure was bungled—she had to remain a week. When she phoned from her hospital bed her parents disowned her.

A beautiful honey locust—one of the few in the city—filtered the sunshine that reached Angela's office. I imagined Katrine staring out at the tree, lost in herself, incapable of response. I imagined Angela waiting without annoyance or resentment, and felt a depth of love I could never plumb when we were actually together—why could I never express my love? Angela knew that

Katrine had to sense in another person complete acceptance, that she could help Katrine only if her love and
conviction were unshakeable. And she would do anything to help those she loved ...

Including me?

One night we lay exhausted under the quilt ... a
wind was stirring the silver maple. The phone rang.
Angela showed no sign of impatience.

—I'm here, Katrine. Try to keep talking.

Angela's voice swam in and out. When she hung up
she had been propped on one elbow for two hours. Her
body was almost rigid.

—My God, it's almost four o'clock. I have to be in at
eight. I have seven hours tomorrow—twenty-four
clients right now. She's in the worst trouble, she means
the most, but she's just one of them ...

—What did Katrine say? Why are you so disturbed?

Katrine had said she was a cosmic error. She had
been a man in other lives and should have been in this
one. This revelation, which I had to badger out of
Angela, had on me a powerful effect—sympathy and
revulsion. I had seen Katrine emerge from Angela's
office and felt the pull of her intense sexuality. She
herself was blind to it ... didn't understand why drivers
pulled over and rolled down the window.

This morning I told Val about her. In the dream I was
making love to Katrine. All the men in the prison were
watching ... Dad was there, too, Wilf, Jay ...

Katrine was a boy.

AFTER Val and I had pumped weight we played chess—
he won all three games. It's odd, having taught him, to
realize he's now a better player than I'll ever be. The
same happened when Dad taught me poker, snooker,
Scrabble, chess. I needed to win more than he did ...
before long I had to be careful to make us seem well
matched. So with Val—he's inspired by cigarettes and
keeps the games close. I don't mind that instead of
asking for tobacco he asks if I want to play chess. I did
the same with Dad—money for the poolroom. But I
wish he'd stop smoking, stop borrowing (two for one),
stop playing spoof and losing even more to Tonio. Debt
is dangerous—I can't make him understand—he must
go through eighty cigarettes a day.

Jay used to stash tennis balls in strategic spots—the
glove compartment of the Healey, his locker at school—
and squeeze them to strengthen his wrists. I carried a
deck of cards and practised dealing bottoms. No guilt or
anxiety cheating Dad—cool purpose. When I had the
deal at poker I could win at will. When he left the
Scrabble board to pour himself a drink I snuck a
glimpse of his letters. I found no way of cheating at
chess ... had to learn how to win. I read books about the
middle game and played with fierce concentration.
When I started beating him I imagined he would take a
parent's satisfaction in seeing his skills passed on. He
seemed not to care one way or the other—finished his
drink and staggered off to bed. Years later Mom told me

he had hated losing. She could tell the moment he entered the bedroom if he'd lost: he would fume and curse. I was startled—was he cursing me or himself?

Ours were games of confrontation—winner and loser. He and Jay had a different rapport. Jay loved model warships and jet fighters and racing cars. He spent hours with a toothpick applying glue to plastic surfaces and fitting them. I helped him a few times but didn't have much patience. One night after dinner I climbed the stairs to his room. I was hoping he'd ask me in—though our rooms were identical his seemed richer and safer than mine. I wanted to lie on his bed . . . watch his tongue flicker in artless concentration. His door was half closed—I stuck my head in. The room had its own unaccountable warmth and bore the sweet smell of glue. Jay and Dad sat at the desk, their heads almost touching in the cone of yellow light from the lamp. They were absorbed in building a destroyer—such an air of compatibility, even sanctity, I didn't dare violate it.

Next time Dad and I played chess I didn't let him win a game. With his money I bought a plastic model Luger. The box promised that the action would duplicate that of a real Luger, the template rising in an inverted V to pull a cartridge into the chamber. The finished gun would shoot plastic bullets ten or twenty feet. Dad loved weapons—when I showed him the kit he said he'd be happy to help. First he was busy and then he was away . . . Jay offered to help but by then I'd lost interest. The box ended up on a closet shelf.

Jay saved his paper earnings and never joined in our money games. Wilf did. On the rare occasions that Wilf, Dad, and I found ourselves together we always ended up playing Scrabble. It seemed unimportant to Wilf whether he or I won so long as Dad lost. We didn't deliberately set each other up for seven-letter words and

triple-word scores but we made nothing easy for Dad.
We played in unstated partnership.

—Eighty-two. Twenty-two plus ten plus fifty.

Wilf rotated the board to read Dad's word.

—Hmm. 'Manting.' May we ask what 'manting'
means, Harold?

—To mant is to stammer. From the Gaelic.

—What do you think, Owen? Shall we challenge?
Let's see what Mr Webster has to say.

—Wait a minute, is it a formal challenge? Which of
you is challenging?

Wilf and I spoke at the same instant:

—I am.

Dad went to fix a drink while Wilf looked it up . . .
stroked his moustache . . . gave me a conspiratorial
smile.

—Sorry, Harold—Webster's Abridged is mum on the
subject of manting.

—What the hell.

Wilf slipped a coaster under Dad's glass while Dad
satisfied himself that his word wasn't there.

—Where's the Oxford?

—Did we not agree on Webster?

—Not if it doesn't have 'manting.' Hell kind of dictionary is that? Where's the Oxford?

—We agreed on Webster, Dad. Your play, Wilf.

Dad removed his letters from the board.

—You little prick. Out for the old man's blood.

The games were always close. Like Wilf I didn't mind
losing so long as Dad lost. He was forever wanting one
more game—despite his superior vocabulary he generally came last and had to pay us both. But he never had
money. Mom wound up paying.

Val loses to Tonio . . . I end up paying.

GILES is a graceful man—once he must have been
alarmingly beautiful. He moves in an ageless way and
his face is as deeply tanned as an actor's. I thought he
was slightly retarded. Playing poker he will gaze at
something invisible to the rest of us and have to be
shouted at. Or bet heavily with two pairs, lose, and try
to collect the pot. Not a cheat—simply unmindful that
three of a kind is the winning hand. Perhaps once he
imagines winning he has trouble giving the further
course of the game its proper meaning. He bows slightly
when you greet him, excuses himself when he gets up.
In and out of institutions. Before tonight I wasn't sure if
he understood why he was in this one. He stopped on
the way to his cell.

—I wish there was a telephone. I really do.

—Who would you call?

—It gives me very great pleasure to use the phone. I'll
tell you my best one, Monkey, it's the one they never got
me for. This goes back to the nineteen-sixties. It worked
wonderfully then. I tried it again in the mid-seventies
but society was changing ... wasn't nearly so
successful.

—Using the directory, I picked out numbers in subur-
ban exchanges and called on weekday afternoons in
good weather. Generally a woman answered. 'Mrs
Kelly?' I'd say. I would introduce myself as Dr Leonard
Fleischer. 'I am a psychiatrist and I must discuss with
you a matter of great importance and confidentiality.'

I'd tell her one of my patients was her husband. The reaction was usually surprise but not disbelief. Occasionally it would go wrong here. 'Like fun he is,' one woman said. 'The bastard's in front of the TV and you couldn't get him away for love or money.' I muttered something about my incompetent receptionist, hung up, and began again.

—Usually, however, the woman admitted she was unaware her husband was seeing a psychiatrist. I told her it was common for the wife to be the last to know when her husband had a problem that had made him seek counselling. In the course of our sessions, I told her, I'd come to know every detail of their lives, including the inhibitions and deficiencies in the intimate relationship. I explained that the husband had a deep-seated problem relating to sexual fantasy, as she might have gathered, and that this problem, in my view, was threatening to make him unstable. It's a great word, unstable. Pronounce it right and it makes people think all sorts of things.

—Naturally the wife is very upset. Generally she asks what she can do to help. It's important that she volunteer—this is the only really tricky moment. I ask if she has read Ellis, Kinsey, Masters and Johnson. The answer is no. I tell her that in my professional opinion she could best assist her husband by having relations—under supervision, of course—with a stranger. I explain that this is an increasingly popular technique in sexual therapy and describe how to go about it.

—Go outside immediately, I said, approach the first man you see—not a neighbour or the postman but a total stranger—and ask him to come inside to help you move a piece of heavy furniture. I asked if she understood, told her I'd give her a few minutes to find someone, and would phone back shortly.

—During the time I was smoothing out the wrinkles I thought this might be where I'd run into problems. Would the woman be tempted to call a friend? The family doctor? Her husband? But I had stressed the need to proceed without the husband's knowledge (just as he had sought therapy without her knowledge) and most women did as instructed. They went outside, approached a stranger, and asked him to help move furniture. Often when I called back the woman had been unsuccessful, so I had her try again. Many women had trouble getting a stranger into the house. Once they got him in, however, they had no trouble getting him to bed.

—It went like this. I phoned back and told the woman I wished to speak to the stranger. I identified myself and outlined the situation, stressing its importance to both the woman and her husband, and lauding the selflessness of the stranger for agreeing to take part. Should have heard them—'Glad to help out, doctor,' that kind of thing. I specified that the sexual activity was to take place very near the receiver so that I could instruct them in detail as the therapy proceeded.

—And they'd go at it, Monkey, they'd ball, with me telling them how. Do such-and-such for three minutes. They'd come back on the line and I'd tell them what was required next. I ran them through the gamut, you name it, urging the stranger not to allow himself orgasm until the therapy was complete. Finally I would tell him that this was the final segment . . . he was free to climax.

—I thanked the stranger for his valuable co-operation. Should have heard some of them—'You're welcome, doctor, I really hope the treatment is successful.' I explained that success would continue to depend partly on him. I stressed that in no circumstances must he give the woman any information about himself or attempt to contact her again. I dismissed him and spoke to the wife. I thanked her for her co-operation and assured her of its therapeutic value. I told her absolutely she must not mention the episode to her husband. It would be psychologically devastating. I myself would inform the husband at the appropriate time.

—After the first few times I started to worry. Was I pressing my luck? Eventually the women would say something to her husband. They would realize they'd been taken. But by whom and for what reason? Would they go to the police? No, you see, here's the beauty of the thing. There was no way to track Dr Fleischer or the stranger (not that finding him would be helpful) and they would only hold themselves up to ridicule and embarrassment by coming forward with the story. In 1966 and 1967 I pulled this off more than three hundred times. It's probably my best scheme. Isn't it elegant?

—Very elegant, but Giles. Why?

—Have you never listened to strangers making love? Imagine what comes over the phone—then they stop and ask what next! It's magical, Monkey, something I could do endlessly. The telephone is what I miss most when I'm institutionalized ... well, goodnight. Sleep well.

GILES, the Hound, Vernon, Tonio, Billie Holiday, Val— how did I end up among them? I have something overwhelming in common with these people—a life absolutely reduced and constricted—yet when I try to understand, to pinpoint moments, the moments are curiously neutral ...

Angela in the rock garden her great-grandfather had built of fieldstone. Arabis, rock phlox, aubrietia, alyssum—the first flowers out of the spring earth. Her teacup cooling on a rickety lawn table. Blue jays skirting the woods ... a black cat appearing in the yellow wall of forsythia ... Mr Berry spotting a humming-bird.

We'd driven over for the day—her parents had returned from Texas with snapshots: Mr Berry pointing out petroglyphs in red rock formations, Mrs Berry in a canvas chair by the Rio Grande, the two of them squinting at the lens in a desert trailer park. Tanned and spirited—thriving on retirement—the opposite of Mom and Dad. They both took a keener interest in me than my own parents did:

—Here we haven't shut up for a minute. How are things at K & K?

—We've picked up a couple of new clients. Home Handyman? Doing their catalogue—I think we have a shot at all their in-house stuff.

—Is this something you look after yourself?

—I'm overseeing Kevin and Susan. They put the catalogue together. I mostly—I winked at her—liaise with the client.

Sure enough, he opened his eyes.

—You liaise, do you?

—Sure I do—haven't you ever liaised?

He allowed his eyes to flutter and close.

—Not yet. Never interfaced with anybody, either. Never even impacted the bottom line.

—The other new one is Lakeview Estates. Prestige

homes west of the city? Doing a print campaign for them, plus the p.r.

—And didn't you have some sort of anniversary do?

Marnie's alarm when the cleaner tried the door—I felt myself flush—reached to pour us all tea.

—Wasn't a big deal. We gathered in the art department, guzzled Torgiano, and listened to McEleney tell us how wonderful we are. I was singled out. I'm one of the dithering old-timers now. Only three of us have been there from the start.

Angela called down in a tone that was light, almost mocking, but a caution to her mother:

—Owen never imagined he'd be there ten years.

—And you never imagined you'd be thirty! When Angela was in her teens, she told me she'd never get older once she reached twenty-one. I said, 'How are you going to manage that, dear?' She said, 'Well, you always say you're only as old as you feel, and I just won't let myself feel older!'

Mr Berry laughed along with his wife, their kind, weathered faces tilted to the sun.

—Well, gracious, you two. Soon you'll be a couple of old fogeys . . .

—Owen's working too hard. That stupid catalogue.

—And you, dear? Busy as ever?

Angela straightened up among the daffodils, pale green shoots about to become yellow trumpets. She touched the back of her hand to her forehead.

—Got another new client. Very nice older woman whose husband died recently. She doesn't have much money—he didn't leave a will, it's all tied up. Have to work something out.

—You remember the value of your services now.

Have you two redrawn your wills yet?

—Hard to find time.

She descended the mossy steps her father had built in the rockery. When she and Sandy were children the steps had seemed a vast, uncharted canyon of flowers and fieldstone . . . now she had to take care not to scrape her arm. She stretched out on the chaise beside mine—four of us all in a row. Something made a soft plunk in the grass. A grey squirrel came down head first . . . bounded across the lawn, its tail mimicking the curve of its body.

—It's lovely here, Mom.

The threadbare spirit of my own family. Dad burned garbage in the fireplace—left scorched debris in the hearth—flicked his cigarette butts in. After Mr Berry swept the hearth he laid a new fire so he had only to strike a match. He kneels on one knee and spreads newspaper on the screen . . . the flames catch with a sucking roar. He rubs his hands and sits in his leather chair, waiting for others to congregate. Miriam comes up from practising and sprawls on the rug. I sprawl beside her—we find faces in the embers. Before long she falls asleep. Mr Berry snaps a Polaroid—he has scores of pictures of Miriam sleeping. I stretch on the sofa to read *National Geographic*. Angela sets cut lilacs on the piano, makes a pot of tea. Late in the afternoon Mr Berry coaxes Miriam and Mrs Berry into a duet, flute and piano, music that delights and saddens me. The Berrys gave me something my own family never did: music, warmth, comfort in front of the fire. Their garden touched me in the same double-edged way.

—What about Craig, dear? How are things with your practice?

—Craig's fine.

She set down her cup, started back into the rockery. Mrs Berry whispered my way, not wishing to perturb her husband.

—Are he and his wife still having trouble?

—I don't know—I don't see him—Angela tells me they've divorced. I gather she's a bit loony.

Mr Berry clapped the arms of his chair. Unkind words were knives to him—he didn't like the turn of the conversation. He didn't approve of divorce . . . failure of any kind.

—Come on, Mother! We're losing our sun. Time to go inside.

—We've not finished our tea. We're enjoying ourselves. You start the barbecue if you're so full of beans.

He busied himself with cups and saucers and the pewter tray. Shifted the picnic table, fired the barbecue he'd built, a wheezing contraption that worked to perfection. Mrs Berry and I chatted while Angela pulled weeds. When the sun went behind the escarpment the air cooled quickly . . . we put on sweaters. Mr Berry led us in grace—he gave the same deep feeling to every word he uttered, whether reading aloud a funny newspaper item, recounting a Pakistani anecdote, or instructing his daughters. He spoke with solemn, dramatic assurance, as if addressing a jury:

> Be present at our table, Lord,
> Be here and everywhere adored,
> God bless us all and grant that we
> May feast in paradise with Thee.

Over the years I had come to recite with them and murmur 'Amen.'

—I'm worried about Miriam. Twice she left her instrument on the subway. She's so scattered, always racing around and forgetting things. Was I like that?

The rich comfort of their laughter—tenor and accompanist, Mr Berry's deep rumbling embroidered by his wife's quick giggles. I couldn't resist coming to Miriam's defence:

—At least she found an apartment with a kitchen sink.

We all laughed with the heartiness we brought to the singing of carols at Christmas.

—Poor old Miriam.

Had she been present Mr Berry would have clapped her between the shoulder blades, his gesture of love and concern. Each daughter was, in her way, a mystery to him. And to me.

—She slept over one night last week. I heard her in the middle of the night. Drinking coffee! And complaining that she couldn't sleep! I don't know when she does sleep.

—How's her job? Hasn't she started at that sandwich place?

—Supposed to be only Saturdays until exams—they've got her on three nights as well. Her exams start this week. She seems to practise whenever she's not working—I don't know how she keeps it up. We offered to help . . . she wants to earn her own money.

Mr Berry had strong views about welfare, and honest toil, and self-reliance.

—Good for her! Nothing wrong with that.

—So long as she doesn't try to do too much.

—Exactly, Mom—I'm worried that she's overdoing herself.

Again I felt the need to stick up for Miriam:

—Sweetie, you're one to talk. How many clients are you seeing?

Mr Berry cupped his ear—in poor light he heard less well.

—What's that? Miriam? Least she's keeping busy—nothing wrong with that.

I cleared the table and loaded the dishwasher—Mrs Berry spooned her fruit cocktail out of a Tupperware cylinder and filled a plate with date squares. When we went out again Mr Berry was lecturing.

—Sheer laziness, now come on . . . going to be thirty . . . these things need to be looked after . . .

Ordinarily Angela was the medium through which they prodded or praised us both, but Mr Berry turned, rather sternly, to me.

—I thought we'd agreed on this. It's something you were going to look after before we went to Texas and still nothing's been done. I know it doesn't seem urgent but Mother and I would feel a good deal better knowing it had been taken care of. How about it?

This was as strongly as he'd ever spoken to me—a reminder that, although Angela and I had never married (a source of bafflement and, I think, regret), he had ceded certain responsibilities to me. That same week we took out life insurance and had our lawyer redraw our wills . . .

A memory that begins with Angela in the garden and ends without her in this cell.

—Tonight. I told them.

—What did you say?

—I says we're not going, me and Monkey. I says when they started putting it together I was doing straight time. But that was a year ago, I says, and now, I says, we could both make parole this summer. I says, that changes things.

—What did they say?

—Gave them smokes—don't worry—it's okay.

—Where did you get smokes?

—Tonio. Owe him sixteen packs next Tuesday.

My chances for escape seem to fall on Tuesday. On a Tuesday Marnie and I went out for the first time, on a Tuesday we first went to bed. On the Tuesday before the weekend at George McEleney's farm she told me he had invited her to lunch. He had mentioned the agency's suite and suggested they might try the room service. She turned it into a joke. He pretended he'd been joking but the incident upset her—and me. My impulse was to cancel out, but it would have been awkward. We'd accepted weeks earlier and I couldn't tell Angela my true reason. Instead I simmered, determined to hide my animosity. Angela was delighted to be setting off on a spring morning . . .

—Sounds like let's pretend.

One summer the four of us drove out to the coast . . . returned by way of California, the southern states, the Atlantic coast. Jay and I fought and played in the back— Mom and Dad fought in the front. Many times we

pitched our tent by the car headlights. Occasional
nights—wonderfully luxurious—we stayed in motels.
Windshield blackened by bugs . . . car overheating . . .
Banff and Jasper . . . Yellowstone . . . Golden Gate Bridge
. . . Grand Canyon . . . the reek of oil refineries in
Louisiana . . . dead alligators on the highway. My sharp-
est memories are of the monuments to wealth—Dad
always stopped. At the Hearst castle our guide was a
middle-aged woman in a pantsuit.

—The lanterns are Tuscan, and these tapestries are
Flemish. The mantel is French, the choir stalls Spanish, the tables Italian—and this gorgeous pool is a copy
of an ancient Roman bath. The huge assembly room
was especially designed to accommodate the medieval
wooden ceiling—these cypress trees were trucked up
fully grown.

After the tour she invited questions. Everyone was
dazzled—everyone but Dad.

—How many people were employed in the construc-
tion of the castle?

—At a guess, five thousand.

—How much were they paid—any idea?

She gave a vague answer about Hearst's generosity.
Dad spat a curse—the guide flinched—all the people
turned to stare. I suppose he wanted to politicize us, but
it backfired. Secretly I yearned to live in opulence and
own as much of California as we could see . . . my
longing in proportion to his contempt. This same envy
welled in me at the ranches of Texas, the plantations of
South Carolina, the cottages of Newport with their
huge solariums and putting-green lawns. I was supposed to despise Hearst but it was Dad who fell in my
esteem. He put us in a succession of thin-walled houses
. . . other people lived in castles.

McEleney's farm was majestic. We turned in the drive, brushed our hair, and presented ourselves at the home of the young Dutch couple who did the farming. The McEleney place stood at the highest point and commanded a magnificent view of woods, ponds, grazing cattle. Split-level house—dramatic and sumptuous, floor-to-ceiling bookshelves, modern art, exotic plants. We had our own suite.

—I wish we could afford a place like this.

—We have a lovely house.

—There's a lot wrong with it.

—We'll get some work done on it. Maybe this summer?

Angela and Brooke got along famously. I found myself constantly with George. Another couple joined us Sunday and the separation continued: men in one conversation, women another. McEleney's face shone with moist colour, as if he had stepped from the shower. I was continually reminded of his overtures to Marnie. Sunday afternoon, after the other guests had left, he asked if I rode. Any of a hundred answers would have ended it there—I could think of none of them.

—I used to ride a little.

He went upstairs . . . returned in jodhpurs, riding hat, gleaming boots. He held a pair of leather gloves in one hand.

—Why don't we take a turn around the property. Perfect day for it.

He was trim and energetic—I was hung-over, forty pounds too heavy, and had no wish to get on a horse. But I could think of no graceful dodge.

—You don't have proper boots, sweetie. You can't go in those shoes.

How fortunate I was to have her, how easily she read

my mind. But McEleney wouldn't be deterred.

—There are boots in the hall closet. I'm sure you'll find something that will fit.

—Owen and I will do the dishes—you and George go for a ride, Brooke. Go on. Let us tidy up.

—Don't be silly, it's a matter of loading the machine. Besides, I loathe riding. Let the men go—you and I will chat.

—I'll saddle the mares. Go find a pair of boots. There are gloves as well. See you at the stable.

Angela sought my eye. I made a sign—perhaps it wouldn't be so bad. I recited this litany up to the moment of mounting Kitty. Only then did I recall my horror of beasts so big and strong—first day in the pit with Vernon—I couldn't believe his strength, how casually he used it.

In open country it was all I could do to appear to be enjoying myself. I fought the mare at every step—found no way to minimize the jolts. When the woods closed around us Kitty fell in behind the other mare and paid me no attention. She broke into a canter when Dewdrop did, slowed when Dewdrop did. I plodded along behind Dewdrop's lathered thighs and ass. Single file at least relieved me of the need to seem casual with the reins. I held tight ... in tricky going I grabbed the horn. McEleney looked back to yell something and caught me. I tried to incorporate my *faux pas* into the act of turning to look behind me—a branch grazed my head. Two inches lower and it would have crowned me.

—Enjoying yourself?

—Great!

The woods opened ... we descended a wash, the mares half-sliding in the loose earth. I had to lean back —almost lost my balance. At the bottom was a broad, swampy creek that gave off a powerful odour of fermentation. McEleney bobbed expertly, kept Dewdrop moving through the muck—Kitty shied violently at the footing. I urged her on, raised my voice, used my heels. She wouldn't budge—I kicked her—she snickered and snapped the reins from my hands. I began rocking and punching her neck, a model of ineptitude. McEleney, in equestrian pose on the far side, eyed me dubiously.

—She doesn't want to go.

—So I gather.

I should never have pretended I knew what I was doing. He had me on his turf and knew it.

—What do I do?

—Make her answer you.

—I don't know how.

—Fod God's sake, take charge! Show her you mean business!

I thumped my heels as hard as I could. Kitty started ... stopped, dislodging me. My weight bore down on one stirrup—she tried to turn—I fought to keep her head forward, scrambling to regain my balance ... she inched back in frightened little stutter steps. McEleney spurred Dewdrop across the creek—see how easily?— and took hold of Kitty's bridle. Terrible crunching of metal on teeth—still she wouldn't move. He spoke soothingly and then stung her. She jerked and stopped, propelling me forward. I found myself embracing her massive neck ... landed on my back, air forced out of me in a prodigious, endless groan. I seemed to remain paralysed a very long time ... would I ever again draw breath? McEleney's face shone down on me, amused, concerned, contemptuous—he knew about Marnie. And knew she'd told me about the company suite.

ONCE, because Val stayed out late, his father locked him in a closet. Another time, when the police brought him home for shoplifting, his father held his hands over a gas flame. For lying he had his mouth filled with Ajax. His childhood was punctuated by swollen cheeks, sore ribs, sprained wrists. His mother helped him invent stories to explain away the injuries. She too was beaten. She once tried to kill the father with a knife—ended up badly cut herself—claimed to have attempted suicide. The father abandoned them and died from something he mistook for heroin. Val speaks of him in tones of tenderness and loss. How could he regard his father with anything but hatred when hatred suffuses my memories of Dad? Compared to Val's father Dad was a model parent. I didn't always bear him ill will ... how did it change?

When Dad was home Mom used to tell him to take me with him. He sometimes took Jay but said I wasn't old enough. One morning on his way out Mom badgered him and he stopped to consider the idea. I stood between them.

—I'll be all day.

—You never spend time with him. He'll enjoy it—the two of you. Take him.

—I have work to do ... meeting in the afternoon.

—He'll find things to do.

—You'll be on your own, dear.

—I don't care.

—What about it? Can you last all day?

—I'll find things to do.

—Just make sure you get him home for dinner.

—Go on, grab your jacket.

—Did you hear me?

Gran and Granddad's favourite shows were *Father Knows Best* and *Perry Mason* ... I imagined the office as a cross between Robert Young's den and Raymond Burr's suite. Dad would use the intercom, smoke a pipe, tilt back and put his feet up. Now and then a secretary —darkly austere like Della Street—would bring him something to sign or to eat.

He parked beside a three-storey building in a part of the city I'd never seen. The ground floor was a travel agency and a dental clinic. The union had the second floor. A red-headed fellow was perched on the desk. When he saw Dad he stood—slyly turned into a man instructing his secretary. He mussed my hair and made my face heat with pride.

—So you're Harold's boy.

—Got his father's good looks.

—One of our boys—he's got an older brother.

While Dad talked to him Lorene bought me a Coke. She didn't seem old enough to have a real job, hardly older than Jay. Curved combs held her blonde hair in a loose pile on her head, tendrils falling toward the collar of her pale-blue kitten sweater. She showed me the offices. The meeting hall had a blackboard, a long wooden table, rows of stacking chairs. On every other chair was a pocked tin ashtray. Stale smoke hung in the air. Double doors opened into a hall leading to the offices of the staff reps. The place had a forlorn, rented feel. I loved it, perhaps because Dad did. At home he had the resignation of a man treading water—here he crackled with unmistakable energy and authority. Others became industrious in his presence. A man in a union windbreaker asked Lorene if Harold was in. He didn't need to see Dad, just needed to know. I understood for the first time that Dad was respected ... Mom's love had roots. She had tried to explain what he did and I was able now to imagine him sneaking into bunkhouses full of Portuguese labourers, asking about Portugal, getting their signatures on cards.

His office was big enough for a scarred desk, a filing cabinet, an extra chair, and a Gestetner machine. On one wall was a map with coloured pins. On the desk were a phone with buttons, a mug of pens and pencils, a stylus for cutting stencils, a card index, an oversized ashtray full of butts, two packs of cigarettes—he bought them by the carton, scattered them so they would always be at hand. A wire basket was heaped with papers and letters. The room seemed hastily assembled and crucially important, like temporary headquarters during war. Or a police station—Stoker's office.

Dad made call after call ... I worked paper-clips until they broke. People came in to ask questions—he told them where to look or who to phone. He had a way of getting rid of them. He said he'd be back in a jiff, popped out, didn't return until lunch. I sat at his desk and pretended I was Dad. Picked up the receiver, punched buttons and tried to say in his pained, almost intimate way, 'Harold Wesley.' I tried 'Wilf Wesley' and 'Owen Wesley' and 'Jay Wesley'—only 'Harold Wesley' sounded right.

When I got bored I went through his drawers. The shallow one held scratch pads, cigarettes, boxes of paper-clips, matches, elastics, cash-register receipts, pencils, a typewriter ribbon. The side drawer held phone books and a paper punch. In the middle drawer were a bottle and a marble pen-stand with two empty sheaths and an engraved plaque: 'To Harold, thanks from Local 216.' The bottom drawer contained an old fedora that belonged to someone whose head was scarcely bigger than mine. The cabinet was full of grievance reports, arbitration hearings, documents of certification. One drawer held reams of paper in several colours, Gestetner stencils, and Gestetner ink like old blood. I unscrewed a bottle ... inhaled the powerful vapour.

For lunch he took me across the street—hot dogs and shakes to go. In the afternoon I sat through a meeting with forty men, mostly Italians, dressed as if for a wedding. They were animated but grew less so in deference to the sobriety of Dad, who wore baggy trousers and a clean white T-shirt. He stood before them, then turned a stacking chair and straddled it. The men voted and got coffee and asked questions. Dad smoked and helped them.

—You have the floor, Franco, go ahead.

—Under the act, that's a decision that should be made by the executive.

—Item sixteen is the grievance filed on behalf of Vittorio Marino. Vic?

The meeting had me squirming. Dad's patience, which at home was undependable, here seemed infinite and genuine. When the meeting broke up he said he had more calls. Everyone had left ... I looked in the offices. They were like his except for photos on the desk, a child's paintings taped to the wall. Only Lorene's desk yielded much—a heart-shaped paperweight, a newspaper horoscope, a box of Tampax. I tried to jimmy the Coke machine and then looked in the washrooms. The women's was identical to the men's except for a second toilet in place of the urinal. It felt dangerous to be in, especially peeing.

Above the back door was a red EXIT sign. The window
was barred, the door locked. I stood on a chair—steel
steps led up to the third floor and down to an unpaved
parking lot. The lane was lined with grey fence and
ramshackle garages. A car turned up the lane with its
lights on. I returned to Dad's office—empty. The lights
were out in the hall, the meeting room, the reception
area. The front door was locked and needed a key. The
back door on the ground floor had the same red EXIT
sign. I returned to the front . . . tried the door again. All I
had to do was figure out the phone. Mom would come
for me. If they were out I'd call Gran and Granddad. If
they didn't hear the phone I'd call the fire department.
If they wouldn't break me out with their axes . . . the
police? Or I could go upstairs, break Dad's window,
jump. I tried to go through my options—I knew they
were plentiful—I forgot where they began. What
brought tears was not panic or fright . . . my own father
had locked me in.

My own father locked me in.

Dad locked me in his world, but he didn't mean to.
And I loved his world—entered it willingly, eagerly. I
bawled and bawled . . . a shadow appeared on the
opaque glass. I shut up. The shadow grew bigger,
blocking the light. A thief, a crazed murderer? I couldn't
call out and betray fear. A key worked one lock . . .
another. When the door opened I slipped through it like
a hungry cat.

—I forgot about you.

—I would have got out by myself—you didn't have to
come back.

He laughed.

—Let's go get ham and eggs. Like ham and eggs?

—We'll be late for dinner.

—Half an hour's not going to make any difference.

You know your mother.

We went across the street and sat on spinning stools. Men came and went through a swinging door between the diner and a room in back. A man with facial eczema sat in the corner dipping toast in coffee, an odd dinner. A fat man at the pay phone made notations on a folded newspaper, holding the receiver by shrugging. The grillman put our food on plates ... the counterman set them in front of us.

—Ham and eggs.

—Much obliged.

—Much obliged.

By the time we got home Mom had had a bath—her face was a lobster colour. She was in her pyjamas ... came partway downstairs. Her questions, made of the simplest words, were masterpieces of intonation.

—Did the meeting go on and on?

—Italians love shooting the shit. Just don't like to decide anything.

I saw by the way he stripped off his windbreaker and flung it on the banister that his listless mood had returned.

—Thank you very much. Am I supposed to hang that up?

—Does it have to be done this minute?

—Do you know what time it is?

He managed to sound both apologetic and sarcastic:

—I know, dear.

—I don't suppose you could have picked up the telephone ...

But her voice had softened—she was speaking to me —Dad's faults grew out of a noble singlemindedness.

—Did you have fun?

If the answer was yes, then thanks were owed her. If no, it was his fault for having kept me out so long. I wanted Dad to take me again ... groped for a reply that wouldn't hint at the remarkable discovery I'd made—away from home, from her, he was altogether different. She waited, hand on the banister ... she would take out our plates or she wouldn't.

—He locked me in. That's why we're late.

She turned and started up the stairs. On the top step she stopped:

—Your dinner's in the oven.

I called after her:

—By mistake.

—HOW was your week?

—On Tuesday we were told. Val didn't have to explain much, it was okay. They made it about fifty yards. Halfway up the duct one of them got stuck. I'd have ended up in dissociation—most frightening thing I can imagine. Thank God we backed out.

—Been writing in your journal?

—I had a dream about Vernon and Palumbo.

—Who are they?

—Vernon's a very strong guy. I taught him to read, him and Val at the same time. I already told you about Palumbo.

—I remember. The one who turned himself in, two years later.

—He whistles after lights out. Sometimes he whistles Dvořák's Ninth. Everybody hates it but he has Vernon to back him up. In the dream we both loved Vernon . . . I was about to kill Palumbo when I woke up.

—Do you know them well?

—Vernon is in the next cell. Palumbo is one of those people you take an immediate dislike to. But I love it when he whistles the 'New World.'

—The others don't like him?

—Everybody's careful with him because of Vernon.

—He and Vernon are close.

—Yes.

—Does their being close affect you?

—It seems pathetic in a way, I don't know . . . I pump iron with Vernon. He can't wait to see Palumbo.

—Does he remind you of anyone?

—He's uneducated, but he can smell weather coming. He knows when a cow is sick.

—Does he have good intuition? Do the right thing?

—When he found out he had cancer he and his girlfriend got hold of a gun . . . ten minutes later they were in the bank. He would never stop to ask himself, 'What's the best way to rob a bank?' He fascinates me.

—I wonder whether you admire the part of him that's unlike Owen. Was the dream sexual?

—It was more like a desire to exclude Palumbo.

—What do you like about Vernon?

—When he's sad it throws a pall over the tier. Happy, he's like a kid at Christmas. One time Billie Holiday tried to show him something on the guitar . . . Vernon ended up smashing it in a rage.

—You'd like to be more like him?

—Maybe. If I could just replace the part of me that closes in on itself, like a black hole.

—Can you locate that part in your body?

—Right now? I'd say my lower back. Kidneys.

—I wonder if there's anything you can do to get it out of your back and kidneys.

—I'm feeling an incredible ... when I get out I'll be like a child again. The world will be magical and new. Oh, how I long for that day.

—That transcendent? I'm reminded of this: 'I'll stop drinking when I get married because once I'm married it will change—I'll no longer be lonely and loneliness causes me to drink.'

—I'm not sure the comparison is apt, Ron. I can't really be someone different among unstable people.

—You admire something in Vernon. I'm not suggesting you be that impulsive, but isn't there a way of expressing yourself? How would the old Owen have reacted in the face of Val's overtures? The Owen who reacted to Angela's affair like a tortoise, showing nothing but shell?

—It's funny, Vernon rarely says a word about Palumbo ... never shows concern. But no one dares mention Palumbo in his presence.

—Is Vernon unaware of the generally negative attitude to Palumbo?

—Generally negative attitude—great!

—*Strongly* negative attitude?

—Sorry, Ron, it struck me as funny. People want to take him down. Vernon is contemptuous of homosexuals, yet he's compelled by Palumbo.

—What in your dream made you so hate Palumbo you'd kill him?

—We were competing for Vernon.

—You had similar dreams about Craig?

—I remember being in Angela's room, looking out her window, fantasizing about how I might kill him. I got

drunk and put sugar in his gas tank, ruined his engine.
I couldn't believe I'd done it, I felt like such an asshole.
They never guessed it was me.

—Did you ever tell him you hated him?

—I heard his voice on the phone. I'd been fired, I was
home. Even when Angela was there, I always answered
—hoping it would be him, so I could get pissed off. He'd
ask formally, 'May I speak to Angela, please?'

—You felt like telling him to fuck off, I imagine.

—He was phoning her—it was her place, too—I didn't
have a right to yell, 'Get out of my life!'

—But what happens to that violent impulse? Where
does it go? When you describe your anger I feel something in my own gut—a pain.

—What would you have done?

—It's important for you to examine what happened.
Otherwise I don't think you'll ever really be rid of it.

—You speak as if anger and frustration are tangible
things. They're just emotions.

—How was your digestion at this time?

—Marnie once asked me, 'How can you drink so
much night after night?' I hadn't realized I drank a lot
because it never affected me. Blankness. What I wanted
from the alcohol was out of reach.

—Do you still have that feeling of blankness?

—In here? Not blankness, emptiness—a lack.

—Can you recall your feelings around the time of the
funeral? Were you shaken? Relieved?

—I'd have to make up an answer—is that shock?

—And the legal procedure? How much do you recall?

—Odd things. The straight chair I sat on, the grain of
the wood. The suit the prosecutor wore day after day . . .
the light in the courtroom. I remember the two young
people who testified that they saw me push her. They

seemed more frightened than I was. This buzzing—a
roar—the toilets—drowned out everything. My lawyer
wanted to argue temporary insanity, which appalled
me.

—Do you remember when sentence was pronounced?

—Something fell away inside. I remember, 'Take it.
Don't break.'

—If you were listening to the judge now, how would
you react?

—He read a long statement which I didn't hear
because of the roar and because I was waiting for the
end of it. I remember he listed the ways I stood to profit.
Disgusted me. I remember the phrase 'precipitated her
death'—unbelievable pun—and 'considered judgment.' I
lost it there . . . told myself, 'Take it.'

—I wonder how Vernon would have reacted.

—Climbed over benches to get at the judge—'I'll kill
you, sonofabitch! Don't forget it.'

—Instead of 'Take it,' let Owen tell the judge how he
feels.

—My lord, I'm afraid . . . you've made a mistake.
You've convicted me of a crime I didn't commit.

—Can't hear you. You're speaking too softly.

—Listen to me! Don't walk out, listen! . . . I said
something like, 'I'm sure you have reason in your own
mind. But I did not do it.'

—Did you feel outraged?

—Not really—in a sense I was guilty—I didn't push
her, but I was one of the forces.

—Do you still feel that responsibility?

—Not . . . entirely.

—How did you feel toward the judge himself? Like
him? Hate him?

—I thought of yelling the sort of things in a gangster film: 'Your days are numbered. Have someone start you car for you.' For a moment I felt I could have strangled the sonofabitch. But he was acting out of obligation, he had no doubt I was guilty.

—Why did you not react when you were found guilty? Or when you were sentenced?

—I had to be a model prisoner.

—Did you appeal your sentence?

—I'm tired, Ron. I'm sick of this. You want me to rework the past ... I want to put it behind me—move on.

—I think you must deal with it before you put it behind you. As long as you don't really know what happened, and why, I think you'll be tormented. The past will drain the present.

—I listen to you—I respect your view. But I could not have killed Angela. I loved her and I'm anything but a violent person.

—I think you have more stored energy than you may realize. In your dream you were about to kill Palumbo. You daydreamed about killing Craig. You could have strangled the judge. I'm afraid we've got to end here ... I have someone waiting.

I left Ron's office unable to think ... stumbled on the stairs. I hadn't eaten properly and I was suddenly famished, how could I bear my incredible hunger? Ron stuck his head out, called after me:

—Owen, I don't know whether you've heard. The correctional staff has agreed to a new contract—there won't be a walkout.

ANGELA loved gemstones ... for a birthday present I
went to her favourite store. I was still in shock from
Craig's letter. I got out of the taxi—a girl handed me a
coupon—free intelligence test, Scientology. The store
was hushed ... made me aware my suit was ready for
the cleaners and my collar too tight to button. The only
other customers were two dark-skinned women, South
American perhaps, exquisitely dressed, chatting gaily
in Spanish and trying on emerald rings. I was attended
by a middle-aged man—Joseph. I said I'd like to look
around, meaning alone.

I had in mind gold but the bracelets and chains were
not special enough, and Angela had inherited gold
jewellery from her grandmother. I looked at sapphires,
purple amethyst, yellow topaz, gleaming peridot, pale
aquamarine. Diamonds in disarray like captured stars
on black velvet. A lapis necklace caught my eye ... an
opal ring ... a brooch of tourmaline in silver. I lasted
half an hour before being hit by the bone-weariness of
shops and museums. Joseph appeared.

—I'm not sure what I want.

—A birthday gift, by any chance?

—Yes. Next Monday.

He consulted his watch.

—The first. Pearl is the birthstone for June.

—It's a thought.

—I adore pearls—the only gem I care for that comes
from something living.

He leaned across the display case.

—As far as I'm concerned you can walk out with the amber and jet and coral—be my guest—so long as I get the pearls. Mineral brilliance, but with that other . . .

He met my eye—I realized he was gay.

—Perhaps you know what I'm getting at.

—I don't know much except how they're formed. Grains of sand.

—Not often a grain of sand, actually. It's a larval worm that penetrates and lodges between the mantle and shell of the oyster. To ease the irritation the oyster discharges a fluid. A pearl is layer on layer of this secretion, which hardens into nacre.

Joseph was so smooth he might have run on ball bearings. He dressed like a daring undertaker: pin-striped suit, magenta shirt, silk tie shot with pink, the knot raised by a silver tie-pin. His hair had been cut to flatter perfect ears and a high handsome forehead. But his hands were big and he's scarred himself plucking his eyebrows. I sensed something of the pretender . . . felt a kinship. I held a string with mock distaste.

—In each of these, there's a tiny worm struggling to get out?

He clapped like a child.

—Marvellous! Actually the larvae are microscopic. To give you an idea, they're no bigger than . . . a single sperm.

To my questions he replied that there were two types of pearl—cyst pearls, in the body of the oyster, and blister pearls, attached to the inside of the shell. He pointed out standard shapes—baroque, button, round, drop, pear-eye—and explained how each was formed. Demonstrated gradations in size, lustre, and orient. Brought out tiny seed pearls and a huge black pearl, which was blue.

—How would I know the real thing?

—Rub these against your tooth. Go ahead.

The pearls grated like tiny files.

—Imitation pearls are smooth. That nacreous skin can't be duplicated. Not yet, at least.

—These are natural, not cultured?

—Cultured, I'm afraid. Most pearls are.

The Japanese, he said, had begun inserting mother-of-pearl seeds into oysters from the mantles of other oysters. The oysters were caged and lowered into the sea ... left undisturbed for years. Ago Bay near Osaka was the centre of the industry ... farms had also been started in Australia and Burma. I asked if pearls tended to appreciate—he considered them a particularly opportune investment because the Japanese, despite producing for export, had only recently begun to prize them.

—It's not the same, knowing they're cultured. I like the idea of divers breaking the surface and gasping, oysters in hand.

Joseph opened a thin drawer and withdrew a string of cream-coloured pearls that caught my breath. I'd have bought them on the spot but they must have cost the earth. Luminescence spilled from his palms.

—Natural pearls are found all over—Tahiti, Gulf of Mexico, the Persian Gulf, near Australia, near Burma, New Guinea, Borneo, Venezuela. In Britain and here in North America fresh-water pearls turn up in rivers. But I think the most beautiful in the world come from the Gulf of Manaar off Sri Lanka. That's where these are from.

—May I?

—Of course I'm prejudiced—I was there when some of these were discovered. Last year I spent a month in Sri Lanka. I was able to go out on a dhow one day and watch the divers ... Unforgettable.

He put them in my cupped hands.

—Tears of the moon. Diving isn't a job for them, it's a divine calling, a mystical thing. They risk their lives. Many divers have drowned ... the waters are infested with sharks. Their attitude goes way back to the local myths and legends. They believe moon and earth were created at the same time, from the same spirit, then set apart. The two bodies stay in sight of each other, helplessly bound together. But they can never get closer, or further apart ... they only serve to remind each other of their separation. The moon is sad and it cries, raining down tears. The tears are in your hands.

Trevi Fountain ... Angela asked why people threw coins—'*Perchè torni*,' a youth told her, '*sempre tu ritorni a Roma*.' She insisted on flinging into the water, one coin at a time, all the change in our pockets. The pearls would be perfect—she'd love the story.

—Dare I ask?

—Thirty-six thousand, six hundred dollars. Plus tax.

He spread his fingertips on the glass, waiting for me to return them.

BY ALMOST any definition Jay is a success. He and Sylvia appear to love each other deeply and have a child they adore. They live in a rambling house of the sort Jay has always admired, full of dark-panelled rooms to which the morning sun is late in coming. He works exceedingly hard at a job he enjoys and that gives him a substantial income, most of which goes to the mortgage. He's putting on weight ... Dad's sprung gut. Drinks vermouth with lunch, doesn't play much squash any more. On weekends he and Sylvia see their friends, couples much like themselves. Why does a life that pleases him have the power to sadden me?

Jonathan?

Today he brought more photographs ... held up each in turn and I marvelled at the child's transformation, always changing and yet immutably Jonathan Wesley. I marvelled that I am this boy's uncle. Dad forced Wilf to the margin of our lives—Jay's efforts to sustain the connection seem to me the highest expression of brotherliness.

At the farm one time I found a tire in the ditch. It wobbled when I tried to roll it and I would have had to drag it had Jay not been there. Slapping it, he made it roll true, true as the spiral he put on a football. Other kids wanted to be on the right side of Jay—Wilf once said the same about Dad. He showed me a photo of himself enfolding his son.

—Don't ever tell him you made a mistake.

—How do you mean?

—Once when Dad was drunk he said to me, 'Getting married and having children was my big mistake.'

—He was always saying stuff like that. Ridiculous stuff. Remember the time he told us, 'All Portuguese are chickenshit—they talk a good game, then they fuck off.' Or the way, when he was drunk, he called Orientals gooks. He was stupid when he was pissed.

—Another time he told me, 'If I could have one wish,

one thing before I die . . .' I thought he was going to say, 'I hope Mom and you boys never get sick a day in your lives,' or, 'you and Jay attain the goals you set for yourselves.' Know what he said? 'I'd take the chairmen of the fifty largest corporations in the country, line them up against the wall, and shoot the fuckers.' Mom said, 'Oh, come on, Dad.' He dismissed her with that chuckle of utter contempt. He looked in my eye and said, 'Don't think I'm not serious.' I hated it when he looked in my eye—I could no more look back than stare at the sun.

—I thought it was the heads of the banks he wanted to line up. One time he nearly froze trying to snowshoe into a mine up north—know that? Trying to organize the place. He was convicted of trespassing.

—Probably drunk. Remember the time we gave him a sixty-dollar bottle of Scotch for his birthday? Saved up for ages—that was a fortune then—he drank it in one sitting.

—At least he enjoyed it. Remember the time he shattered the toilet bowl with a hammer because the board had disallowed an application for certification? Remember what he said to the plumber? The guy scratched his chin and said, 'What happened anyway? This toilet's not very old.' Dad said, 'We're a family that enjoys lentils.'

—The first time Angela met him he was in for a convention. You remember, we had dinner that night. The men were in his hotel room, drinking and shooting the shit. Poor Angela was petrified, never seen anything like it. Somebody was ranting about what crooks politicians are. Angela's father had been mayor and he'd run for the House. Angela got so offended she managed to speak up. Instead of defending her father she told them about one of the kids she was tutoring, a retarded girl whose dream was to go into public life. It was a moving story of impossible aspiration ... she had a room of piss artists staring into their drinks. Dad waited till she finished, then said, 'This girl sounds like Cabinet material.'

—You've got to admit he came up with some good lines.

Jay was suddenly overwhelmed. I hated to see the strength of Dad's memory in him—felt angered by his sadness.

—He was a prick! An asshole! He never remembered our birthdays! He forgot their anniversary! He hurt people! Remember we went to Wilf's and on the way home Mom asked him, 'Did you like the sole, dear?' Dad said, 'Our one hope is world government and Wilf's worried about whether to put a sprig of parsley on the fish.'

—Remember when you asked why he'd decided to quit the labour movement and move out west?

—He said, 'Drinking takes most of your time if you're going to do it justice.' Funny, but not true. The point is he never disclosed the central facts of his life, not to me anyway. Not to anybody, I bet. His jokes were lies— nothing's wrong, grief and pain don't exist. He never did tell me why he quit the union. Tell you?

—He didn't quit, O. He was fired.

—Fired! Was he? I see what you mean about following in his footsteps ...

—Listen, made up your mind about the pearls?

—You always ask, know that? Almost every time you come.

—I don't like having them around the house.

—I don't want to sell them ... maybe ... I don't know.

—Hey, remember his social-climber line? Dad had to go to a christening, remember? Uncle Don had slept in his suit. He rubbed his eyes and said, 'A what?' 'A christening,' said Dad. 'My godson is being christened.' Don said, 'What kind of depraved individuals would want Harold Wesley to be their child's godfather?' Dad got that twinkle. Scratching his feet, half-pissed at ten in the morning, he said, 'Obviously, Don, social climbers.'

—Who's Jonathan's godfather?

—Doesn't have one, O. Not yet. Sylvia and I were just talking about it. We thought it should be one of his uncles. Got any suggestions?

My brother.

FIRED. When people screamed 'Surprise!' I almost took a fit. Corks popped ... Marnie led a chorus of 'Happy Birthday.' The only one missing was McEleney. The party was great fun except that I had so much wine I was a wreck by the time I arrived at Angela's office.

I'd given her my present in the morning—carried two mugs up to the bedroom as if they were brimming with hot coffee ... handed her the one with the pearls. At dinner I told her the story Joseph had told me. We

started talking about ourselves, the past year, the
coming year. But I was drunk and wanted only to
celebrate. A heart-to-heart talk would bring me around
to children . . .

On Friday of that week I was about to leave when my
intercom sounded. It was six: I'd thought I was the last.

—Got a minute, Owen? I'd like to see you.

McEleney closed his door behind me. Out the window
new leaves wove a green veil that would soon make it
impossible to see into the ravine. A truck blocked traffic
but no one would let it turn. A streetcar was stopped in
its tracks—ding ding ding—I felt a surge of panic.
Usually McEleney sat on the chair and I took the sofa.
This time he sat at his rosewood desk. The wall behind
him was covered with bright lithographs and
silkscreens. Beneath them, beneath his tan, he seemed
pale. He took off his glasses to rub his eyes.

—Headache?

—I've had a migraine.

We had hardly said a word since the débâcle at his
farm. Angela and I had invited them to dinner but
they'd declined. Sometimes, when he didn't have a
lunch, he'd suggest we go for steaks. We played spoof
for the cheque (I suspected him of charging it to
expenses when he lost). We hadn't done that lately . . . I
regretted it. We'd become friends, to the extent men do
in offices. I spoke with an ironical gravity.

—Wanted to see me?

Still he didn't put on his glasses. He looked naked and
vulnerable. His eyes were small and recessed, distinct
as headlights at dawn. He was not happy this sunny
afternoon—Brooke, himself, business? Me? He cleared
his throat.

—It's been exactly a year . . .

Only then did it click. He'd decided some time ago but you do the deed on Friday.

—Less than outstanding year. I was brought in to assess the operation . . . come up with ways of slimming it. I've had a good hard look . . . time for a major reorganization.

—Spare me euphemisms, George.

He gave me a look—I felt oddly sympathetic—wasn't easy for him.

—This business is changing. The agency was capitalized because the parent envisioned a growing need for its own publications wing. Not enough thought was given to how it ought to be staffed, its association with the parent, where the competition would come from, or how the economy was going to perform.

He put his glasses back on—once again he projected smoothness and infallibility. Shortly after he took over I had told him frankly I didn't aspire to his job because it involved even more lying than my own and because I'd hate firing people. When I told Angela she gave me hell. Just because you'd hate to, she said, doesn't mean you couldn't do it. That didn't clear the air—I pressed her until she cried in anger:

—George McEleney's ears stick out but there's no reason to tell him! Just because it's true doesn't mean you have to say so. You're so candid about some things. Others things—like what your anger is all about, like what's happening to us—you refuse to talk about!

—Frankly disastrous year. The gentlemen in their wisdom pin the blame where it's easily pinned. I myself feel we're not doing that—

—Is it because I whip your ass at darts?

—Owen . . . I'd like you to start looking elsewhere.

A lump rose in my throat—I feigned nonchalance—

said nothing in hopes of making him uncomfortable. He only studied me . . . made me uncomfortable.

—Why me? Why not Rudy? Now there's somebody who deserves the sack. He carries a picture of his sailboat in his wallet. Wears polyester underwear. He says 'knock knock' instead of knocking.

—I've thought long and hard, believe me.

—I've given my working life to this place. Any point asking you to reconsider?

—You're going, Owen. That's what you have to work with. How and when and why—it's up to you. You're a capable copywriter and ideas person—loyal—you've helped Bob and Susan. At least you don't have a family to support . . . I know Angela's doing well . . . I don't think you'll have trouble finding something.

—Like hell! This little scene is being played all over and you know it. Don't hand me that shit!

—I don't intend to make it difficult—I'll help any way I can. I want you happy with the terms we settle on.

—When did you have in mind?

—I thought we could talk about it . . . end of next month?

—I've never been fired, George. Never even worked anywhere else so I don't know the drill. What does one do—our secret, that it? I find an offer too good to refuse? Will you have a send-off? Break out the Torgiano? 'Sorry to see him go, fine fellow, three cheers for Owen.'

—I know it sounds lame, but I like you and Angela both. I'm acting as president of K & K . . . this goes against my own feelings.

—Sure, nothing personal. Only why me instead of Rudy? You owe me a straight answer.

—I think you need a change. I get the feeling you despise your work. You seem to me profoundly unhappy, and your attitude has an effect on the others.

—Hell, no! I'm fascinated by the stuff you send my way. Home Handyman catalogue? Loved hearing from them ten times a day. We had a ball stripping in changes, working every night so it would be ready in time for the mail strike. What did they do with it, dump it in the ravine?

—You should have been generating your own accounts.

—Or Lakeview. I got so involved I actually looked at the houses.

—So Marnie said.

There was something in his pronunciation of her name . . .

—What else did she say?

—That has nothing to do with this.

—What has nothing to do with what?

—Your . . . situation with Marnie. Whatever it may be.

—Sounds like you have an idea . . .

He didn't like this—shifted in his chair, glanced out the window—couldn't back down now.

—Frankly, I expect you're sleeping with her.

—But that has nothing to do with this.

—Believe me, if you were less cynical I'd overlook any . . . personal indiscretions.

—Like the company suite?

McEleney went crimson—I felt despicable—men make war with the weapons at hand: spears, rocks, women. He inhaled through his nose . . . on the exhalation he seemed at last to relax. It was settled. Never again would we exchange a friendly word.

—I hope we'll be able to come to an arrangement. If not, we'll leave it to the lawyers.

He stood up—I was already on my feet, grabbing his
tie, hitting his nose, shattering his glasses ... a vivid
instant, but only in my mind. I strolled out like a man
without a care, turned at the door, and said, as I did
every Friday:

—Have a nice weekend, George. Say hi to Brooke.

He left me with the lacerated feeling that I'd brought
it on myself, but I can't see how.

What did Yoshino say? 'I think you can do more by
seeing, at every instant, how you create your world.'

TONIGHT I won all Vernon's tobacco and gave it to Val.
Impossible to lose to Vernon—his cards show on his
face. He starts with a sense of expectancy. Takes his
cards one by one and you see a progressive weakening.
(Opposite of Dad—gloating over nothing.) When he
catches a pair there's contentment about the eyes ...
offset by a softening of enthusiasm. Better than a pair
and he debates aloud whether to fold.

—The hell, boys, let's see where the strength is.

To see myself as I see Vernon. Tonight, last deal, he
called for blind baseball. The Hound sighed.

—Tell me the rules again.

—Threes and nines wild, first four gets a free card, next four has to match the pot, next four has to double it. Turn up a red king you lose automatic unless you get the other red king, then you win automatic. Three wild cards in a row you win automatic. You keep turning till you beat the last hand.

—That's not poker, that's bullshit.

—Want me to tell you again?

—Save your breath—deal me out.

—Sit out, lose your place to Boomerang.

—It's not poker when you don't see your cards.

—You see 'em all right. They're right in front of you. Jack diamonds is still jack diamonds, front or back.

Giles surprised everyone:

—That's the attraction of poker, it requires belief in good fortune. You invent your own fortune.

Vernon ended up with four aces. We folded one by one, until only the Hound was left. His last card, a nine, filled a royal flush. He reached for the pot—Vernon grabbed his bony wrist.

—That ain't no royal.

—Course it is. This nine is wild, right?

—Right . . .

—Ace of spades. Royal flush.

—You can't make it the ace, I got the ace right here.

—Threes and nines are wild. This three is the ten of spades. This nine is the ace of spades. Gives me a royal —puts away your lousy aces.

—You can't make a wild card same as a card I got. Can't be two the same.

—Don't be a bonehead.

Vernon kept his grip on the Hound's wrist and looked to Tonio. Shrug, smiling. Vernon looked to me.

—Who wins, Monkey?

—Well, I always understood—

Tonio slapped the table, making the pot jump. He wasn't smiling.

—The Hound.

Billie Holiday reached to shove the pot at the Hound—Vernon seized his wrist, too—Billie in one hand, Hound in the other:

—Is he right, Monkey?

The tier went silent. The veins in Vernon's temple were lit up. Tonio, smiling, unwrapped a stick of gum, waiting for my answer. Everyone was waiting.

—Tonio's the expert.

MARNIE seemed genuinely ashamed of her face without make-up and no amount of reassurance was enough. Her attention to appearance—the wrinkle that had to be ironed, the hours in the bathroom—came to seem a kind of desperation. So too in bed. I liked to think I alone inspired her pyrotechnics but I knew she had been as passionate with others, and would be again. She was thirty-three and joked about being an older woman. Perhaps those liquid eyes were fixed on the gap between singledom and spinsterhood.

Her moods were mercurial and had a forcefulness I came to fear. So exaggerated was her elation at a gift or a kind word that I began to withhold them. She was given to worrying ... the worry always seemed to outweigh the cause. Once in a motel room she lost a contact lens. We searched in the worn carpeting ... her distaste built up until she no longer knew what she was doing and erupted with such force she might have been watching the ground open beneath her. She struggled for breath—tried to stop her tears with fists. Soothing her was like throwing water on an electrical fire. She could only sob and gulp air until the mood played itself out. Afterwards her face looked hopeless and asymmetrical. To the bathroom she took her make-up bag.

The second time we drove out to Lakeview was the night we broke off. I had not come up with a concept acceptable to the client ... thought a second visit to the site might stimulate my imagination. Now that I'd been fired I felt a real commitment to the project. I'd told McEleney but no one else that I didn't intend to return to the agency after my month in France. I planned to tell Angela while we were away—we'd sort out everything free of daily entanglements—and to break the news to Marnie over dinner.

K & K had handled the launching of a seafood place near Lakeview Estates and there were discount vouchers. I suggested we drive out, take another look at the houses, then have dinner at the Lobster Pot. Dusk was falling—the lake appeared dead but curiously beautiful—we sped past fast-food places, industrial parks, businesses impossible to divine: Nutone, Isolation Systems, Colquitt Inc. The development consisted of skeletal structures on an unpaved, bulb-shaped road. In three weeks the builders seemed to have made no progress—

nothing had changed but the foliage. Beyond the trees was a warehousing complex. The tractor trailers and docks would soon be obscured, the bucolic illusion complete.

Marnie and I crossed the threshold of the same framed house as last time. The breeze was chilly and tugged at loose ends of tarpaper. The floor was sawdust and wood rubble. In the falling dark, moving from one room to the next, I felt the most acute melancholy. She took my hand. I tried to imagine drapes . . . kids . . . this was as close as we would come. Not that I wanted to marry Marnie — I simply had no access to my feeling for her—Angela somehow stood in the way.

Why did I have no access to my feeling for Marnie? For Angela? Why had I never had access?

I felt ashamed of myself, sorry for Marnie, enraged at Angela. But that was ridiculous—it wasn't anyone's fault. My inability to love wasn't Angela's fault, or Dad's, or Mom's, or Marnie's . . .

—Looking for a prestige home at an affordable price?

—Who isn't?

—Easy reach of everything?

—Sounds terrific.

—In a setting of natural beauty, only minutes from downtown?

—Where can I buy one?

—Lakeview Estates. Affordable luxury. Let's get the hell out.

The Lobster Pot had an air of newness and optimism and eventual failure. The three or four other couples seemed distinctly unhappy. The waiter tried to seat us at the worst table. I wanted a double martini—the restaurant served only beer and wine—I drank two litres . . . longed for drunkenness but the core of sobriety would not give in. I struggled with the best way to put it

... if I said I'd been fired, she would surely blame herself. If I told her I was quitting, she would assume it was because of her. I said nothing. At the end of the meal I presented my voucher. The waiter didn't know what it was. He consulted the owner and then presented the cheque. Free meal, exorbitant wine—a perfect microcosm—everyone felt cheated.

—Why did you tell McEleney we went out to the site?
—Did I say something wrong?
—Why did you tell him?
—Oh, did I do something wrong?

Rain. Tires hissed ... wipers played a lulling rhythm. I lit a cigarette—she waved at the smoke and gave me her little lecture about heart disease, lung cancer, emphysema. I put my arm around her shoulder ... stiff, unhappy. Rain bombarded the car. We had to slow past a tractor trailer on it side. A beacon whirled in the darkness—flares lit the highway—disaster all round. I pulled up to her building. Rain pattered against the hood—cleansing, musical, a little lonely. The whole world seemed a creation of my own despair. I cut the engine to listen.

—Owen, I don't know if I can go on like this.

Her words sounded rehearsed ... calmly spoken, but the front of her dress rose and fell with her breathing.

—I tried to explain. Remember?
—We never go anywhere and you're about to spend a month in France ... with her. You love me but you won't spend the night—not one night—because you have to get home. You're going to have adventures with her and then you'll be back in your house together ... I'm supposed to pick up where we left off?

I pledge to share this life with you, I vow ...

—I'm sorry.

She was nodding—tears ran from her closed eyes. We

sat on opposite sides of the seat, listening to the tick of
the cooling engine.

I ASKED Val about the scars on his arm. They're crude
and deep and vaguely representational, like something
on the wall of a cave.

—Did your father do that?

—I did it, Monkey. After they took me off chlorpromazine. You heard about the hacks, huh? The union signed
a new contract.

—My father organized unions for a living. The only
things that seemed to have meaning for him had to do
with work. When my brother was in university he got
Dad to answer a questionnaire. The questionnaire was
to be filled in by heads of families of various ethnic,
racial and cultural origins—an anthropology project.
One of the questions was something like, 'What are you
proudest of?' Dad said, 'That's easy—organizing
Wesco.'

—What's that?

—Wesco was a steel company. Dad was instrumental
in getting the union certified and he helped negotiate
the first collective agreement. Organizing the place was
difficult. The owner, a man named Singer, fired work-

ers suspected of union activity. The workers were mostly Portuguese and Italian, some illegal immigrants, with little English and no understanding of their rights under law. The working conditions at Wesco were appalling, the wages half those in unionized plants. Dad was young then ... took him and Uncle Don three years to get the union certified. During negotiation of the first contract Singer tried to bribe Dad. Dad pressed charges but Singer had friends and the case was thrown out. The negotiations were bitter and protracted. Dad was threatened by anonymous callers. It was terrifying, I remember, they tried to keep it from us but we knew what was happening. The union's offices got torched, Dad's car got run off the road. Singer spent a fortune on lawyers ... the negotiations dragged on.

—Finally the union and the company signed a collective agreement. Singer rented a floor of one of the hotels and filled it with oysters, crab, salmon, booze, and women. He invited everyone involved in the negotiations on either side. Dad did not attend. He would have preferred to slit Singer's throat. He said to Mom, 'I put three years of my life into that place and to him it's a fucking *game*.'

—Jay's project was supposed to demonstrate that in every culture the family was central. All the other people who answered his questionnaire said something about being proudest of their families. Mom and I were watching TV when Jay asked Dad these questions. Dad was reading, he said without looking up, 'That's easy—organizing Wesco.' Mom gave me a soothing look. I told my brother I thought Dad's answer had been pathetic. 'Did you?' said Jay. 'I thought it was kind of neat.'

Val started doing isometrics. He spoke to the rhythm of exertion:

—I used to get a certain allowance from my mother.

She usually give it to me on the Monday but she started forgetting. I'd wait till she was in the bath—sometimes wait until Tuesday or Wednesday. I'd call through the door, 'I need my allowance.' She'd call back, 'My wallet's in my purse. My purse is in the bedroom.' I'd take what I figured I could get away with—usually change—if she had small bills I might grab two, three extra bucks. Now and then I'd grab a fin.

He stopped exercising—sat beside me—his scars shone.

—One night she woke me up. She'd been out—pretty good glow on—made me sit down in the kitchen. I knew this was it. I thought she was going to say, 'I could have sworn I had an extra five. You don't know nothing about that, do you?' Instead she took a piece of paper from the cupboard—'I don't know when you started but here's what you've stole in the last four months.' It was a list: September 12, two dollars and twenty cents, September 20, five dollars. She said, 'You owe me a hundred and five dollars and eighty cents, buster. I want it next week or I'm calling the cops.' Sounded so casual—'It's in my purse. My purse is in the bedroom.' First B and E I ever did went to paying her back. She thought it was my old man beating me that made me run away. After that shit I didn't want nothing to do with her. Ever.

My teeth ached. I went to the bars, started doing isometrics.

—I've only ever been to one dentist in my life. He had three daughters and one of them hanged herself in her room. I had an appointment a few weeks later and while he had his back to me I told him I was sorry. He gave a laugh not much like a laugh at all. He said, 'Things

don't always work out the way you think they should,'
and he began probing my teeth. The office had an
atmosphere of grief to which I was utterly susceptible. I
kept my eyes closed—turned the headphones to ten—he
found no bad spots and cleaned my teeth. His wife, who
was his receptionist, handed me the bill in a self-ad-
dressed envelope. I was almost out the door when she
slid the glass partition—'Owen, I wondered, would you
mind witnessing our signatures?' On the wall of her
cubbyhole were school portraits of the girls. I watched
Dr McGibbon and his wife sign three copies of a
document pertaining to their daughter, then I signed
each copy.

—I knew very little about him. I had never seen him
out of his smock and had never met the daughter. He
knew of me only what one can learn from a few
questions once or twice a year. There seemed no reason
to be moved except that he had put in place every one of
the fillings in my teeth. Why should my dentist's
daughter's suicide have been more wrenching than—
say—news of my father's death ... or the judge's
pronouncement of sentence? I can't—

—Abandoned farms do that to me, house boarded up
and the barn caving in. See a lot of that where I come
from, people have walked away. Emmylou does it to me
sometimes. Put your arms around me, Monkey.

—Val, listen. There's something we—

—Put your arms around me.

Today I did.

ON THE plane I told Angela I'd decided to leave K & K. But I could see she knew I'd been fired.

—Maybe it wouldn't be such a bad thing to pursue something new. I'm making enough for us both. It wouldn't have to be lucrative.

I thought of Mom's small, carefully managed inheritance—her resentment of Dad's 'early retirement.'

—That's a nice thing to say. But what makes you think I want to be dependent on you?

—Come on, sweetie, you helped support me all the way through school.

—I have no intention of living off you.

—I'm just saying we'd have enough, if you wanted to do something that didn't pay as well.

—Let's just drop it, OK?

When the lights were extinguished we sank into a dull sleep. Lightning struck the wing of the aircraft, my nightmare. Everyone dozed uneasily after that. 'Perhaps your dream has something to tell you . . .' The captain woke us, pointing out the green sweep of Ireland. Paris was blanketed by fog expected to lift soon. We circled for an hour . . . ran short of fuel. The plane returned to Heathrow and put down in the chilly morning. We waited. We were not allowed to disembark. At intervals the captain announced that the fog had not yet lifted—the no-smoking sign was kept on—strangers began quarrelling. With Marnie I would have suggested a rendezvous in the washroom. Her eyes would have lit up...

When we landed in Paris we had been twenty-two hours in our seats—missed the connecting flight— finally set down in the south just in time to watch our bus pull away. Taxi-drivers were staging some sort of protest, refused to accept fares. We waited for public transit and boarded along with three times as many people as the bus was meant to convey. The crush was terrifying—the bus swayed ponderously—the highway bisected a valley of lavender fields, the journey seemed endless ...

We followed our map through foul-smelling streets. North African men, huddled under streetlamps, studied her. She took no notice—I was the one who was disturbed—the opposite of our first evenings on Yonge Street, our reactions reversed.

Finally we found the building. The massive door hung open, disclosing an interior courtyard. A German shepherd began barking—Tuffy throwing himself at the gate—the noise reverberating fiercely. The staircase was pitch black—I felt the wall like a blind man, took forever to find the right door. Our flat, thank God, was spacious and clean. At long last we slept. But I dreamed the building was on fire ... Angela was smouldering in my arms. 'Tell me, Owen, why do you think we dream?'

Awoke, totally disoriented, to the scent of smoke— fires in the hills. That summer was the worst on record. The news each night showed charred devastation and men in blue work clothes digging trenches. Each morning after shopping at the market we went to the public pool and lounged in the sun. Water bombers droned overhead, lumbering down to the Mediterranean and back into the haze. The planes swung low and discharged what looked like fuzzy tentacles of mist. But this was no more than a holding action, a fire died only when it ran out of combustible ground or the wind whipped the flames back on themselves. One day a verdant hill turned black in a slow eclipse before our eyes. Nothing to do but let things run their natural course . . .

—What are you going to do, Owen? What are we going to do? We need to talk . . .

—Let's just get used to being here first.

After the pool each day we had a nap. In late afternoon we opened wine and sat on the balcony . . . tried to talk. How might our lives change after the holiday? We assured one another of our determination to stay together. But she was not prepared to sacrifice her involvement with Craig and I kept waiting for her to suggest that we split up. I told myself to get used to the idea—pain established itself behind my eyes. Yet I felt buoyed by the foreignness of life and tried to keep her spirits up. Then, after a few glasses of wine, I'd sink into depression and her mood would lighten . . . ends of a teeter-totter.

Evenings we strolled the main boulevard, took a café table. The street was an uproarious pageant of motor-bikes, dogs, musicians, white-aproned waiters, stifled cars, and tourists. The animation was a relief and here, for a short time each night, we were absorbed. We sat contentedly, as we had as students, in the park, enraptured by what seemed a show especially staged for us. Plane trees formed graceful arches overhead, filtering the light of the moon.

It wasn't like the park at all. I was afraid . . . of what was happening, was going to happen. I couldn't talk for fear of what she might say.

One of the street people was an emaciated boy who looked Scandinavian. He resembled me, in features and complexion, though he had Angela's angular frame. His jeans were caked with dirt, his bare feet the colour of coal. His long hair was stringy and matted. He appeared at a late hour with a container of clear fluid and a swabbed baton. Directly in front of us, he guzzled, ignited the bulb with a cigarette lighter, tilted back his head, raised the torch to his lips—blew a roaring flame twenty feet in the air ... then another, smaller burst. People gasped in astonishment. A waiter hurried over to berate him but the boy had an oblivious composure no amount of harassment could affect. He wandered among the tables begging coins, an alarming look in his eye.

I gave him two francs. He stared at Angela with the blunt, direct expression of a madman. People turned to look. I asked him what he wanted—this seemed to reach him—he shuffled off, muttering in a language I couldn't understand. She thought he was thanking us. It sounded to me like contempt.

From our balcony we could see over the wall of the city's most expensive hotel. On the terrace, waiters in white stood in the shade of oleander. A plump, hairy man was the only guest. He was teaching his twin daughters to swim, supporting one in each hand. They kicked and splashed ... remained in place.

—How are we going to work things out?

—You mean work it out so you can spend more time with him?

—Owen ...

—I saw you writing postcards, the way you put the one to your parents on top. And why did you encourage the lunatic kid? I hated the way he stared at you.

—He wasn't bothering us.

—He bothered me. He was right out of it.

—Owen, I've been wondering if it might be better . . . living apart. Would that make things easier? . . . I'm just trying to think through the possibilities.

The ache located itself behind my eyes, I gazed at the turquoise pool, fell into one of the long silences that had seemed, at first, the opposite of estrangement. Marnie and I would have made love . . .

I still had said nothing about Marnie. I must have been holding her in reserve, a high trump, unsure how and when to play it. The café seemed the place, but the firebreather appeared soon after we sat down. I knew he was making his way toward us, the purpose of his nightly appearance. I knew he was the one setting fires in the hills, imagined him arrested, sent off in chains . . .

The sparrows, Vernon's moans, Palumbo whistling the 'New World'—waiting . . .

The evening before we left for Marseilles, as we waited for the firebreather, I finally told her about Marnie. Implying that I, not she, had ended the affair. Why this lie? Because I didn't want Angela to feel responsible? Or was I ashamed to have lost control of the affair? Did I want Angela to know I would sacrifice any other relationship to protect what we shared? Or did I want her to know that I expected her to do the same?

A stupendous illumination lit up the night. Our table was close to the sidewalk—the street was crowded—a crowd of people moved with him. He caught sight of Angela and set down his container of fluid, hyperventilating, eyes fixed on her. I don't know what possessed me, I was enraged, I found myself on my feet, yelling in his face:

—You bastard! Get out of here! Leave us alone!

Others were startled, but the boy continued as if I weren't there. I had the distinct sense that by intervening I could forestall tragedy . . . felt suddenly foolish at the spectacle I'd caused, sheepishly took my seat. Angela gripped my arm—hurting me—gazed at the boy in horror. When he lit his bulb a silence fell . . . the circle expanded . . . a dog sniffed at his feet as he brandished the torch. He cocked his head back, brought it to his lips . . . tripped backwards over the dog, instead of the flame-thrower surge there was a dull explosion, his head a falling sun engulfed by fiery tongues, hitting the concrete with the dull thud of a melon. How abruptly it happens—the falls—Val's embrace—and yet it unfolds in slow motion . . .

A Frenchman beat the flames with his jacket, people came hurrying, Angela was crying, an ambulance wailed. Traffic was so congested the ambulance was abandoned. The boy was carried away on a stretcher raised above the heads of the crowd . . .

I stayed up, sitting in the chair, drinking Pernod, watching Angela, who thrashed in her sleep. I awoke, chilled and stiff, to find her watching me . . .

We learned from the newspaper that the boy had died. He had carried no identification—the police were appealing to anyone who knew him.

—I knew it was going to happen. When I yelled at him. . . .

—I was dreaming, I have cramps and a terrible headache.

I wanted to talk now, to raise the subject of children, suggest we resume making love.

—Starting your period?

She looked at me as if I'd uttered an absurdity.

—Owen, I haven't had a period for two years.

FOR a pack of cigarettes, Val will hold his finger in the flame of his lighter for as long as it takes him to recite the alphabet backwards. He doesn't hurry ... this leisurely quality is the key. When the Hound wins at poker he has Val do his trick, watches as raptly as a child. The Hound borrows Val's lighter and tries it himself ... yowls, jerks his finger away, pesters Val for the secret.

—What do you do? Coat your finger first? What with?

—Not even close.

—Give you another pack.

—The secret of life for a pack of smokes?

—Like firewalkers, right? Your finger don't burn because you're protected by spirits, right? Do it again.

—For another pack.

He did his trick four times tonight ... different fingers. Afterwards I lay with him. Imagine: being with another man, on a cot, in a prison cell—hard to conceive and yet there I was. I'd have thought it would cause me panic and distress but it has the opposite effect. The sense of oddness arises now, later. Is happiness no more than a capacity to entertain contradictions? Holding him soothes me, even when he himself is far from happy. I studied the winged snake on his arm, imagining the needle's stab of ink. All Val's wounds. I kissed his finger—he flinched.

—What the hell is your secret, anyway?

—I'm in a fix—I owe Tonio.

—I've got five packs I didn't tell you about. Probably win another five tonight.

—But I need thirty-two by Tuesday. Wednesday it's sixty-four. Got off Percodan, got off chlorpromazine, but I can't seem to kick smokes.

—You don't want to be in that bastard's bad books. I hate it that you're always in debt to him.

—It's my problem.

—I don't want anything to happen to you . . .

—I'll tell you, on one condition—promise you won't tell nobody. It's my only money-maker right now.

—Tell me what?

—The secret—the lighter—it hurts like hell—I just don't let on.

—How have you been?

—What I was going to say to Val, remember? Didn't work that way.

—There's a new side to the relationship now?

—Changed my mind, I guess. Or my mind changed itself.

—Did you enjoy it? Were you there with him, or not there?

—It was intense ... I felt odd afterwards. It was something I hadn't been in control of.

—You often think of things as happening without your control. If your mind isn't here, does that allow things to happen?

—I always liked to control things—which restaurant we'd go to, the colour scheme of my office. The summer before her death I got the sense that things were happening, I wasn't controlling anything.

—Which feeling did you have with Val?

—I didn't make a choice. In fact, I had made the opposite choice.

—We seem to come back to the part of yourself you're not always connected to. Do you know that part—the old Owen—better now?

—Strangely enough, I don't worry about the implications.

—You've obviously dealt with it at some level. Otherwise how could you be accepting of something that used to frighten and disgust you?

—If I can't take things as they come ...

—I'm reminded of Angela's death, how obscure that period remains for you. It's as if one Owen does things and the other acknowledges them or refuses to. Maybe with Val the two have come together.

—You make it sound as if I'm schizophrenic. Christ, does it say that in a file somewhere? Am I schizophrenic?

—Part of you has gone unacknowledged for a long time. You've become skilful at canning it and ignoring it. I see our goal here as integrating your past, present and future. That doesn't mean I view you as schizophrenic. I hope you'll walk out of here in tune with yourself rather than as someone composed of parts.

—Such as queer and straight?

—I hope you understand that your experience means nothing to me in a moral sense. It's whether you embrace it and include it in the richness of yourself.

—I feel surprisingly good about it.

—Let's go back to the question of why you used to repress a part of yourself. Who's in that can? Are you getting to know that Owen?

—Ron, you piss me off sometimes. This makes me clench my teeth. The two Owens shit—I don't buy it.

—When you bought the pearls one could say there were contending voices. You chose to act on the voice that said, 'Buy them, Angela will adore them,' rather than the one that said, 'They're expensive, you can't afford them, you're in debt.' Like everyone else, you have many facets. It's important to integrate them.

—Myself and my father. Seeing myself as part of a continuum—I used to deny the connection altogether. Is that the sort of thing?

—I think you're finding parts of yourself that have been repressed. The animality—isn't that what came through with Marnie, and now with Val? Your need became so strong that it broke through. Because you allowed it to break through. Tell me about the relation with Val. Been dreaming about him?

—Sleeping and waking aren't distinctive sometimes. You hear in your sleep—doze on your feet—I'm remembering the time before her death.

—I think you're making tremendous progress. It pleases me no end. Do you have that feeling?

—At the start I told myself, 'You're here, adapt or it will break you.' And I did adapt. But lately it's felt slow and deadening. In a way Val only makes that feeling more acute. Oh, how I long to be in a room with art on

the walls. God. I'd like to be in front of the fire with
Angela's family, or having a beer with Jay and Mom and
my nephew. Christ, am I crying? I don't have the
sensation of crying, just the tears. That's why I'm
laughing. Isn't that funny?

—It must be very difficult at times.

—I remember an old film, a comedy, Harold Lloyd
maybe. He's hanging onto the minute hand of a huge
clock. Each minute, the hand moves. You mustn't step
back and ask, 'Where's the hand now?' But I am
stepping back, I feel stuck.

—Yet amazing things seem to be happening. You
don't seem stuck.

—Think so?

—When we first met I don't think you'd have allowed
yourself to have sex with a man. If you did, I don't think
you'd have told anyone, perhaps not even your journal. I
think many things, including your journal, are helping
you see yourself in a new way.

—I suppose so.

—Back to whether this was something you wanted or
something that happened to you. The notion of control.

—You know when you try to join like poles of
magnets? The repulsion is incredibly strong—one of
them flips—the attraction is equally strong. It was like
that.

—It's important to see that you wanted this and got
it. As opposed to, 'I didn't want it, wasn't really me.' No
difference in what happened, only in your attitude
toward it. Self-acceptance.

—But to fully accept that I'm here seems to me an
admission of defeat. What sustains me is knowing I'll
walk out. That moment will be . . . however you define
transcendence.

—I'm not saying this is a place anyone ought to choose. I'm not denying it will be wonderful to be among people you love, in a room full of art and Persian carpets. But I've seen men emerge imprisoned—they take with them an invisible cell. People who are apparently free and happy commit suicide.

—I want to be in the world. Trains, mountains, wine.

—While you're here, the way to escape is to be fully here. Does that make sense? When you feel something's wrong, look inside to see what's causing the feeling. That's the process you've begun and must take to its conclusion.

—I don't know ...

—How does Val fit into your thinking? Your future?

—Perhaps I could be switched to a women's prison to serve out my term. Could you arrange it, Ron?

—I'll see what I can do.

—What would have made me shy away was fear and contempt, plus a preference for women. Now I've lost the fear—the contempt—the question doesn't weigh on me.

—I asked whether you'd decided to try this or whether it had happened, or been forced on you. This has been strong in you, this idea of an overwhelming force. I'm not saying there are no external influences, but a lot of men here think of themselves as not responsible for what they've done. It seems to me a futile way of looking at things.

—What do other inmates talk about?

—Wives. Children. Fathers. Mothers. I can't really generalize. There are levels of awareness. Some people begin with a distorted view of themselves, others have a high degree of self-knowledge. What they have in common is some sort of disconnectedness—a need to get in touch with themselves. Why does he rape? Why is he driven to steal? Why does he hate blacks? I see my role as a catalyst, helping precipitate the gaining of self-knowledge. Everyone has his own solution inside him. I'm sure of that, though I don't mean to discount the considerable, often devastating effects of poverty and abuse and racism and neglect.

—It's amazing to think that you're involved with other inmates. That I'm one of twenty people you see. I think of Angela . . .

—You understand, Owen, this is a job, pure and simple. You also understand that I like you very much, and feel affinities between us. I am constantly sorting out my own life and much of what we talk about is illuminating to me. I want to help you work out a mechanism by which you can look at yourself. I can't stress enough how important it is that you eventually take over my role.

—Tell me something. Why do you do this?

—I enjoy it and it seems to be what I do best.

—But why, when there are no solutions? Only another maze.

—It seems to me that the mysteriousness of life will not yield to faith or intuition, or any form of rational inquiry. And that this—not famine or illness or pestilence—causes the greatest pain and bewilderment. One can deny the mysteriousness of life, or fear it, or one can embrace it. It seems to me it ought to be embraced, that we ought to help one another embrace the mysteriousness of life. Perhaps this is just another way of saying that we ought to do all that we can to find our illumination in love. To love everyone, everything we encounter. This is what I believe I ought to be doing, and somebody pays me.

—How little I understood Angela's work.

—I'm sure you're aware, having lived with a therapist, that it's often fairly easy to do the work and yet impossible to apply the insights to one's own situation. I've certainly found this.

—Angela didn't have much use for psychiatrists. She disapproved of their tendency to prescribe medication.

—Medication has its place, particularly in an institution such as this.

—I'd hate to be looking forward to the trolley each morning.

—Weren't you like that? A joint or two, a vodka?

—I once shared a highrise with a guy with delirium tremens. All night he'd pound the mattress. His body fired on its own—legs and arms jerking, head bobbing, body twitching. He yelled, 'Give me my Thorazine! You took my Thorazine!'

—I'd like you to think about this idea of control. You might consider that you are responsible for the fact that you're here. That no big, invisible machine put you in this situation—you brought it on yourself. See yourself as the instigator rather than as a helpless victim.

—I am a victim. I'm not criminally responsible for her death—no way—perhaps I could have prevented it . . . that's not the same.

—I'm suggesting it might be fruitful—as an exercise —to view yourself in a new, completely responsible way. See every element of your life as your own doing. Try it. See what happens.

IN MARSEILLES we took the first hotel we came on ... high on a hill, the city sloping down to the harbour and rising again to the burnished majesty of Notre Dame de la Garde. The streets were various and exhilarating—old women washing rags in one block, fashionable shops in the next. We wandered through a textile market that meandered half a mile. Another market offered nothing but garlic, all colours and sizes. By the old port we took a café table and sipped beer. The masts of moored yachts formed a swaying forest ... the lanyards set up a chorus of pings that carried across the water. A siren pierced the stillness—a police van sped by, right out of a Belmondo film. A gnarled little man with a basket hooked over his arm put three salted peanuts on our table.

—He'll be back, selling them.

—Isn't this a wonderful city?

—Just what we needed. That poor kid in Aix drove me crazy. I'm sorry, Ange ... the way I've been lately.

The gnarled man reappeared, dragging himself from table to table, with bags of peanuts for sale.

—Told you.

—Let's get some, they were good.

—Oldest sales gimmick in the book.

She laughed:

—Well, it worked on me. I want some.

She signalled the little man, who made his lopsided way to our table.

—*Non, merci.* Sorry.

—What's the matter with you?

—Why are you buying them? Because you want them, or you know it pisses me off? You don't even like peanuts.

—One bag, please.

—You wouldn't have bought them if I hadn't said anything.

Sulking, sniping, touring the old fort, wandering out the sea wall—ancient smells of salt breeze and urine. We came on a lee where people were sunbathing, climbed down the rocks and found our own spot. Angela stripped, abandoning herself to the sun. Against pale breasts, the v of skin in her unbuttoned blouse looked reddened and rough. Her buttocks seemed doughy, the shaved skin of her armpits raw. Love is a brimming cup ... one day you find nothing but gritty residue. I ached for Marnie.

—You're going to get burned.

Tourist boats cruised back and forth from Château d'If. Sun on the water—a million gold coins—I stretched in the warmth and began to feel a kind of fatalistic contentment. Everything would work out in the end, or wouldn't ...

Our room, top floor, seemed cramped and gloomy until I opened the shutters. Tile roofs formed a patchwork stairway down to the harbour and the glittering sea. Gulls wheeled overhead ... their cries mingled with the faint din of traffic, children, dogs. The sun was dissolving behind the gauze settling over the harbour. I sat on the bed, touched her breast—put a white mark in the red.

—I told you. Does it hurt?

—I don't feel it.

—What's wrong, sweetie? Not enjoying yourself?

—When are we going to talk?

—Over dinner. Let's eat and talk.

We headed for the old port ... mounds of mussels, squid, clams, prawns, tile fish ... shills promising the best bouillabaisse in Marseilles. The streets that ran back from the harbour grew narrow—our footsteps echoed. Through a café window we spotted men sharing a giant bowl of mussels—the omen.

The place was full of North African men. They took notice—I felt uncomfortable—she, oddly, seemed at ease. When I ordered a second litre of wine the proprietor said the man in the corner wished to buy it for us. An intense-looking North African raised his glass, beaming. We called our thanks and drank to him—the serendipity of travel. He was by himself ... I invited him to join us. Angela gave me a quick worried look. It angered me.

—For Christ's sake, relax. Let it flow.

He spoke little English, my French was better than Angela's, so I translated back and forth. We told him about ourselves and asked about his life. Nourredine— from a village near Algiers—in Marseilles five years. Somehow it became a conversation between them. She wondered if he had found happiness in France. No, the opposite. He and many other young men from his village had come to work. When he saw the villas and cars and well-fed people his mouth fell open. He poured concrete in a sewage tunnel, lived in a barracks near the site, started work at five-thirty. The labourers were North African, the foremen French. She asked if he had a family. Wife and two children, boy and girl—he hadn't seen them since coming to Marseilles. His family lived with his parents. Each month he sent money but it was

not enough. He was ashamed of not having visited them
... afraid of losing them. And what about us—did either
of us have children? He took us for brother and sister ...

Late every afternoon he came to the café. Free meal
for odd jobs. He spent his little money on wine and
anisette. The café gave him a sense of warmth and
acceptance—Angela's family, warmth in front of the
fire. When the café closed he went home and listened to
Arabic music on his transistor until he fell asleep. Arose
each morning at four for his ritual evocation of Islam
and home.

I ordered more wine. As he grew drunk he became
more emotional. He was cut off, all alone. She asked if
he had photographs of his family. No, pictures made
him cry because he knew he would never go back. In
truth he no longer sent money, that had been a lie, he'd
stopped sending money two years ago. He spent all his
money in the café. If he returned to Algeria he had to
take presents for his wife, children, parents, and brothers, or he would be a disgrace. They would think he had
drunk wine and run with women, never thinking of
them. He thought of them constantly ... when he left
for work he pretended to kiss them goodbye, when he
said his prayers he included a prayer for each of them.
At night, listening to his radio, his mind flew over the
Mediterranean ... home, arms full of presents. Once, he
said, he did buy presents—a dress for his wife, trousers
for his brother, pretty things for his children. Someone
in the barracks stole them.

He kept saying he was afraid. What he feared most
was dying in France. To die alone in a foreign land—
that brought him back to the café and the anisette.
When you die in Algeria—his eyes ignited like sparklers
—your family is with you. You leave them a word, what

you've learned from life. In Marseilles there would be no one to listen. He was like a tree forced to grow unsupported—it begins to bend, each year gets more crooked. He himself was now so crooked he told lies to strangers who shared their wine. No one stole his presents, he said, that too had been a lie. He never bought presents, only wished he had.

I wished I hadn't invited him to our table—grew fearful and suspicious—where was this going? His story seemed melodramatic, unconvincing. What else was lies? But I could see from the way Angela held herself that she was deeply moved. She asked why, if France was awful, he didn't return home. He was afraid his wife had been unfaithful. If she had gone with another man it was his fault ... he had left her alone. Perhaps his mother watched over her—perhaps she watched over herself—hoping was better than knowing. She asked if he couldn't bring his family to France. The authorities wouldn't permit it, they wanted labourers and no one else. Besides, where would they live? His room was a closet—all he could find—in an unheated basement, an abandoned building full of cockroaches and rats.

He'd said he lived in a barracks—Angela didn't seem to notice—I tried to interrupt but he was spewing an impassioned monologue. He wanted his children to grow up proud to be Algerian. Bringing them to Marseilles would only lock them in the prison he was in. He wanted his son to be a professional man, a doctor or lawyer, with riches and happiness. He would work ten lifetimes to save his son.

Angela wanted to know if he had friends in Marseilles. A few, like himself—he gestured around the café. Had he no French friends after five years? He laughed grimly—the French didn't like North Africans. On the street youths he had never seen asked him why he didn't stay in his own country. The police stopped him to check papers, sometimes three or four times a day.

Angela was incredulous, close to tears. Her empathy was frightening, the way she so willingly entered his lies, his life. Has no one ever invited you home—your foreman, the people here at the café? No, he said, never. You learn to accept this, but not on holidays. You watch others return to their families ... you're unable to return to your own. He rested his forehead on the table, spoke in a choked whisper.

—The shame of my life.

I translated—but Angela was already reaching across to touch his shoulder, reassure him. He looked up at her and spoke in English.

—Lose man. Nourredine, lose man.

—We're your friends. Friends.

—*Amis*—I spoke bitterly—*nous sommes amis.*

He insisted on joining hands and drinking some sort of toast. I did not want to be saddled with him and gave Angela a stern look. She was engrossed ... it was my own fault.

Tomorrow is Saturday, he resumed—Saturdays were worst. He cleaned his room on Saturday and knew for certain he was a lost man. It was shameful to do the cleaning. A man's wife should do his washing and cleaning. He could not watch his children grow, he didn't send money home, he was afraid of dying in France—and he had to do his own cleaning. He said this last with deep remorse ... I couldn't help smiling.

He beamed in return—sprang from his chair and took my hand, wanting me to go with him. Where? Come, you'll see. I jerked free, said I wasn't going anywhere without Angela.

He took her hand and gently pulled her to her feet. Wait, then, he said, he'd go with her instead. I told him no ... was this going to get unpleasant? He was small but wiry and strong. Perhaps I could use my weight to advantage. I thought, I wouldn't mind this, wouldn't mind fighting over her—fear, exhilaration ...

Yet she, to my astonishment, said it was all right.

—What are you doing?

—I'll be back in a while.

—This is Marseilles, for Christ's sake! You can't even find your way back to the hotel.

—Wait here—don't worry.

What could have possessed her? Was this the same person who had clutched my arm on Yonge Street, barely able to endure the appraisal of strangers? Before I could think what to do they had gone. I sat paralysed a moment ... hurried out to the street. It was narrow, poorly lit—I wasn't sure which way they had turned. I drank wine, trying to appear unconcerned—couldn't think—the jukebox was playing Algerian music. The men seemed to be regarding me with contempt. I looked up—they snickered and looked away. How would I find her? The police? What if his whole story had been a lie? There were thousands of men in the city who looked like him. What if he wanted love and she'd given inadvertent consent? A man whose greatest shame was doing his own housework. I asked the proprietor where Nourredine had gone. He answered with a smile, an exaggerated shrug. I heard laughter behind me and spun round, ready to fight. A table of men pretended to be laughing among themselves.

I rushed into the street . . . turned this way and that, helpless. Come back, I prayed—and she appeared round the corner and waved. I felt disappointment. Disappointment! He wore a child's grin—they hurried toward me. She extended her hand like a bride. We moved into the light of the café window. A bit of glass in an adjustable band—the sort of ring children find in boxes of confection.

—Nourredine picked it out. It shows our friendship.

He was nodding, beaming. He held something out to me—a ballpoint—he said he hoped I would not forget him. While I admired the pen he embraced me. I had never been embraced by a man . . . I felt his heart beneath his ribs, the surge. He kissed me on the lips . . .

Back at the hotel we stood at the window, gazed at the flickering city. Traffic seemed thin and forlorn—moon a dull smudge—a lighted ship was bulling its way toward open water. I'd been disappointed!

—I was in a panic. This sounds stupid, but for a minute after you went with him I was afraid I'd never see you again. God.

—I know you as I know my soul . . .

—I love you with an ancient heart . . .

I kissed her, and for the first time in years we made love. It was awkward, strange. I imagined myself as Craig, wondered how she was with him—the way Marnie was with me? I tried to keep my eyes open . . . if I closed them I thought of Nourredine, the force of his heart. I pretended she was Marnie—pretended I was Nourredine—tried to make it anything but what it was.

Simple, stunning, tragic. It wouldn't have been my fault, anyone's. A young woman disappears in a foreign city.

BEFORE his hearing Val was so nervous he couldn't eat. Couldn't even smoke. He did isometrics in my cell, breathing in a shallow, fitful way that sounded like panic. He was hoping for limited day parole or, if lucky, day parole. Fifteen minutes in front of the board—full parole! The news ought to have delighted him and saddened me but it's had the opposite effect. In the yard we found a sunny spot and sat by the wall. But before I could ask him about the hearing Billie Holiday appeared.

—The big day, right, Val?

—What do you want?

—Make it? 'Speck you would—model inmate like yourself. Wouldn't want nothing to fuck it up now, would you.

Billie's laugh—broken glass—he hurried after Tonio.

—What's he talking about? Cigarettes?

—I got other things to think about.

—Worried about making the adjustment?

—No money, no trade. They'll be on my ass the moment I step out. I'll come back—always do.

—As a famous prison philosopher once said, trying to cheer up his best buddy, 'What the hell kind of attitude is that?'

Val threw back his head and laughed, face to the sun.

—This one time, Monkey, I went to Florida with a good, loving woman. Stayed at this condominium. We ate dinners, took the sun, screwed ourselves silly. I got unhappier every day. Couldn't figure out what was wrong. We pretended nothing was wrong—nothing should have been wrong. Then I started to notice everybody in the building, on the beach, in the shopping plazas, everybody else in the state of Florida seemed to have some health problem. They shuffled along, their ankles were swollen, they had arthritis and diabetes, and it made me ashamed of good health. Should have made me thankful . . . it made me ashamed.

—Angela and I went to Florida once. Got a rental car at the airport and drove for hours. It was hot. We were tired and we started arguing about where we were going. At a gas station we told the guy we were looking for an unspoiled area, some place that wasn't completely built up. Older fellow—a cap and a deep tan—he said, 'You're about thirty years too late.' He told us to drive out to a certain key. We followed his instructions and found ourselves at a beach where, right then, there was no trace of other people. We were in time for sunset. That morning we'd been in a foot of snow . . . now we were watching the sun sink into the Gulf. The sky was the colour of salmon. Birds of all sorts were flying across it, silhouettes against this marvellous sky—cormorants, herons, pelicans, gulls of different kinds, many species I didn't recognize. They kept coming, until there seemed an infinity of birds. They seemed to be coming from the same place and heading for the same place. We'd spent all afternoon locating ourselves on a map and arguing about whether to turn left or right. The birds were so sure of purpose . . . their common intent was thrilling.

Val shielded his eyes, squinted toward the guard tower.

—I feel the walls, Monkey. I'm afraid I'll take them with me when I leave.

—Think of the things you'll be free to do again.

—Oh, man, it's great at first.

—Made any plans?

—I can't travel on parole, probably get around that. I'd like to go to England. My ex-old lady is English ... got relatives there. I could get a work permit. Legal junk, too, comes to that.

—I wish you were going with more optimism.

—This is my ninth bit ... in and out is how I spend my life. It's stamped on my soul. Sooner or later I get lost out there.

—Funny, I was just talking to my brother about the time we got lost. We lived in this little town—middle of nowhere. My father was organizing the smelter. Jay and I used to go into the woods searching for rotted pines. You could spot them by the dull colour of the needles. The trees looked sound but you could topple them with a push. One day after school we wandered into the woods. Got tired of playing ... realized we were lost. Dad had drilled into us rules for survival. Find a stream and follow it. Blaze a trail—it's impossible to walk a straight line. Certain types of moss are edible. A hole dug deep enough eventually fills with water. Wet wool retains its insulating properties. The flesh of any animal can be eaten. I rhymed off these idiot phrases over and over ... sat on the forest floor, bawling. Jay made me promise to stay put. He found the way out and came back for me. It felt like I'd been lost for hours, days—we weren't even late for dinner.

Val draped his arm around me.

—Good we got together, anyways.

—Wish I could do something to help.

—Whatever happens, we'll stay in touch.

—Course we will.

Awkward silence—we both looked away, wondering if this were true. Then the buzzer, signalling the end of yard.

DAD met Angela four times. Val's nervousness before his hearing reminded me of my own, back then—I so wanted them to like each other. We were in second year —he came east for a party convention—Jay called him and arranged things.

The din of Dad's room was audible all the way from the elevator. I gave her a squeeze, rapped on the numbered door—had to pound. Uncle Frank opened it ... fifteen or twenty men were drinking from dixie cups, laughing and shouting, old cronies. I introduced her to Dad.

—Pleased to meet you, Mr Wesley.

—Likewise, dear, but call me Harold. Angela or Andrea?

He introduced us around—many of the men were 'uncles.' Space was made on one of the beds ... cups of rye appeared in our hands. Overwhelmed by noise and smoke, she sat there in watery-eyed wonder—I put a comforting arm around her. When Uncle Frank went to the door I thought we'd see Jay. It was Uncle Don ... ageless, silver-haired, moustache and a rogue air. With a woman who must have had a picture of a flamenco dancer taped to her mirror.

—The Silver Fox!

—Hope I'm still chasing it at his age!

—I've met the gal ... but who's the old geezer with her?

Amid the wisecrack greetings I heard Dad.

—Don! You old bastard!

Joy was a rare and extraordinary thing to see in Dad. Delight transformed his face—Don's too—as they shook hands. The mentor—one of the very few people to whom Dad in any way deferred. Don gestured with his cigar and announced to the assembly:

—This, boys, is the redoubtable Marlene. Anybody care to go on picket duty with the old girl before we say goodnight?

—You remember Owen, the younger boy. This is his girlfriend Andrea.

Don negotiated toward us in a manner that bespoke age and alcohol. He grasped my hand, squeezing to make me squeeze, as he'd done for as long as I could remember. Long retired, he could have crushed my fingers in his ham fist. Each time we met I felt older, no wiser ... he stayed exactly the same.

—Good God, son, don't ask me to wrist-wrestle. Good to see you. Nailed any groundhogs lately?

He released my hand for hers, raising it in gallant fashion to his lips.

—My pleasure, Andrea. Sorry, dear, I hope I didn't offend you. I should be wearing my tie with chauvinist pigs on it. I won't tell you who gave it to me.

Angela didn't say a great deal at dinner. Neither did Jay's girlfriend, a dentist's daughter. Dad washed down duck à l'orange with Cointreau on the rocks. He insisted on paying but had only a credit card the waiter didn't like the looks of. The maître d' made a call—had a word with Dad—looked very dubious but finally relented. Back at the room Dad kicked off his shoes to scratch his feet. Produced from his toilet kit two joints—handed one to each girl—struck a match.

—Legalize it. Who the fuck are they kidding?

That was her introduction. She didn't see him again for years. I had to go west on business and asked her along. She cancelled her Friday appointments and we spent three days at the house. The first two seemed endlessly social. Wilf was around, neighbours dropped by, Mom threw a party on Saturday so we could meet their friends. Two-thirty seemed an odd hour, but perhaps it made clear there would be no food. I tried to have fun—to appreciate Mom's efforts—but didn't feel I had much in common with their friends. Only man in the room who paid forty dollars for a haircut.

On Sunday after lunch Wilf said goodbye—Mom took Tuffy and went to play tennis—we found ourselves alone with Dad. Twice I had stayed up with him, drinking, playing chess and Scrabble—we had no more to say. She had connected with Mom and with Wilf but hadn't said two words to Dad. She motioned me into the kitchen.

—I don't know what to say to him.

—Just start a conversation. Or don't if you don't want to—he doesn't care.

He'd pulled on khaki pants and a T-shirt. Scratching between his toes, book in his lap, beer in hand. Angela leafed through magazines.

—How have you been, Mr Wesley? We're leaving tonight ... haven't had much chance to talk.

His eyes addressed her—his glasses were still aimed at his book.

—What have you been up to, Andrea?

—Well, I'm working on my doctorate. I'm tutoring to earn a bit of money and I'm about to go into private practice with my thesis supervisor, Craig Hartling.

He set the book aside.

—What do you mean by private practice? Tutoring?

She perched on the edge of the sofa.

—Not exactly. I'm seeing three kids right now, all bright children doing poorly at school. They've been diagnosed as having a learning disability ... I don't really think any of them has a learning problem as such. Part of it is that the school system tends to alienate bright kids pretty quickly. But in each case poor schoolwork seems to be a symptom rather than the problem. I think there are emotional difficulties behind the so-called learning disabilities.

—What makes you think so?

She laughed from nervousness and modesty.

—Well, one girl—she's twelve, bright, wealthy family, always being shuttled off to camp or grandparents' cottage or aunt's house—she said to me, 'Angela, why do you want me to get a good report? So they'll take me at boarding school?' The practice Craig and I are starting will be geared toward those kinds of situation. I hope so, anyway—I hope people will come. I think there's a need for what we have in mind.

—Help yourself to anything, won't you. There's Scotch in the cupboard.

He took up his book, leaving her there, on the edge of

the sofa. When Mom got back, Tuffy bounded upstairs. Dad set down his book to pet him. 'Who's a good dog.' He ended up rolling on the floor with the dog, rubbing its belly . . .

Then when? I guess the year she defended her thesis and he left the union. We flew out a day after Jay and Sylvia to spend New Year's. Dad had been dropped by chest pains—when he picked us up his angina had been diagnosed. He shook her hand and then mine. Tried to take our bags. In the no-parking zone in front of the terminal the Chrysler had a ticket. He cursed, crumpled it into his pocket. Angela sat between us. We chatted pleasantly . . . the holiday, the fierce weather back east, the prospects of a spring election.

—Owen tells me you've left the union.

He honked at somebody.

—As far as I'm concerned they can go fuck themselves, the whole bunch of them, if you'll pardon the expression.

He twisted around to change lanes. We all twisted back, then forward again.

—Mother tells me you two are buying a house.

—Already bought it. It's being renovated. We take possession June first—our birthday—come visit us.

—How's the tutoring going, Andrea?

—Angela, Dad. Jesus Christ.

He'd hit the ramp too fast and had to brake sharply, crushing us together.

—Sorry, Angela.

—I don't do tutoring any more. My partner still does some educational work . . . my clients are mostly adults now. Two of them are a married couple I see separately. Boy, that's something.

—That so.

He turned in to a mall. Lanes and parking places were indicated in yellow but vehicles moved about unpredictably, like ants. A black van nearly clipped us ... Dad never saw it.

—What the hell are we doing?

He pulled up at the liquor store.

—Can you drink with your angina?

—Listen to him. Sounds like his mother.

Angela and I got out and stretched our legs. The snow peak of Baker shone in the distance ... white ceramic. The air, bright and chilly, bore the sulphurous pulp stink I could never get used to—acrid, invisible. Dad felt in his trousers.

—We'll look after it, Mr Wesley. I'd like to contribute something.

He zipped his windbreaker, pulled it taut on his belly.

—Suit yourself. And call me Harold, dear, nobody calls me Mr Wesley. What do you smoke?

—She doesn't smoke. I'm trying to quit—we could quit together.

—Pick up light rum, will you? Jay likes light rum.

The last time was two summers before his death. We'd been visiting friends in San Francisco. I had a day at home before she arrived—Wilf and I met her at the airport—Wilf hugged her. We arrived home as Mom was taking a roast from the oven. Dad carved, cursing the dull knife.

—How's the tutoring going, Angela?

God, he infuriated me! She was invited to symposia to give papers on the acquisition of metaphor in children. Taught two courses. Had a thriving practice. She was sought after by journalists wanting quotes. She'd flown in from Seattle—could spare only one day, having clients, students, and a TV interview awaiting her.

—For Christ's sake, Dad, she hasn't done tutoring for years. Years! She's a psychologist. A fucking therapist! Can't you get that through your thick fucking skull?

—It's true, my practice is mainly individual counselling now. I'm also seeing a number of couples and getting really interested in relationship counselling.

Dad loaded margarine on roast potato.

—What kind of people?

—All kinds ... let's see. One couple owns several clothing boutiques. Things aren't going well and their business problems are getting confused with their personal stuff. I see a physicist at the university and his friend, a realtor. I seem to have a lot of gay people at the moment.

Wilf raised his eyebrows and his glass.

—The most interesting to me is a woman in her early twenties. Her doctor has her on three different medications. Been dependent for years now, ever since she got married. Working with her is exhausting but it's wonderful ... the progress. She's separated and her husband is suing for custody of the children. Terribly difficult situation.

Mom shook her head, clucked:

—I'm sure it is.

Dad sluiced down the last of his pork and lit a cigarette, which triggered a fit of coughing. We waited —he coughed and coughed. Finally, red-faced, wet-eyed, panting, he looked squarely at Angela for perhaps the first time in his life.

—Ever wonder if you're wasting your time?

CORSICA—no one could remember such unrelenting heat. Sleep was impossible. Exertion of any kind required iron will. The air seemed not to cool at night, merely to grow perfectly still. The sea was as warm as bathwater—our skin dried instantly—the salty residue chafed thighs and armpits. Flies bit our ankles, I lost my sunglasses, Angela suffered wracking cramps. In the afternoons we went our separate ways—Angela climbed down and poked among the tide pools, I sat on the terrace drinking coffee and brandy and watching the men play boules. Each night at dinner, when we tried to deal with things—Craig, ourselves—the words flared like sparks, threatening to ignite something lethal but unseen.

—Keep talking, Owen. Please. Don't go into a shell.

—Fuck it! We say the same things over and over . . .

—Maybe we should think about seeing someone when we get back.

—I went to a shrink last year—I never told you—it was useless.

At night a wind rattled the windows . . . waves thundered against the cliffs. The proprietor's dogs slept on the terrace below our room, howling and whimpering. I wanted to shoot the dogs. I found myself awake in the dark, listening, waiting for morning to show through the shutters, the mirthless singsong of the old, goatish woman who brought us *café au lait:*

—*Bonjour, monsieur madame, vous avez dormi bien?*
— *Très bien. Merci, madame.*

After lunch on our last day we flagged the bus. The ride up had been mortifying enough. Now, in the outside lane, we seemed to be seated out over the edge of the cliffs. When we arrived at the ship we were nervous wrecks. Boarded early—watched the embarkation of trucks, cars, tourist buses, far more than the hold seemed able to accommodate. A voice on the PA urged passengers to eat promptly—the dining-room would close soon after departure. A queue stretched half-way round the second deck and we congratulated ourselves on having got our own dinner—found a lee and had cheese, baguettes and wine. The sun slipped behind barren mountains ...

Angela found it moving to set out by water and we joined the other passengers at the rail, bidding farewell to strangers in the falling dark ... people ashore waved back, as people have waved at ships through the ages, gradually diminishing to nothing. Up the coast, beyond the harbour, a lighthouse blinked its warning.

In open water the ship took on a pounding rhythm. We moved to the top deck to watch spray break over the lower decks. The bow sliced through a swell and smashed down, sending up huge diaphanous wings of water. Great fun, until a swell lifted the ship right out of the sea. The hull slammed with a shock I felt in my spine—the spray hit like a firehose—knocked us both off our feet. We might have been swept away! I might have been washed overboard. She might have been. Nothing I or anyone else could have done—that simple. I'd return home in grief, be treated with pity. No one's doing, no one's fault ...

—Owen!

—You go. I'll be down in a minute.

—Come on! What are you waiting for?

Inside, the ship's motion seemed grotesquely exaggerated—a couple made their way past us like children in a funhouse. We went to the common room—dozens of rows of people, nervously gripping the arms of their seats. The ship's progress was an unremittent battering. We went on deck and lurched like drunks, looping steps and truncated ones, bracing against each other and the railing. The sea churned and roared. Better to return to the common room and ride it out. People were pale and sweaty . . . children were crying.

—This is awful. How are we going to get through it?

—I don't know.

Each time the hull crashed down, the floors, the staircase, even the hallways warped. A woman next to us got to her feet—gripped each seat in turn, shakily made her way out. Her face beneath her black hair looked like a death mask. Other people began hurrying out. Others took out sickness bags. The room filled with the sound of discreet vomiting. I looked at Angela's watch—we'd been at sea only thirty minutes.

—I forget how long it takes.

—Twelve hours. Maybe we'd be better off in the cabin.

We staggered to our cabin—opened the door—a groaning man had vomited all over everything. We returned to the common room, where politeness had given way to desperation. The bags had run out—people were using corners and ashtrays. Out on deck people were gathered at the rail in postures of agony. No moon or stars . . . nothing seemed to exist beyond the reach of the stern lights. The ship crashed and shuddered—the wake churned with phosphorescence—I elbowed a space and heaved up, which in turn set off Angela.

Sooner or later everyone was ill and each person's manner seemed a clear indicator of personality. A black youth with a backpack ran at the railing and stopped abruptly—projectile vomiting at its finest—then lit a cigarette. A Frenchwoman with two crying girls gagged over the railing without interrupting her reassurances. An old woman in a sari lay curled in a ball behind the anchor, moaning and chanting . . .

Beyond exhaustion—an alternating limbo of anguish and heightened clarity. The deck was no less rank than the cabin but we hadn't the strength to move. At last we fell asleep, huddling for warmth . . . I dreamed we were at the rail, I reach for her, too late—she's gone, I cry out, my voice drowned by the roar . . .

Perhaps your dream has something to tell you.

We came to stiff and chilled, jolted awake by the PA— awash in nausea and misery, we were informed that breakfast was being served. We arrived three hours late at Marseilles, which caused us to miss the direct train. The milk run took all day—we got caught in rush-hour traffic—missed our plane. The quickest way home would be to fly to Heathrow and catch the first transatlantic flight in the morning. On the way to London we slept so profoundly the stewardess who woke us was plainly alarmed. Zombies, we made our way through customs, found ourselves in a waiting lounge.

By now the disorientation was complete. Our flight, I gathered, would leave at nine in the morning. Angela's watch said six o'clock—the terminal offered no clues. People in suits, shorts, sweat clothes, and jellabas passed by in states of haste, fatigue, and irritation. One airport clock said 4:42, the other 11:16. I roused myself to look out—planes in different colour schemes were in various stages of takeoff and landing. The sky was a continuation of the tarmac . . . some quality of illumination suggested early afternoon. Six o'clock, five-thirty, 4:42, or 11:16?

—Watch our bags, sweetie. I'm going to phone, if I can find one that works. Be right back.

I didn't know whether to try Jay at home or his office. I called the house—he answered in the bright, breathless voice of someone trying to sound awake. My voice echoing off fainter voices, all of us tangled together in a cable on the ocean floor . . .

—Congratulations, your number has been selected at random. Tell me the exact time at Heathrow airport and how to get the hell out of here and you'll win a lifetime supply of detergent samples. Perfect for batting practice, sliding under buses—

—Where are you, O? Can you hear?

—Talk slowly.

—Nobody knew how to reach you. It's Dad.

—Dad?

After a moment my voice, pale and tangled, came back at me:

—Dad?

TERRIBLE night—vomiting and shivering—poor bastard. I saw it before it happened, in my mind. Did I make it happen?

No more Palumbo. No more Dvořák.

On Saturday afternoon one of the great blues singers gave a concert here. The diamond on his little finger may have been worth more than the limousine in which he arrived. No matter. The honesty of his suffering was transparent—no inmate was unmoved. After each number we cheered and applauded like lovesick teenagers. He took his time, coaxing from his guitar impossibly attenuated accompaniments to his sweet croak. Performed more than three hours—stopped, I think, only because of exhaustion. Sweat streamed down his face. His handkerchief was saturated and he had soaked through his cobalt-blue suit. He stepped out of his guitar as Marnie stepped out of a dress. Holding the instrument to one side, he bowed deeply, an overweight man whose heels met at ninety degrees.

—Thank you so much, gentlemen, been a great audience.

Though he may have said the same thing after other performances I'm certain he has not often said it with the same feeling. He went off drying his head with a towel ... we filed out in an air of solemn privilege. No allusion had been made to the venue or the regulation issue. I had a feeling, as I once had with Angela, and sometimes have with Val, of expansive calm and possibility ...

The show last night—three men in drag. Two of them minced and prattled, vacant parodies, but Denise was compelling. High heels, brunette wig, dress made of sweatshirt material. It's not that she's convincing as a woman but rather that she—he—is unconvincing as a man. She played a veteran hooker instructing two girls just starting out. She filled me with longing and guilt.

—Never go with anybody shaves his skull. Never go with anybody has a ship tattoed on his back.

She rhymed off succinct descriptions of a couple of dozen men who had sought her favour. We howled and cheered . . . looked around for the victim. By the end of her list the gym was in glorious uproar.

—How do you decide to go with a guy?

—You make discreet inquiries . . . that the telephone? Show you what I mean. Hi, this is Denise, I'm not in at the moment but if you'd like to leave your name, passport number, Visa number and expiry date, date of birth, height, weight, eye colour, hair colour, distinguishing marks, occupation, gross income, marital status, sexual preference, communicable diseases, drug addictions, history of mental illness, religious affiliation, astrological sign, criminal record, last known whereabouts, aliases, shoe size, favourite colour, goals in life, three references, and a short message, I'll get back soon as possible.

When the gym is full and we all stamp and clap in unison a resonance is set up that seems to include even the inanimate. The noise rises up to the vaulted dome, swelling and tumbling back on itself like the music of a fountain. Stacking chairs shake . . . the wooden stage trembles . . . the whole place becomes caught up in sympathetic vibration. The power of the moment—I thought of Ron.

—Perhaps the way to free yourself is to be fully here.

I see it—at the concert, watching the skit, in Val's arms, talking to Ron—I see it. But if I allowed myself— a convict with a male lover . . . if I entered fully into my life, this life, how would I ever get out?

Vernon came on, the last act, and launched into songs we had heard many times. Shouts, jeers—he carried on oblivious . . . the mood shifted to irritation. A couple of his numbers require chord changes that take longer to execute than his tempo allows. He holds the transitional note—his thick fingers make their way—not so inept as to be comic, merely annoying. During 'Moonshadow' the disgruntlement rose ... he abandoned the song in mid-line and shouted into the microphone.

—Shut up! Just one more and I guarantee you ain't heard it because I wrote it myself and I never done it in public. It's called 'You're What Life's All About' and it's dedicated to my best friend. For you, Mario.

While he strummed bland choruses I felt growing dread. Men mumbled, fidgeted. Palumbo was seated on the far side of the gym. He smiled up at Vernon, lowered his eyes coquettishly. The race for the exit. We're supposed to count off but the hacks get out first, the line turned into a crush at the door ... Palumbo's dirty ponytail ... I saw it happen before I saw the knife— complex moment of clarity and fear, Palumbo twisting down, sagging, the strangest expression on his face. Men flowed around him like a river around a boulder— no way of stopping—I almost tripped on him—saw the shiv and then I was through. The inmate ahead said, 'Four!' The hacks didn't know. I said, 'Five!' Somebody said, 'Six!' 'Seven!' 'Eight!' Hold on, hold on ...

Nothing in my stomach and still retching. Retching on the ship with Angela ... retching at Heathrow when I found out Dad was dead, stumbling back to Angela, both of us dazed—what's going on?—our lives unravelling around us.

Val came down to my cell, wiped my forehead, laid his cool palm on my solar plexus.

—Sounds like an overdose, Monkey.

Of what?

OUR plane seemed to remain in daylight for days, suspended over the ocean. My head was all angles and corners. I rambled on about Dad, accustoming myself, I suppose, to the idea that he was gone.

—The bastard—took him twelve years to get your name straight.

—Sweetie, your father.

—Let's face it, he was a selfish prick. I'm not saying I didn't love him, I'm just being objective. I wonder what the funeral was like. I wish I could have heard what people said about him.

I was drinking screwdrivers, using our last English money—when the plane thumped down I was raging drunk. Angela was in a state that made me think of her taxing weeks—the verge of nausea, light-headed, chalky white lines under her eyes. When the limousine reached the house I felt unbelievable relief, could have wept. But then, while we fumbled for keys, an awful awareness ... my dream—taking possession, finding the place ruined—haven't had the dream for months. Nothing seemed awry—neighbours had kept our grass trimmed and the porch free of flyers—yet we opened the door with dread ...

A strangely extended moment of incomprehension ... the drawers of the desk were upended on the floor, contents littered all over, yet it didn't register for the longest time. Burglary—not only burglary, the house

had been defiled. Jam on the walls of the living-room—
every picture destroyed—glass shattered, art punctured
with a knife—mayonnaise on the chesterfield and the
wall behind it—Tiffany lamp in pieces—firescreen
kicked in—candlesticks gone—track lights wrenched
out of the ceiling—sideboard upended, every piece of
crystal and china broken. The dining-room table had
gouges in it, the silver had been taken.

We thought of them at the same instant.

—Did you take them?

—I hid them in the closet.

There was hope, it all came down to this—if they'd
been overlooked we might salvage something, begin
again. Panic—the pillows had been slit open—fluffy
down everywhere—a terrible odour from the closet—
someone had urinated on our clothing.

The pearls were gone.

The other night on the big screen we saw war footage
of Russian peasants leaving their destroyed village. Not
hurrying. Not crying or even talking, simply walking
away with what was left of their lives. Val found their
conduct unbelievable, thought the documentary had
been faked, but Angela did something similar. Went
downstairs and, amid the rubble of the kitchen, looked
up a phone number, dialled, told someone she would
have to cancel an appointment. She called five people,
calmly explaining that she would like to reschedule—
made notes in her day book, put it back in her bag. And
only then cried.

Every room had been ransacked. She'd hidden jewellery in an Ajax container under the bathroom sink—the
Ajax was all over the floor. Shampoo, cosmetics, shaving cream all over. The television had been disconnected, brought to the top of the stairs and—too big to

take?—smashed. Linen yanked from the closet, blanket boxes upended, books pulled from shelves. On the third floor our records and tapes were all over—tape deck, stereo, speakers—massive things—were gone. The filing cabinet had been jimmied—papers, bills, receipts strewn about—photographs on the walls had been ruined—a crystal vase she gave me had been smashed against the brick—sofa slit, stuffing pulled out. The phone, ripped out, had been used to gouge the walls. A half-empty gallon of cedar stain, which I'd left on the deck, had been poured over chairs, sofa, and rug.

—Why do you think these things happen? Do you think your external life has nothing to do with the life you create for yourself?

I would happily have drenched the place in gasoline and struck a match. We could have moved in with Jay and Sylvia, taken an apartment, pitched a tent—anything but deal with this. The police had to be called, of course, we had to compose ourselves and begin to consider how we would go about remaking a habitable home. I had to find a job—she had to resume her work— we still had to do what the trip had not helped us do, sort out our life together. We climbed stairs, wandered from room to room, looking for a place to sit. Kept having to step over the mattress, so we hoisted it back in place. And there, on the floor, was the black case that had contained the pearls. She opened it.

—Tears of the moon.

How could they still be there amid the desecration? She held them in cupped hands ... their beauty was extraordinary. In the chaos and destruction of our lives they seemed to embody all that is pure and abiding. Palumbo is gone and yet today, in the yard, I heard someone whistling the Largo from the 'New World.'

—If we could have asked for one thing . . .
I took them and fastened them around her neck.

THE last time I saw Dad he shocked me. I'd been vague about which flight I'd be on, not wanting to be met at the airport. Told Mom I had business on the Friday but would spend the weekend with them. I hurried through the terminal in that purposeful way of travellers with no one to meet them. A broad-shouldered, almost un-recognizable fellow blocked my way. I was startled. Angina was driving him into himself. His skin usually had a seashell hue . . . it was chalky grey. He had new glasses, the sort that darken in sunlight, and a puffed hairdo. Too many strands had been arched over the crown, not disguising the thinness but emphasizing it. His sideburns were in stages, the bottom half still growing in. His shirt was the colour of rusted steel, his slacks the colour of beef, his tie bright brown. His jacket incorporated all these tones and more. His shoes and belt were white.

—Dad.
He stuck out his hand, chuckled.
—The harried businessman. Where's your bag?
—I checked it.
—Bar's upstairs.

In the darkened lounge we sat by the glazed window. On the tarmac below us a crewman with flashlights was waving in a DC-10. The plane seemed impossibly cumbersome. The pilot's head looked no bigger than a cocktail onion. The crewman seemed angry and impatient . . .

—How are you? How's Angela?

—Fine.

The waitress set down paper doilies and drinks.

—Cheers.

—Cheers.

He downed his martini in one sustained grimace.

—Look, I know you weren't expecting me. But I wanted to see you before you got to the house.

—What for?

He took out a loaded pipe, struck a match, held it over the bowl. The flame turned upside down and raged.

—I thought the doctor told you to quit.

I waited for him to tell me I sounded like my mother. He expelled a prodigious cloud of smoke . . . let out an involuntary sigh.

—I've decided to leave your mother.

My eyes bounced around the room. Three men were making cracks about a woman at the bar. High boots, huge purse. She may have been enjoying their remarks. The waitress was sharing a cigarette with the bartender. I remember the airport lounge very well: burned into my mind.

—For someone else?

Must have come out too loud—waitress and bartender both looked our way, alarmed. Dad thought they were asking if we wanted another—drew a little circle in the air.

—Who is she?

—You don't know her—doesn't matter.

—*Who is she?*

—Lorene McKinnon. She's worked on several campaigns out here. Used to work in the provincial office, now she works for the fed. She's a very ... bright woman.

Unlike your mother, he meant. Sweet soul though she was, Mom read Harold Robbins and said to the television, 'Oh, come on, Merv.' Did the plumbing and finances, knew when a lamp needed rewiring, raised two boys on her own ... wasn't very bright. Couldn't have told you what month Hitler invaded Poland or the terms of the Taft-Hartley Act. Dad believed you broadened your understanding with facts. 'You sound like your mother.' 'You know your mother.' On one level he and I had conspired against her. But he believed I was like her—narrow mind focused on the wrong things—and to injure her, forsake her, was to inflict the same on me.

—I've met Lorene. I met her when I was a kid. You've been balling her all these years? You rotten prick!

The waitress set down drinks.

—Everything all right here?

Dad gave her a look—she fled—he blew a slow pennant of smoke in the air.

—I know. I know. But I wanted to tell you before you got to the house.

—Where did you get those clothes?

He drained his martini, amused.

—What's wrong with them?

—You look like a blind man someone played a joke on.

A softening of his mouth ... implied smile. I couldn't hurt him, didn't know how—what touched or pleased or stung him was a mystery. He reached for the check.

—Sixteen bucks for four bourbons—shitty bourbon.

Dad, who'd drink anything, the connoisseur. He peeled off a twenty, disclosing a five. I snatched the check, to remind him he had no job.

—I'll put it on expenses.

—The hell you will.

—Have you told Jay yet?

Perhaps this hit home. He shook his head ... flicked the twenty with his knuckle. His glasses gave his eyes an odd convexity, a frailty I'd never noticed. Dad, sixty.

—I'm not telling him, if that's what you hope.

—Let's get out of here. Come on, your bag will be down. I'll drop you at your hotel.

I didn't want to spend another minute in his presence. I needed to be alone, to let it register.

—I've got a rental car.

But he came with me to the Budget counter, and I had to pretend I'd made a reservation that they'd screwed up.

Next day after seeing my client I drove up the valley. I turned in and saw Mom on hands and knees in the garden ... shorts and sunhat. Even after she got to her feet—in stages, like a pack animal—she seemed bent over. At my approach the dog slammed against the gate, barking.

—Oh, come on, Tuffy, you remember Owen.

I gave her a hug, smelled elderly sweat and the garden. The muscles in her back were as taut as a drawn bow. The dog wedged his narrow skull between us.

—Nice of you to take the time, dear.

—You look well, Mom.

She looked older but there was, as always, a liveliness about the eyes. Mom's eyes ... the deep blue of Persian carpets. No matter how dirty or worn, the blue has a radiance that suggests authenticity and worth. Rich, like Marnie's. Clear, like Angela's. The dog drove his skull between my thighs and lifted. I patted his neck, to no avail—I clubbed his head.

—He's just being friendly.

The kitchen, the depleting force of the familiar: his boots, her rackets in their presses, the extraordinary chaos of the breakfast nook. The roasting pan, licked clean, on the floor beside Tuffy's bowl. Old newspapers stacked waist-high in the corner. Buckling linoleum in the hall, the living-room arranged around the television, a cabinet model the size of a coffin. An allergy could not have drained me as suddenly. She came into the bedroom with clean towels, and the bourbon I'd left in the kitchen—Dickel, present for Dad. She closed her hand on mine.

—Don't let him get at this. Doctor told him to stay off the booze. It's what'll kill him.

I wasn't sure if she knew he had met me. I turned my back on her, to put things in a drawer lined with yellowed newspaper.

—Where is he?

—Where do you think?

—What's going on, anyway?

—Didn't he tell you?

—A bit. What are you going to do?

She sat on the bed.

—He's got it in his thick skull this Lorene—she didn't pronounce so much as sneer her name—is just the thing now that he's almost sixty.

I sat beside her, my weight drawing us closer.

—Told me he's leaving.

Mom laughed, a sound not like laughter at all.

—She's younger than Jay. Who's kidding who?

I made a noise of failed comprehension.

—He and Lorene—sneer—are going to buy a condominium. Tell you? This seems to be the latest plan.

—What will you do?

—What the hell is he going to do with his books and tools and guns? All the crap he's been collecting over the years. 'For the boys,' he says when I ask why he's ordering more bloody books, 'they're not for me, dear, they're for the boys.' Is he going to put his crap in the little condominium? You can bet it'll be little. Know what the housing market's been doing out here this spring?

Mom got to her feet, an act requiring effort, and went to the window. Baker on a sunny day—it's why they bought the house, the one thing they agreed on. That and Jay.

—Where are they going to get money? She's a secretary with a teenaged daughter. Am I supposed to come through? Ha!

—What if he does?

—He's not stupid.

She looked out at the snow peak, lost a moment, sun on her face, and it seemed to me he was stupid, incredibly stupid, for not seeing his effect on those who loved him. I wanted to hug Mom but we had no mechanism for hugs beyond greeting and parting. I wanted to tell her about Marnie, about Angela, my fears and confusions. She clucked, and I knew she was going to say something about Jay.

—That's what you've walked into, dear. How's big brother?

—He's fine. What about you—have you ever gone outside your marriage?

—Of course not. Not that I haven't had opportunities

... every woman does. There's a fellow at the tennis
club ... and of course the men, when they'd get a few
drinks in them and we'd all be dancing with one
another ...

She fell silent, an astonished silence, it seemed to me,
perhaps seeing that she had indeed had opportunities—
other women might have made their lives differently.
She shrugged.

—Your father and I took a vow. Anyway, dear, I'm
glad we've had a chance to talk.

She didn't seem glad, ending the conversation to peel
potatoes. Dad wouldn't eat potatoes that hadn't been
peeled.

He came home for dinner and hung around Saturday.
No allusion was made to Lorene, or the separation. I felt
as if I'd never left home—at the same time it was as if I
were from another planet. I caught the plane Sunday
morning. Dad's announced date of departure came and
went. More angina. The doctor told him a bypass might
give him ten years. He wanted to think about it ...
while we were in Europe, he had the heart attacks. By
the time I phoned from Heathrow he was smoke and
ash.

What do I think I missed out on? What do I imagine
he'd have said on his deathbed? That he was disappointed in me, proud of me? I'd been right in believing
that he considered Jay the special one? He'd made
mistakes he hoped I wouldn't repeat? His life and Mom's
hadn't worked out as they might have wished and, so
far as he could tell, this made them no different from
anyone else? After Jay and I left home—or, rather,
stayed behind—he and Mom had no reason to be
together other than habit and fear, lives as tangled as
vines?

What would I have said to him? That I'd hated the

sense of imminent battle between them? I felt like the
scout who looks over the valley that will become the
scene of the massacre? I wished we'd been able to talk?
It disturbed me that his life was something to which I
wasn't given access? I resented his absence? I hated him
for his treatment of Wilf, his slighting of Angela, his
unabashed love of Jay? I felt an overwhelming need for
reconciliation, a final accounting?

At the time I didn't. And by then it was probably too
late. Perhaps my mistake is to think anything would
have changed if I'd been there at the end.

—You got involved in her family, O, but when did she
ever show any interest in Syl and me, or Mom and Dad?

—Give him this—he bowed to no one. He thought the
world was a fucked-up place and he felt he ought to
spend his time unfucking it.

—He was just a guy doing the best he could. Doing
what he thought was right.

Maybe Jay's right. Maybe I should just let it go. Let
Dad go. Stop blaming him.

I THOUGHT Vernon would be devastated—told him I was
sorry—he grinned and rubbed his neck.

—Told him he was stupid, Monkey. I go, 'Who do you

think you are, four tiers of men don't want to know.' He goes, 'There's no law against whistling.' I go, 'It's your funeral, buddy.' My exact words. Where's Tonio? Guys ready for a little game?

The Hound collapsed in the yard and was taken to the infirmary. This afternoon he was back on the range, good as new, he said ... more woebegone than ever: emaciated, sunken-eyed, rash raging over his forehead. Val asked what the problem had been.

—No problem, just an inadequate level of bodily fluids.

Giles told me he kept a dog in his cell, a cross between a Doberman and a German shepherd. I asked what it ate.

—I bring stuff up from the mess. But that's between you and me. I haven't told anybody but you.

This afternoon we got our commissary orders. I waited, waited, waited ... how long could I go? Finally, after supper, my resistance broke down. I told myself to savour it. Be fully here. Only a snack, but this was going to be a supreme experience, more enjoyable for having been deferred. I had a choney bar in one hand, diet soda in the other ... I happened to read the candy wrapper: 'Congratulations. You are a discriminating chocolate lover. You have selected Nestlé, a superior quality chocolate.' And the soda tin: 'Warning. This product may be hazardous to your health. It contains saccharine, which has been shown to cause cancer in laboratory animals.'

Giles gave me pruno tonight and started talking.

—I always wanted to understand computers. I'm in some and once you're in, you're in. I wouldn't mind finding out. I know three guys on this range alone who know practically everything about them. Only reason I haven't learned about computers yet is because I can whenever I want. There's no rush. I'm doing six and I can learn about computers any time.

—Here, Monkey, have more juice. Once I was on the plane with a well-known actress. The flight was late and everybody had a connecting flight to catch. When we touched down the guy on the PA told us to remain seated until we came to a stop in front of the terminal building. Everybody was in a hurry and they began clicking open their belts and standing up to get their stuff out of the overhead bins. Purser came on again, telling them to sit down and buckle up for their own safety. They ignored him. The plane braked . . . actress was thrown into the seat arm. Cut her lip and broke off two front teeth.

—I found out later she sued the airline. And collected. The judge ruled they should have done more to ensure that she stayed in her seat. Like that bartender found responsible for an accident caused by a customer who drove off loaded, remember? That's what you have to remember. You think Giles is crazy . . . I know something about grinders. You're here for your own good.

Before lockup Billie Holiday asked me to put my cock through the bars. He always says the same thing.

—Just once, Monkey. Let me cop it once . . . one time . . . never bother you again.

—Learn yoga, Billie, cop yourself.

Usually he laughs like a lunatic and moves on. Tonight he looked like a man told the hour of his death. Palumbo—the look on Angela's face—the toilets roared.

Tears brimmed in Billie's eyes. In mine.

OOOOOOOOOOOO

—How was your week?

—I saw a man get taken down. Mario Palumbo.

—Vernon's lover?

—In the ribs, then his stomach got slit open, he tried to hold himself together. Not a sound—looked surprised, that's all.

—It must have been upsetting.

—Happened so quickly. His guts were in his hands, glistening like jewels. When I got back to my cell I felt pain in my kidney. I started shaking and throwing up.

—What happened when Angela died? Did you see her body?

—I took off—help—that surge you get. I freaked out.

—Do you remember what you felt through it all?

—I remember questions, certain things—the rescue basket they used, the prowl car I sat in.

—Did you experience the same detachment when you saw Palumbo stabbed? Functioning, but not there?

—Nausea swept through me. I couldn't stop because of the crush. There was no stopping, I had to keep going.

—Did they question you?

—If I'd seen anything, I said no, he was down when I got to him.

—Tell me about the pain in your kidney. What did it feel like?

—Once I was on my motorcycle, drizzly night, I

realized a taxi was going to cut me off. I braked, the bike slid, I watched it smash. Later I realized I was hurt.

—Angela?

—You know the way falling water mesmerizes you? You see yourself in it, swept away. I knew what was going to happen but I couldn't do anything.

—She looked at you?

—I reached to grab her. The two witnesses, what could they see? They didn't know ... I knew, I reached for her, they got it backwards. She moved first, I moved to stop her.

—You have a clear recollection of that moment?

—The roar of the water, I thought, 'Christ, no,' she was gone.

—In your cell, after the stabbing, did Angela enter your mind?

—The same suddenness, helplessness, disbelief. I knew, before, that something was about to happen.

—Have you talked about it to anyone?

—Val. He had his hearing, he's out at the end of next month.

—How do you feel about that?

—It means I have a good chance, too—they need the space ... I dreamed about Val last night. A restaurant, somewhere posh, waiters in tuxedos, someone playing piano. Val and I were waiting to get in, wearing regulation issue. There was a red-velvet rope, and the maître d' took it down to let someone out. He said, 'It's crowded tonight, perhaps another time would be better.' I said, 'We'll wait.' He was strong, like a bouncer, broken nose. A battle of wills. I thought he was going to unload on me. Instead he unhooked the rope.

—Who was the maître d'?

—Muscular, broken nose, about my size. A part of

myself, maybe? Refusing to open the rope, then opening it?

—I want to tell you again how well I think you're doing—being direct with Val, overcoming things that in the past may have kept you from acting on what you felt. It's great to see it happening.

—Things are coming together all at once, same way they fell apart.

—Why did all those unpleasant things happen?

—Getting burgled, for example? We were a day late because we missed our flight. The house was done, in other words, while we were stuck in London. We should have been back.

—Do you attribute all this to anything in particular?

—The poorer people resented all the disposal bins, skylights, the affluence. I suppose our house got burgled because of the discrepancy.

—I'm not making my question clear. You must have felt, 'Something's going wrong here.' Did you ever relate it to yourself?

—It becomes almost comical. You lock your keys in the car. A policeman sees you with a coat hanger, wants you to prove you're not stealing the car, you've left your wallet in the house, the house key is locked in the car. Why do you think things happen?

—Some people might have looked at these 'accidents' as a message to deal with the problem.

—We never really had a chance to sort things out— something always got in the way. We stopped trying—I stopped. I never started.

—I think when you avoid something important, you create conditions in which intrusions flourish and multiply.

—Like people in high-stress jobs being more subject

to heart attacks? Angela had a client who developed multiple sclerosis just before her husband told her he was leaving her—I see the link—but those are internal things.

—Do you think what happens to you bears no relation to your internal state? Everything is pure hazard?

—I have trouble seeing all that led to her death in those terms.

—Perhaps it's a useful way of looking at things. The pearls, too, the one thing of value left in your house. Why, when you were overextended, did you purchase such an expensive gift?

—I knew she would cherish them. I wanted her to know how much she meant to me. I knew she'd love the myth. All those reasons.

—Did you have a premonition of losing her, of needing to give her an extravagant gift to ensure her love?

—I thought, 'They're perfect.' Funny, I thought that before the guy told me it's actually a larval worm in the centre of a pearl, not a grain of sand. They're beautiful if you don't think about what's at the centre.

—There was a lot of pressure on you that summer. Being fired. Your lover. Her lover. Your tax investigation. How did you deal with all that?

—I couldn't. Didn't.

—I'd like to suggest something. In your stifled situation—your frustration with work, the duplicity of your affair, your sense that Angela was moving away—there was something very appealing. Putting yourself in debt, feeling she was changing and succeeding while you were stuck—in all this you found something attractive. You discover she has a lover and yet fail to object. Being downtrodden must have corresponded to the way you viewed yourself.

—I took the subway, sat at a desk, had a mortgage. I owed money, I drank, I got interested in someone else. Life.

—Part of you recognized what you were doing, and objected. But you switched that off.

—If I did, why? Why lock myself in a shitty job, in a life with a woman whose success I resented and who was deceiving me?

—Owen, let's abolish 'if.' Who chose your situation but you?

—But I don't understand why I'd do something that, on one level, I didn't want to do. Can you explain that?

—I can tell you my own experience. When I let go, stop reacting, whether with my wife, this job, or my aspirations, the process gains momentum. It's not easy to change the course of your life. It's evolution rather than epiphany. Your life with Angela didn't start the way it ended.

—That's right, it almost grew backwards. But why?

—I don't think you should count on discovering a neat answer. Just try to be aware of motivation and feelings. Why did you sink deeper into yourself, further from her? Why did you break with Marnie if you loved her? Little signals were there all along.

—I know—canoeing—even if rapids are a long way off, something subtle begins to change—the sound and colour of the water, the current ... the way her voice changed on the phone with him.

—At the same time, of course, you have to be sensitive to your present life. How you react, and why, to the man offering heroin, the possibility of escape, your involvement with Val.

—It seems futile.

—It feels that way to you now, but it's not futile. To

me your progress is very clear and satisfying. You seem to be beginning to open yourself, to embrace the mysteriousness of life. You are not the same person who walked in and said he wanted a way of killing an hour.

THE process that brought me here—I think of it as coercive and myself as inhibited by grief—not fully resistant—but when I think specifically about what happened, my role seems almost co-operative. There are men doing harsh terms for minor drug and property offences and for the sort of morals offences that make up part of any adolescent's education. There are men who were railroaded. In my case the police were scrupulous and considerate, the judge had an air of probity, even the prosecuting attorney took pains to point out my co-operativeness. What coerced me?

Some days after the interment I was roused in mid-afternoon—knuckles on the door. Who would knock when there was a bell? I stumbled downstairs—found myself facing two men with that unmistakable air. They had parked in the no-parking zone in front of the house. My comings and goings were scrutinized and I poked my head out to see which neighbours were watching.

The older man, a lieutenant, Stoker, had eyes of such brown they seemed black. I was aware at once of the intelligence behind them. He understood it was a trying time, he said, but details had to be tidied up ... a few questions. I made coffee and we sat on stools in the kitchen. Simplest to start at the beginning. How long had Angela and I known one another? Toward the end how had things been going? A kind of buzzing in my ears. Had she seemed disturbed for some time? Late October seemed an odd season for camping—whose idea had it been? I answered through the buzzing. Why that park? Had we known the forecast called for rain? Was there a particular purpose to the trip? What were the 'things' we planned to talk over?

Stoker lit a plastic-tipped cigarillo—sweet smell. His partner, a jug-eared man, wrinkled his nose in comic distaste. He kept sitting forward as if to withdraw something from his pocket, grimacing ... back pain? Stoker was a big, loose fellow who squinted when he listened and seemed to compute every word. I liked him and disliked his partner. I pointed out that I had answered these questions many times—only then understood that my answers were being compared. Offended, I told them I needed to lie down. At the door Stoker asked exactly how Angela had gone. Lead with the left foot or right? Buzzing ... I had trouble hearing him. Did she actually leap, or was it more like a fall? Was her back to me? Did she make a sound? When I reached for her, did I touch her arm or not? The buzzing was a roar. When I ran along the bank what had I been intending? I tried to answer over the roar, conscious of describing not the events but the reconstruction I'd given at the scene. He thanked me ... I waited shakily for the slam of car doors.

Next morning they were back. This time they ran the

wheels up on the sidewalk. I suggested the living-room and brought them coffee. Stoker commented on the firescreen, an antique piece Angela had found. He looked around the room—lost in himself—wondering whether he could live in the house? An oddly melancholic moment.

—Nice place.

—We were burgled in July. The house was vandalized.

—Riverdale's the area for it.

The questions were gentle, well directed. Had Angela and I been in the house long? We owned it jointly? Buzzing. Did we share expenses or have some other arrangement? A joint bank account? Too personal to ask why we'd not married? The circumstances in which I'd left my job? I was able to give answers without quite hearing the questions. His manner seemed inquisitive rather than probing ... I imagined that if we had happened to find ourselves side by side at the ballgame we would have taken turns getting beer and agreed that the umpire was calling high strikes. I imagined him as someone who'd go alone to the stadium, who reflected my own desolation—perhaps that's why I failed to grasp my situation until after their second interrogation.

I couldn't reach Jay so I called Brian Littlewood. We'd two or three times received announcements to the effect that Harkins Littlewood & Perras had joined Fortier Sullivan and would be known hereafter as Harkins Littlewood Sullivan & Partners. Littlewood had moved again since redoing our wills ... his new office, in one of the jutting towers, looked as if it could, over lunch, be removed in its entirety and installed elsewhere. I despise lawyers, as Dad did.

Littlewood and Angela had rented in the same building when they were both starting out—just how long ago was brought home by desktop photographs of his four children, all of whom appeared to have his chinless confidence. One of the girls had been a client of Angela's —school problems, I think. Littlewood seemed uncomfortable as I described Stoker's visits. Ate a pastrami sandwich at his desk. When I asked his advice he rolled backwards in his chair, as far as the little wheels would take him . . . balled up his paper napkin . . . smoothed it again.

—I'm not sure I'm right. Frankly.

—What do you mean?

—Sharon and I were delighted with the help Angela gave Sherry. I'm not sure I could . . . Owen, look, put yourself—

I stormed past his frost-headed receptionist, his rented art and rented furniture and rented plants. Trembling, I called Jay. He was disturbed and said he'd call back with the name of a criminal specialist. The word, sent over the phone, sent a shiver through me. When, toward five, the phone rang, I expected Jay.

—Bob Stoker. More questions, I'm afraid . . . could you possibly drop by the office?

Even that was a courtesy. He could have said 'the station.'

—Do you want me to come now?

The desk sergeant told me where to find him—I took the stairs—on the landing I passed two detectives with a wiry man in a singlet. The man was demented or perhaps desperately tired. For a joke he lunged menacingly at me—tripped—didn't go down because the detective to whom he was cuffed jerked him like a yo-yo. It might have dislocated his shoulder . . .

The incident shook me—I was relieved to see Stoker. He was in a cluttered, two-man office, typing with forefingers. Took no notice until he had finished, separated copies, signed them and put them in baskets. He raised his eyebrows in surprise—already!—and offered coffee.

Stoker reminded me of Dad. He disposed of callers with the same efficiency ... his office had much in common with union halls, committee rooms, campaign headquarters. The metal furniture was cheap and mismatched, the lighting harsh. There were maps on the walls and the measured confusion that comes from more to do than will ever get done. I didn't feel out of place. He seemed to understand. I may have been a suspect but I was not the man in the singlet. He may have been a cop but was not about to bully me or exploit my fragility.

—This other fellow. Hartling. Craig Hartling.

—Yes?

I knew Hartling, did I? Buzzing. I had been aware of their involvement? How did he figure in things? Did his name come up that weekend, in the park?

Stoker wore a revolver under his arm, handcuffs in the small of his back. He went to the window ... leaned on his fists. No view really, traffic and a row of squat buildings across the street. Night had fallen and Stoker, gazing out, seemed to me inexplicably mournful. Nothing mattered—I was no less unhappy in this office than I would have been anywhere else—he turned to me.

—When did you decide to go for a walk? Whose idea was that?

I answered over the growing roar:

—We walked a lot that weekend.

—Did you notice the warning signs at the top of the gorge?

Incredible, I thought, he'd driven all the way down to the park, just to look around. He really thinks I'm lying.

—We climbed down from the campsites, not the picnic area.

—Why did you head toward the falls?

—I don't know—we could hear the roar.

—Was it foggy when you got there?

—I don't think so . . . the fog burned off as the sun got higher. There was a cloud of mist over the falls.

—There you are, two feet from the drop. Wired on coffee, pissed off, haven't slept . . .

The roar was in my ears.

—It was too loud to think. Incredible roar of water . . .

—She just goes? No warning? That it?

—I'm going to tell you something . . . it passed through my mind how easy it would be to push her, or be pushed, or to jump. For something to happen. But then I was reaching for her—I knew, we often knew at the same instant—I lost my balance, I came close to going with her! Maybe it would have been better . . .

Stoker ignored my self-pity—lit a cigarillo—rolled it in his mouth like a toothpick. He sat on his desk, set the cigarillo in an ashtray.

—Here's the thing. I can't help imagining what might have happened if she'd been planning to tell you she wanted to separate . . .

I know you as I know my soul . . .

—We weren't about to separate.

—She would have wanted a neutral place. Place you could argue and fight and talk it through.

—We didn't fight.

—I have two kids, OK? Boy fifteen and girl twelve. They're what I love in this world and they're what keep me from going crazy. You could go crazy doing what I do, easy. My kids and ex-wife live with another fellow on the force now.

—That's too bad.

—In your case, what, twelve years? First girlfriend? Ouch.

—Something like that.

He made swirling motions.

—The night my wife told me she wanted out, I remember—pillow on her face, shut her up, hunt the fucker and shoot him in the shorts. 'You're a cop,' I told myself.

—Angela and I . . .

But what was I going to say to a lieutenant in the homicide division? The first time I heard the 'New World' I nearly wept and I still cannot hear it without being stirred. The first time I saw Angela it defied what my life to that point had taught me. She was the one in whose presence my heart opened.

—I imagine that wracked feeling in my gut. I'm not saying I'd think, 'There's a way to stop her.' I'm not saying it would occur to you that it might look like suicide. Or that you'd just redrawn your wills . . .

—Stop it!

—I don't think I'd even consider the insurance, the house, the cars, the pearls, the tax problems, the borrowed—

—Shut up! You're insulting me. You're talking to yourself. This has got nothing to do with me or what happened, this is you.

—That's right. I talk to myself, try to figure things out. I talk to other people, too . . . like the couple who happened to be watching you from the railway overpass. Ask them what they saw, if that helps me get it straight . . .

—Look . . . I'm sorry . . . I need to call my brother.
He stood, gestured at the phone on his desk.
—Please. Dial nine to get out . . .

IN THE pit this morning, after Vernon and Val had gone
back to the range, I did more curls with dumbbells. I'd
planned on fifty reps—got thinking—lost count. I
wanted to test my limit, decided to keep on until I could
do no more. My left arm began lagging a little and I had
to focus to keep both arms moving in time. Through
this concentration I felt growing heat in my left palm,
not of friction but of gathering force. When it seemed I
could do no more I told myself to do another ten.
Finishing the last—bringing the weights to my shoulders, my final drop of strength—my left palm crackled
like static electricity. My left arm and shoulder trembled in a way that was unlike spasms of muscular
exhaustion.

I set the dumbbells down to study my left palm. It
looked identical to the right but some form of energy
was leaving the tips of my fingers. I had no control of it.
I extended my arm as if to direct the discharge and the
force for a moment became visible. Streaks of wispy

fluff faded like an aura a few inches beyond my fingertips ...

Angela—Yugoslavia—our week in the socialist republic seemed oddly prolonged, unrelieved by the sight of a single lighted face. Ticket takers and passport police were glum and hostile. Hotel clerks were glum and unhelpful. Mothers in parks swatted glumly at their children. This glumness had on me an effect that would have been devastating if I hadn't been with her. She believed there are marvels beneath even the glummest of surfaces. I did not, and that, perhaps was the source ...

We spent our last morning on a bench in a park in Zagreb, before a graceful fountain in a circular bed of tulips. The benches were full of glum people. The walk was patrolled by agents of the state who sent packing derelicts trying to sleep and lovers trying to fondle. Sparrows fed and drank, moving in a threadbare gang between the path and the fountain. I happened to be watching the sparrows' flight at the moment a cat, hiding in the tulips, leapt straight up, three feet in the air, and nabbed one of the birds. It happened in a second and then the cat was gone. I turned to the glum fellow beside me. He had noticed nothing. I looked at the faces on all the benches and could find no trace of amazement. Must have been a hundred people and yet no one else but Angela had seen the mortal ballet. It seemed that if she not been with me I might not have seen it or would have dismissed it as hallucination. Perhaps it would not have taken place. It seemed my life was nothing more than a creation of her capacity for wonder and love ...

I recalled where I was. In the pit were ten or twelve others ... no one had taken any notice. I let my hand fall to my side and shook it. It tingled. I sat on a bench and there came to mind the shiv. I pictured it on the floor inside the door . . . knew it was Tonio who had used it on Palumbo. Then, tonight, Val asked me:

—Who you figure stuck Palumbo?

—I can only guess. Who do you think?

—Tonio. Billie Holiday told me.

We had a few minutes—neck massage—Val's strong, scarred, tender hands.

—These muscles are looser, Monkey. No more knots. Billie said, 'Too bad about the wop. Man took care of it himself.' I told Billie to tell Tonio I didn't have cigarettes but I was working on it. He says, 'Work fast, friend. See what happens if you fuck with the man?'

—Subtle, isn't he? Told anybody you made parole?

—You don't have to tell Tonio.

His fingers sent a jolt of pain down through my shoulders and back, up into my skull.

—That hurts. Be careful of him, Val.

Yet I know I'm the one who must be careful.

THE day before we went camping we were awakened by a vibration rattling the windows. I leapt out of bed. Parked in front was a flatbed truck with a crane and an aerial pod such as firemen use on burning buildings. Half a dozen men were putting on hardhats, oiling chainsaws.

We had had dealings with the city about our sewage system—a silver maple grew in front of our house and the tree's roots had penetrated the drainage tiles. Sewage backed up into the basement. We had to have the tiles replaced at great cost—the tree was on city property—we lodged a claim. A succession of inspectors and assistant inspectors came, made inspections, filed reports. One of them noticed a small hole in the maple where the trunk branched in two, seven or eight feet above the ground. He borrowed my ladder and inspected the hole. A few mornings later a crew from the department of public works arrived and probed the hole with a measuring device. We both had to leave for work before they finished. When we got home we found a numbered tag nailed to the tree trunk and a business card in our mailbox. I phoned the inspector—the silver maple had been found to have a rotted core. The tree was a danger to pedestrians and parked cars, had to come down. Amid all the upheaval I'd forgotten or put it out of mind. And now here were the men with their chainsaws ...

I pulled on jeans and hurried out. The leader was a wiry, freckled man in a peaked cap. The city had hired his company to take down the tree. Couldn't it be pruned or helped in some other way? After all, it gave every appearance of health. It bore abundantly in spring and had an aura of strength and robustness. I told him we would take responsibility for any damage the tree might inflict. He used our phone to call someone at City Hall. Two wary men arrived in a blue sedan. The one who did the talking had a Scots accent and a clipboard. I pleaded, argued, cajoled—he was adamant. Despite the appearance of soundness, he said, the tree was gravely afflicted—the two main branches could split apart.

Angela tried to explain the importance of the silver maple. She described its beauty through the seasons, the shade it provided, the birds it attracted. She asked him to cross the street and regard the tree with her. Attempting to persuade a man with a clipboard that our tree ought to be preserved for its beauty—how I cherished her at that moment!

He was soothing and patronizing. The city didn't remove trees for no reason and this one had a priority rating. Look for yourself—he waved his clipboard— here's the report. The city could not afford to pay damages caused by decayed trees. She said we'd sign an agreement assuming responsibility. Right, I said, we'll take responsibility. It had never been done—he wasn't empowered to authorize such an agreement.

We had lived on the street seven years but knew only immediate neighbours. People we had glimpsed—getting in cars, sweeping porches, trimming hedges—gathered in front of our house. Gloria, the fat woman whose love letters we had intercepted, stopped and ate rolls as she watched. The widow who walked her poodles morning and night silenced the yapping dogs long enough to ask what was happening. Shook her head as if envious.

—What are we going to do? The tree can't come down.

—Look at them! It's coming down! What do you want me to do? Wave a shotgun at them? You're so bloody unrealistic.

Her eyes shone with water.

—You don't have to yell at me.

—I'm sorry, sweetie, it's not you I'm mad at.

—What are you mad at?

—Would you stop asking me that! Christ! Anything I say, you use it against me.

Angela went inside. The air filled with fumes and the whine of chainsaws. A teenager was hoisted in the aerial pod—he fastened his belt to one top branch and a steel cable to another—wielded the chainsaw expertly, severed branch after branch. The crane lowered each branch to the street, the others cut it into firewood. The silver maple was eighty or ninety years old ... so perfectly proportioned it disguised its tremendous bulk. The operation was as brutal and stunning as an amputation. By the time the men stopped to eat sandwiches the tree had been reduced to its major limbs. By early afternoon it was a squat silhouette against the sky. When the cutters reached the afflicted portion, chainsaws ripped the punky wood as if it were wet bread. The stump was four feet in diameter ... only the outside inch was healthy. The centre was so rotten you could scoop it by hand.

—It looked good from the outside. She wasn't interested in your family, your work. She didn't want your children. What was at the centre?

They climbed in their trucks and drove off. One of the vehicles had leaked oil on the sidewalk. Butts and empty bottles on the lawn—sawdust everywhere—our gloriosa daisies had been trampled. Our house seemed suddenly barren and exposed. The maple had extended in three directions, filling the space with graceful intention ... now it had contracted to a single plane.

—Did you ever relate it to yourself? Why did these things happen? Do you think what happens bears no relation to your internal state?

'Maybe it's rotten, but we'll take responsibility.' We

never did, not until too late. In the morning we set off camping in a mood of despondency. She gazed back at the house, as if setting it in memory. Where once a tree had effected splendid transactions with sunlight and breeze, now we had a grotesque stump and a promise ... one day the stump would be removed, a seedling planted in its place.

NEW dream—flying—no wings, no plane, no nothing—just flying.

I told Val. He laughed: 'Take me for a ride sometime.'

Haven't seen Tonio for two days. I feel his presence.

I remember Dad's last words to me. Wilf had come to the house and he and Dad baited each other over dinner. The three of us played Scrabble. Mom washed dishes and then sat in front of the television. Wilf said good-night ... Mom ran a bath. She and Dad exchanged a look before she went to bed. The night had become chilly—Dad made a fire. The grate was an elaborate, two-tiered contraption of which he seemed inordinately proud. He'd just got it, he said, the finest grate made. The logs were damp, though, and every few minutes he went to poke them. Tuffy had sprawled in front of the fire ... each time Dad knelt down he rubbed the dog's belly, scratched its ear.

—Who's a good dog? You love the fire, don't you ...

Something about the way he spoke to the dog infuriated me. I got the Dickel from my bedroom.

—Here, Dad. This is to help you commit suicide.

—Hot dog! Can't get this stuff out here.

We played chess for ten dollars and Scrabble for a dollar a point. He got so drunk he kept forgetting what he owed me. Finally we cut cards until he had won back what he'd lost. I poured the last of the bottle. While Dad was playing with the dog he said over his shoulder:

—I'm glad you were able to make it out for the weekend.

I'd never heard such a sentiment from him. It took a moment to think of something to say.

—Me too, Dad.

He poked the charred logs ... the fire was beyond reviving. He stroked the dog.

—I'll get more wood. You've got to see this thing when it gets going. It really throws off heat.

—I'm sure it does, but I can see it next time. I've got a plane at nine—it's almost three-thirty.

—The harried businessman.

—What's this businessman shit? Disappointed I didn't grow up to be a union organizer? Is that our problem? You disapprove of what I do? If everybody was a union organizer there wouldn't be anybody to organize.

He was surprised.

—I don't care what you do, believe me.

—Of course, why would you? I'm only your son.

When he was drunk his forehead had a peculiar glaze ... the skin beneath his eyes seemed to loosen. He looked at me levelly:

—If anybody harmed you I'd kill him. Believe me. You are my son.

I drained my glass and got up.

—Jay's your son. I'm your other son. Goodbye, Dad—see you next time I get out.

He got to his feet—toppled—gripped a chair back.

—I'll get up in the morning to say goodbye.

—You don't need to.

—I said I'll get up.

—Suit yourself. Goodnight.

I started downstairs and heard a crash. Dad and the chair were on the floor, his head awkwardly propped against one leg. His drink was all over ... he held the glass aloft as if he hadn't spilled a drop.

Mom called through the bedroom door:

—What's going on out there, you two?

—Nothing, dear.

My father, sixty, angina, a slave to his addictions. Puffed hairdo, tinted glasses, young girlfriend. Unaware of the name of the woman I loved. Rubbing the dog's belly and telling me, at Mom's urging, he's glad I made it out. I felt a tender surge of pity or love ...

—Are you all right?

He was short of breath but didn't seem in pain. Now that he'd changed into a T-shirt, his puffed hair seemed ludicrous. He gazed at me, to make me look away. I would have helped him but he didn't want help.

—You think I'm wasting my life, don't you. Well, I think you're pathetic.

He'd got himself into a sitting position, on the floor, he was smiling, gripping his empty glass, shaking his head ...

—I hope one day you'll understand why I like to get drunk, Owen. And why I've only ever really cared about one thing.

PAIN.

TRIED to sit up. Faint. In and out.

CAN'T breathe. Right eye shut. No feeling in left thumb.

SLEPT last night. Skull and face ache. Sat up and took a little soup . . . suddenly aware of the intravenous.

People on either side. The Indian kid seems to have broken feet or ankles . . . medication keeps him out. The fellow on the other side is emaciated and grey-haired. Nodded when he saw I was functioning.

FELLOW beside me nodded again this morning. I said hello—my face hurt, my voice sounded hollow. Older fellow . . . terrible respiratory problem.

—Is it Tuesday?

—Thursday. Must have been. Quite a scrap. Been out three days. They operated.

I've missed my appointment with Ron.

Jay must have come on Sunday—I wonder what they told him.

Does Val know where I am?

Tonio—the bastard—did I hurt him as badly as he's hurt me?

—Been here long? You?

—Six weeks.

—What's your trouble?

—They don't know yet. Or else not saying.

Said his name was Norman—told me about himself in bursts, drawing breath:

—I left the East at sixteen. Didn't come back for. Thirty-eight years. Ended up in a lumber camp. Worked as a hauler. Good money but I broke my leg twice. Started working as a chef. Cooked for sixty men. That's when I started drinking. Sobered up during the day. Made mountains of food. Then I got into the sauce. I had to get up at four. I know about hangovers.

—After two years I got tired of it. Stole money and went to the Yukon. Bought an interest in a restaurant. I was the cook. Met a gal. Kept me sober two years with her love. We had a little girl. Never married. Had a drink on my birthday. Drank for a year. Cost me everything. Ask me where they are now. Timbuktu.

—Had a buddy. Went on a bender. Found myself in detox. Dried out for a year. Learning to be sober was. Like learning to walk again. Went from picking fruit and pumping gas. To running my own laundromat. Be surprised how quarters add up. Put together down payment on a motel. Work it right you can milk it. Four years I owned it outright. Twenty suits in the closet. Continental Mark IV. Look at me now you'd never believe it. Thing could fly.

—Met a gal and married her. Turned out we had the same secret . . . got into it together. Tried to kill me with scissors. They put her away. Put me in to dry out. Come

back here. Couldn't find much. Welfare. Started again
... take what I could get. I've drunk Elvis Presley
records. Haven't touched a thing in. Eight months and
two weeks. And three days. Story of my life. Can't stay
off the booze.

—What are you here for?

—Uttering.

—A bad cheque?

—Money orders. Six years.

—Six years for forged money orders?

—Sixteenth offence. And you? You the guy who.
Killed his wife?

No nurses, no charts, no medicinal smells. Except
that everyone is ill or injured it isn't like a hospital at
all. The doctor looks like the guy the bus-driver kicks
out at the end of the line. A hack asked when twenty-
two would be on his feet.

—What sort of activity?

—He's going downstairs for ten days.

—In the morning.

Norman's bed is twenty-three. The Indian kid is
twenty-one. A spasm of pain twisted my face, a prayer
rose in my heart. Make it a mistake, don't let me be
twenty-two.

—First trip to the penthouse?

—What's it like?

It made him laugh, horrible, racking noise. He apologized by his tone of voice.

—Don't know what to tell you, son. Never sailed
across the ocean. Never walked on the moon. For me,
isolation. Was like nothing else. Course, I was coming.
Off the booze at the time.

He drew a rasping breath, held it a moment ...

—I didn't come out the. Same fellow I went in.

THE dissociation wing is the basement of the services building—a structure of forbidding simplicity—the original prison. I was signed into custody of dissociation hacks and searched from toes to teeth. Stepping into my issue I felt a pang ... Marnie had a way of smiling when I stepped into my pants. Two hacks accompanied me down a staircase as narrow as something you'd pay admission to enter in England. Iron door. A rapping of keys brought an eye to the peephole—keys worked locks —the door creaked ponderously. We passed through and the station hack passed the other way. (To keep the door between us?) The corridor was a catacomb, so chilly and fetid I wanted to fight for my life. The door impacted its housing with a sound that rang in my marrow. Felt thoroughly drained ... wanted to cry. Tried to keep my shoulders loose, my step light. Scuffle of boots, dripping water, three men breathing, oddly amplified ...

How could my life have come to this?

The corridor ended at a door of shatterproof acrylic:

—Six six two one three nine in the company of Beauchamp and Dawkins.

The door opened with a click and clicked shut behind us. Cells were spaced not to face one another—one door was ajar—I went to it smartly. This, I understood from the hacks' concentration, was the threshold men were reluctant to cross. It seemed I ought to say something ... turning, I felt a billy at the juncture of neck and shoulder. Crumpling, twisting to my knees, I was propelled into the cell—the lock was shot—fireflies whirled.

My anger drained as my circumstances registered. Iron cot embedded in the floor, caged bulb in the ceiling, thin ventilation duct in an upper corner and a slot in the base of the door. Mingled odours of nerves and sweat and human waste. My shoulder throbbed, my neck stiffened, I felt my frightening depletion. The cot (steel frame and pallet) seemed to harden at my touch. I sat. In the floor a hole gurgled. My heart beat wildly and I sought to calm it by timing the interval between gurgles ... reps ... thousand one, thousand two ...

I knew the ruses of time, knew a day could be long and short—interminable in passing and then, past, because it had no substance, thin as a wafer. No matter how many were stacked up they never gained substance. Each day took me further from my life but didn't bring me closer to anything. At keep-lock each night I had a sense of accomplishment ... nothing had been accomplished. Two hundred forty hours, two-twenty, perhaps two hundred ... I thought longingly of Val and tried to imagine where he was and what he was doing. Imagined cellhouse routine, felt it vividly, as a man accustomed to his hat will feel it in place after removing it. Tried to anticipate the tray (no appetite—ate nothing). Reconstructed my cell, one end to the other, each thing in place, then the other way in case I'd missed anything. The bulb became oppressive—I began concentrating my energies to make it burn out. My efforts were unsuccessful but I attributed to them preparatory significance. I inspected the walls inch by inch, studying the marks others had made—with what implement? Amid drawings and obscenities, outrage and defiance and simple historical record—'Rudy King, July 1961'—I found these words painstakingly etched in stone:

> Solitude gives birth to the original in
> us, to beauty unfamiliar and perilous.

From the moment I'd learned I was headed here I'd told myself, meet it head on. Deprivation = new growth, like cutting back a plant. My optimism failed, my resolve felt impossible. The cell seemed suited only to testing the depth of my fear. I lay on the cot between fever and chills, so cold one minute it seemed I'd never get warm, basting the next, sweat chilling me as it dried. So weak—California—Mom and Jay had gone back to the room, Dad was reading on the beach. I swam a few strokes. When I tried to touch bottom my feet were jerked as if a rug had been pulled. Borne by confounding forces—the waves were moving toward shore, yet I wasn't going with them. The force that ought to have been taking me to safety was taking me away ... I could have lost myself, not gone under and then, majestic indifference, been cast ashore, but taken down and not heard from again.

I would be taken down only if I wished to be.

This realization moved me bodily—I hit the floor, on my damaged shoulder. Howled. Suddenly, marvellously, nothing stood between pain and lamentation. I moaned and whimpered. I thought of what lay in the way of richness—the isolation door, acrylic gate, iron door, the services gate, cyclone fence, unauthorized zone, twenty-foot walls of fieldstone surmounted by loops of barbed wire, the towers manned by hacks with binoculars and automatic weapons—and suddenly, marvellously, I understood I had chosen my life.

I had chosen my life.

—View yourself in a new, completely responsible way—see what happens.

I understood that my life had not been forced on me. It had not happened to me. I had chosen it as you choose one thoroughfare or one suit of clothes over another. I struggled to my feet and spread my arms. Pain gave clarity—I understood that if responsibility was mine alone and not partly Angela's and Marnie's, Jay's and Dad's, Mom's, McEleney's, Tonio's, Val's, and Ron's . . . if my life was a wilful act and the world an imaginative response to it, then every word I had ever uttered had been not so much an engraving of the moment as a message to the future from the past—every thought, every action was a declaration of intent. I felt the walls like a blind man . . . the idea was stunning: the power to put them up was the power to take them down. I thought, or said, or perhaps I shouted:

—Ron's been trying to help me see!

A cocoon . . . you'll emerge when you're ready. How the caterpillar must long to emerge, and fly! The air was as charged as crystal. Silence and thunder, a man beaten, dripping water . . . a voice so forceful I didn't recognize it at first as my own. A rat emerged and inspected the cell as if I weren't there—no pitchforks, no rifle butt—just a creature grooming itself and then disappearing. The cot rose under me, a tide, bearing me away, waves of sickness—I knew where I was going— felt her presence before I could see her.

—Oh, sweetie. You're so hot.

—If only it had happened some other way. An accident . . .

—I'm not sure there are accidents. Do you think it was an accident we found one another?

—It didn't seem like it, we didn't even need words.

—When we needed the words, the words weren't there.

—I was always afraid of what might come out ...

—Or the pearls—an accident that they weren't taken along with our things?

—I thought we'd grow old together ... one of those couples who die within a week. But I had to go on alone. Because of you. You're why I'm here! It's your fault!

—When you need me I'll be with you.

—I've needed you all this time!

—No, it was best this way.

—If you hadn't jumped off I'd be free—in the world— not locked in this place! I hate you for that! You're why I'm here! I hate you!

—Now you can be free.

—I hate you for leaving me!

—What if I hadn't ...

—You must have known what would happen—did you? That I'd be blamed? All this pain ...

—There was something wrong.

—I know, but what? I know you as I know my soul ...

—If we'd connected later—after trials and disappointments.

—After I'd found my own ...

—Strength of your own?

—I relied on you, I relied on Jay. I blamed Dad. I blamed McEleney. Now I see—and yet I'm still blaming you.

—Now you're free.

Her head on my shoulder, my arm around her—how long, how many nights or years? It didn't seem something to be measured that way ...

—Now we ...

Her face was alarmed:

—Be ready! They're coming to let you out.

—Wait!

—I can't.

—Meet me in the park!

A key worked the lock—the door squealed on its hinges—two hacks assessed me cautiously.

—Moving day, pal. We'll have your calls forwarded.

—YOU'RE out.

—Wait! I'll see you in the park!

—Can you get to your feet?

—The park! I'll be there!

—Up we get.

I felt uncertain standing. Pain located itself in my cheek, neck, shoulder—I was exhausted but keen as a blade. In the corridor I reeled like a drunk, on the narrow stairs I fell backwards into the arms of hacks. At the gate I was signed over to cellhouse hacks— emerged into morning as one through the mirror—a sense of having glimpsed the heart of things, of eternity beginning in me and extending out in every direction. Someone on yard detail was a genius—the lawns and shrubs were flawless. A trusty stopped raking to mop his forehead with a sleeve—gazed at me, a trim, older man with cropped hair. The tines of his rake gathered light and sent a sunburst. I waved, I called to him.

—Did you do this? Did you? The grounds are marvellous!

He lit a cigarette and watched me go . . . seeing what? A black-eyed man in filthy issue, nose plastered, blinking in wonder, stumbling between hacks as bored as the Italians on the bus we once rode through Calabria . . . on spectacular vistas of lemon trees, cliffs, and glittering sea they pulled the curtains—wilful blindness! When I looked toward administration the lawns flared, a continuous wave that kept pace with me. Pigeons, from perches beneath the overhanging roof, had streaked the stone grey and white—like the green wash on statues, like the rust that bleeds from ocean liners, the streaks testified to history, endurance, the backward weather of time.

This morning pigeon droppings roused me!

Somewhere a gas mower coughed and sputtered to life. A prison van was making its way from the gates to the reception building—poor bastards handcuffed in the dark. The vehicle's rear end rose abruptly as a badger's as it started down the ramp. Just clear of the roof the moon had risen, pale but distinct in the blue dome of sky.

Even if she did know, look what's come of it . . .

In the cellhouse gate two hacks were playing checkers. Another sat smoking a cigarette, legs apart, arms dangling, staring at the floor. Another was asleep on the narrow bench, snoring delicately, hands crossed on his chest. A plug-in fan swung back and forth, rattling in the middle of each pass.

—At least you do it in one go. Twelve years in this joint—four-year stretch, eight hours at a time. Sign in.

I'd entered the cellhouse a thousand times before, yet today it offered up all manner of revelations. The machined geometry of the tier housings—awesome! The ring of boots on steel stairs—piercing! The colour of regulation issue, drab olive I would have said, in fact a complex blue-green. I gazed through steel mesh— down below a dozen men, skins and shirts, were using a ball made of elastic bands to play a cross between handball and dodgeball, a game fitted brilliantly to its circumstances. They cursed, shouted, cheered in excitement—I was moved by the adaptability and perseverance of human beings.

From the tier my absence might have been minutes. The din—deafening! The imprint of human hands at chest level on the bars—wrenching! Vernon, Giles, and the Hound playing poker—a skit! Giles was gazing off, not quite in the realm of events, his eyes blue eggs in a nest of wrinkles. Having seen Giles's cards, the Hound made an exaggerated show of looking away. He held his own hand tight to his chest, facial tic out of control. Vernon tentatively embraced the pot, the winner until proven otherwise.

Someone I'd not seen was in Tonio's cell. Boomerang was gazing in contentment at the ceiling. He called to me—I didn't stop—I wanted to get to my cell ... letters and cards taped to the walls, blue-and-white checked blanket, the undulation worn into the floor one step at a time. A cigarette—smoke moved through me like fog rolling over a golf course—it spun me, dizzied me, as if I'd gulped alcohol. I sank into the cot's embrace. A tinny radio on another tier was playing a golden oldie. There she was, just a-walkin' down the street. I studied my surroundings, each object in turn ... the book, I'd forgotten!—a paperback *Shogun* that Val found in the showers and gave me on my birthday. Dry at last, risen like a loaf of bread.

At that blissful instant he appeared, his shining face more familiar to me than my own. Water shone in his eyes when he saw my bandages. Water came to mine when he told me in the morning he'd be gone. How miraculous it all seemed today! The warmth and compliance of his body, the idea that he'll be out, the news that Tonio has been transferred to special handling—as if I'd willed it all—this marvellous sense of expectancy and attunement.

Two men laughing and dancing in a prison cell. Do-wah diddy diddy dum diddy-do.

—WHAT happened?

—I never realized how much a broken nose hurts.

—What was the fight about?

—They were threatening Val. I'm lucky neither of them had a blade.

—How did you get involved?

—I was passing Val's cell and saw what was going on. He owed cigarettes. I piped up, Billie came at me but I nailed him. He hit the bars, got his hand up and snapped his wrist—bone was sticking out. Tonio hit me in the face but I hit him, a good one.

—Besides pain, what did you feel afterwards?

—I always thought of myself as a coward, afraid of this place—it was exhilarating to realize I could fight.

—Did you have flashes, connections?

—In the infirmary I had a vision of myself back in the world. You know the kind of guy you see in winter sometimes, jeans jacket, dented nose, a muscular guy who doesn't seem to feel the cold? He fishes a cigarette out of his pocket without taking out the pack—a yardbird. I used to be an account executive at a public-relations agency.

—Is there a change on the inside as well? I see something very positive in the change. I'm not urging you to fight anyone you disagree with, but I think it's sometimes valuable to act instead of keeping everything locked in.

—If I'd stopped to think ... but I didn't—that made the difference.

—Perhaps the next thing you'll learn, as you tap into that powerful energy, is how to use it. How did Val react to what happened?

—He's out.

—Was it difficult saying goodbye?

—Sad, but quite wonderful. He's not optimistic, I wish I could help him. It makes me aware my time is coming.

—Your nose and eyes suggest your depth of feeling for him.

—I hope the doctor knew what I'm supposed to look like.

—Are you afraid of looking different?

—When I see myself, the swelling and discolouration

... I look grotesque. If I'm lucky there'll only be a little scar.

—Have you thought of Angela lately?

—Isolation was an amazing experience for me, Ron. I can't really explain, but I connected with her. We fought, we came to an understanding ...

—Your energy seems very different.

—I've not really lost her, you see. The park ...

—Did you deal with that last weekend? Tell me about that.

—We saw Canada geese, we could hear their lonely honk.

—Things between you—were the channels open or blocked?

—Craig had told her he was involved with someone else. She told me Sunday night, in the tent. He'd given her an ultimatum: break off with Owen or I'll break off with you.

—What was your reaction?

—I began to realize how close she felt to Craig. When I understood how deeply she cared for him, my feeling wasn't sympathy and understanding, it was pain and fear. Something traumatic was happening to her that had nothing to do with me.

—I'd like you to lie down, breathe deeply, and recall the way you felt, sights and smells from that weekend.

—Nights were cold. Mornings were chilly and damp. The day warmed up, more like summer than late October. Our time was the routine—the fire, wood, making coffee—and these precarious discussions.

—What exactly did she say about Craig?

—I'd asked her, 'What's going on?' Meaning, 'Have you broken with him yet?' When I asked on Sunday night she said: 'He's given me a choice. He's involved with someone else.' I asked her reply. She said, 'I want us all to make this work—we could if it was what we all wanted.'

—Did you believe her?

—Did I believe she said that to Craig?

—Yes, and did you believe it was what she really wanted?

—I had this knot inside me, I was afraid she was trying to find a gentle way to break it. I'm getting a headache. The pain in my cheekbones is moving into my skull.

—What was your attitude to Craig? Were you still, on one level, trying to ignore him?

—I wanted him out of my life. I've got an awful headache, Ron. I need to sit up.

—Try to stick with this. It's important.

—She was saying, 'I won't leave you,' but I was hearing, 'I won't leave Craig.' We'd promised each other you see . . .

—What did that suggest to you?

—I was locked in myself, I didn't see until that weekend how tortured *she* was.

—What were you feeling that you weren't telling her? Think of your headache now as the things you tucked away that weekend.

—Like seeing Palumbo get knifed, the disbelief. Horror, anger . . .

—What were you doing with this anger?

—Sunday night we didn't sleep. We were cold, exhausted. When the sun came up we had coffee and walked, to rejuvenate ourselves.

—That weekend was to be decisive, one way or the other. What it boiled down to was that she had to choose.

—We were locked in and had to find some way out.

—And you believed she'd choose Craig . . .

—She got more and more distant . . .

—Did you talk as you walked along the bank?

—It was beautiful—the river sliding along, the mist rising, the sound of the falls . . .

—Heading for the falls. Exhausted. Spaced out. Not quite believing what was happening. And all the time, in the pit of your stomach, you have this feeling you're going to lose her.

—She reassured me we'd be together no matter what.

—How did you interpret her phrase—no matter what?

—Once in high-school physics we were learning the structure of the atom. At root, said the teacher, is a simple fact: the electron is attracted to the nucleus. Someone asked why. What is electrostatic attraction? 'Who knows?' said the teacher. 'It's there. A force that defies further description.'

—How long did you walk before you reached the falls?

—An hour, maybe? We threw stones, we found swallows' nests in the cliffs. As we got closer the river picked up speed . . .

—What happened at the brink?

—The river wasn't deep but it had real force. It feels like something's trying to pull you over.

—You felt that force?

—My broken nose! The maître d' in the dream! Who opens the velvet rope! I dreamed it, remember?

—You felt the force trying to pull you over . . .

—She was looking at me and I knew. I reached for her, too late.

—Is that what you wanted to happen, or what you tried to prevent?

—You fucker! I tried to stop her! She looked at me as if she didn't know who I was. I reached for her ... almost went off myself. She was gone, I was still there. My headache ... our time must be over.

—Did you reach for her, Owen, or did you push her?

—I saw what was going to happen but there was nothing I could do, Palumbo getting knifed, slow motion —by the time you react it's over. So that's it—that's what happened—you wanted to know, now you know.

—How did it really happen?

—What did you say, Ron?

—How did it really happen?

—How did it happen?

—Yes, Owen. What really happened at the top of the falls?

—I ... I tried to push her off.

—Did you succeed?

—No ... she had already jumped.

GOT back—heard Vernon crashing around—I was dizzy, exhausted. I wanted to smoke and think, tried to communicate in a glance but a moment after I lay down he stuck his head in. The veins in his temple were lit up.

—Talk to you, Monkey?

—What's happened?

—See the lineup for Sunday?

—I didn't know it was posted.

—I ain't on it. I read it three times. I signed up two weeks ago. I go, 'What's going on here? Got to be a mistake.'

—Did you find out?

—This afternoon I catch up with Turnbull in the yard. He goes, 'What can we do for you today?' I go, 'As if you don't know.' He goes, 'You're not the only talent in the grinder, Vernon. Others have to have a chance.' I go, 'Fine with me, but I want to sing too.' He goes, 'Last three times you done the same songs. People don't like the same all the time.' I go, 'Bullshit, ever listen to the radio?' He goes, 'The radio's not the same as live.' I go, 'I got four I never played before.' He goes, 'What are they?' I go, 'Think I'm lying, sonofabitch?' He goes, 'I don't see why a performer'd be reluctant to tell the co-ordinator his songs.' I go, 'Cherry Cherry, You're So Vain, Love the One You're With, and Peace Train.' He goes, 'Yeah, well, Sunday's booked, Vernon.' I go, 'Never heard that one before.' He goes, 'Two-hour show, right? We got two hours booked solid.' I go, 'How come you said it's 'cause I ain't got new songs?' He goes, 'Well, I was concerned about that, too.' I go, 'Lying sonofabitch, you don't want me 'cause you don't like my singing.' He goes, 'The list's made up. The lineup's posted.' I go, 'Why do you think I come to you?' He goes, 'It's too late for this month.' I go, 'You mean to tell me you couldn't squeeze in a lousy couple of songs?' He goes, 'Solid, Vernon, I swear it.' I go, 'We'll see about this, you sonofabitch!'

—What should I do, Monkey? I want to sing.

I told him he had to find his own way—sounded like a

Kung Fu rerun—but he does. So does Val.

Poor Val—out there somewhere, starting from scratch. I wish he wasn't broke, jobless, pessimistic. Wish there was something I could do.

JAY seemed preoccupied today—when I said so he told me about friends of theirs we met three or four times. Bill had a knack with penny stocks and supplemented his substantial income as a pediatrician. He decided to take the game seriously and borrowed a quarter million dollars—invested in a bull market—before long his stocks were worth upwards of six hundred thousand. Didn't tell Jay, or Jennifer, or anyone else. When he'd made a million he intended to break the good news and retire.

Jay's heartbreaking when he's saddened. He took off his glasses to rub his eyes with the heels of his hands.

—If he'd told me—any of his friends—we would have told him the same thing. Sell to the value of the loan, for Christ's sake, fool around with the rest.

The pendulum began to swing back—prices fell abruptly—Bill began frantically selling this, buying that. Soon his portfolio was worth less than the original quarter million. Interest rates were climbing and his monthly obligation at the bank became, as Jay put it, significant. He confided in his receptionist, they began an affair. A few weeks later he disclosed the affair to Jennifer, implying it was what had been making him distraught. He said he realized what a fool he'd been and asked forgiveness. Jennifer reacted with vehemence, said she wanted a divorce, insisted he move out. At this juncture Sylvia and Jay learned about Bill's affair. Bill began staying at his receptionist's apartment—this brought home what a mistake he'd made. He pleaded with Jennifer, begged her to reconsider, but she had engaged a lawyer and was suing for divorce. Bill told Jay the story—money as well as love—and asked his advice. Jay thought Bill ought to tell Jennifer exactly what had happened. Bill confessed the whole mess—penny stocks and borrowed money—but it further enraged Jennifer. The marriage was shot, she told him, and insisted that they communicate through their lawyers.

—What's Bill doing now?

—He lives in a furnished studio in one of those apartment hotels. The bar is full of expensive hookers and guys with coke spoons on gold chains. He's fighting a custody battle with Jennifer, trying to keep the bank at bay, hoping to move to Arizona and find work in one of those clinics that *60 Minutes* is always exposing. We don't play racketball any more. He's taken it into his head that my advice ruined his marriage. Sylvia thinks Bill's a total jerk. I suppose he is, but what am I supposed to do—renounce him?

I thought of Jay's fidelity to me, to Dad, to his friends and family, and marvelled at his predisposition to goodness. Certain people seem to me links in a moral chain ... I have the good fortune to have one such person for a brother. I realized, talking to him, that I'd always thought of Angela in the same way.

When I gave Jay power of attorney he agreed to say nothing until I asked. After selling the house and paying my taxes and debts he was to manipulate the rest with a view to making it grow and no worries about whether, in the process, it disappeared altogether. Today I told him that, for my hearing, I needed to know. He flushed —embarrassment, I imagined—I'd forgotten Jay does not embarrass easily.

—You told me to pretend it was Monopoly money.

—I'm not going to blame you—it's not important.

—Said you didn't care if you wound up with nothing. I was to do whatever I figured might work out.

—What happened?

A beaming grin.

—The house went for a good price and I've managed the proceeds. In the time you've been here, your net worth has doubled.

—Great help that should be! My hearing's Friday.

—If it goes well, when will you get out?

—End of the month. Everybody seems to be making it—they need the space.

—Perfect. Mom's coming on the twenty-eighth. The guest room's finished and it's yours as long as you want it. Maybe, though, way your portfolio's been going, you ought to think about applying for an extension of sentence.

—And maybe you don't want me out because I'll discover you've been fiddling my money.

He adjusted his glasses.

—Do I look stupid enough to pull something on a crazed murderer?

No one else in the world could have said that. We

laughed today, my brother and I, we laughed! Laughed so hard others couldn't help joining in—laughed as we laughed on the bucket seats, Jay steering with his foot, passing a quart of chocolate milk back and forth and firing papers as the Healey gathered speed and our lives seemed the endless unfolding of possibility . . .

He took a chamois from his pocket, carefully unfolded it . . .

Tears of the moon.

—What do you want me to do with these?

I thought it was the acrylic, the distortion, the way I was looking at them—asked Jay to move them closer—it made no difference. I remembered them as breathtaking. They were just a string of pearls—had I really paid so dearly for them?

—Still want me to be Jonathan's godfather? Sure it's all right with Sylvia?

—Damn right.

—Then here's what I want you to do. Those are worth something like thirty-six thousand . . .

—No, they're not—I had them appraised.

—Oh, no. I got taken?

—Not at all. They're worth about fifty.

He remembered where he was—looked around the visiting room, refolded the chamois, slipped the pearls in his pocket. Spoke softly into the receiver:

—Guys in here who'd kill for fifty dollars . . .

—Here's what I want you to do. Besides you and Mom and Angela, I also borrowed from the Berrys—I need to repay them. Five thousand. Maybe you could do that . . .

—I've already paid back Mom and myself. Angela's parents—maybe that's something you should do.

—You're right, I'll wait till I'm out. Then write them, make sure they're willing to see me . . .

—So I sell the pearls for what they'll bring . . .

—And divide the money in two. Half goes into a trust fund for your—for *my* godson.

—O, are you sure?

—It's my money, isn't it?

—Fair enough, but that's also something you could do when you get out. What about the other half?

—I want you to take care of a friend of mine.

—You could do that as well.

—I would, but he needs help right away. I'll give you his address. I'd like you to work something out so that he's looked after. Something each month, done in a way that he doesn't know who it's from.

THE first time I saw Billie Holiday he raised one hand, palm out, like an Indian chief—he kept it there as he approached. His right arm was encased in plaster in a sling. Men in the chow line nudged one another hopefully. Billie spoke loudly enough for everyone to hear—the hacks stopped doing head count.

—I don't bear no grudge. I got nothing against you for the scuffle, Monkey. Nothing against Val for them smokes. They were Tonio's smokes and he ain't a factor no more. Val ain't a factor no more. You got nothing to fear from me. Billie Holiday behind you.

In the pit this morning I found him drumming the light bag one-handed. There were a dozen regulars and a freckle-faced man I'd not seen before, sturdy and squat as a pressure cooker. He had the good bar. When he set it down I asked if he was through. He went red and cursed me—I could have it when he was finished and not before and if I wanted—

Billie slipped between us.

—'Scuse me, friend, been here long? Ever hear what happened to a friend of mine? Yapped at somebody one day, didn't think nothing of it. Few days later he's minding his own business, eating a Mars bar. In and out, quick as that ... think the sucker knew what hit him?

At yard this afternoon the Hound called me over. He dismissed one of his runners with a backhand motion.

—Lovely afternoon, Monkey. I find myself in a position to help a few people who like to relax. Maybe you like to relax.

He extended a closed fist—a Baggie with a quarter ounce.

—Thai ... top of the line. Compliments of the house.

I studied the Hound's face. His rash was all over his forehead ... his tic jerked him like a slap. I looked to the men walking round and round, the wall looming behind them, the pale moon ... felt part of some larger alignment, an incandescent being in a world of incandescence. I am locating in myself a strength I don't understand—the others have begun to give substance to it. I must be sure of my purpose, impeccable in my relations ...

After supper Vernon was back.

—I go, 'You got no right excluding me cause you don't like my singing. Show's open to any inmate wishing to showcase his performing talent, says on the poster.' He goes, 'It's not that, Vernon. Others have to have a turn. You been on before and you'll be on again.' I go, 'I've got another new one—five new songs. Joy to the World, a classic.' he goes, 'Next month. This Sunday's out.' I go, 'Says you, you sonofabitch.' He goes, 'Vernon, everybody knows his spot. We already had rehearsal.' I go, 'We'll see about this, you sonofabitch.' But I don't know what to do next. What do I do, Monkey?

Before lockup Billie Holiday stopped by my cell. His cast has begun to give off an odour of deterioration. Without Tonio he's like a child. He spoke softly, intimately.

—Found out the sucker in the weight pit . . . doing six and he ain't no debutante. B-Range, name of Morrison. Friend of mine tells me—

—Why you telling me, Billie? Everybody telling me, asking me, giving me—why?

He jerked this way and that, looked at everything but my face. Cleaned crusted matter from the corner of his eye.

—Shit, Monkey! What you 'speck? You the man now or ain't you?

OF ALL the grim duties associated with her death, the most daunting was the need to go through her things. I took her keys and drove to her office—front room, second floor of a converted mansion. I had trouble with the main doors. Fumbled at her waiting room, again at the locked door to her office. It was Sunday—the dwelling had an air of great tranquillity—my heart wouldn't stop racing. I busied myself. I watered her plants, read the titles of her books, swept the hearth, studied the prints on the walls. I made tea and lit the candle she liked to burn. I sat in each chair in turn, imagining myself as Angela or as one or another of the clients she had described to me. The room was exquisite in its simplicity but I couldn't absorb its ambience.

She did her phoning and correspondence at a cherry-wood secretary that had been her grandmother's. The upright portion was divided into rows of pigeon-holes. I started at the upper left cubicle—she didn't store things alphabetically, or chronologically, or in any apparent ranking of importance. She used a system I couldn't figure out although it had been perfectly obvious to her. There were recipes, barrettes, candle stubs, a pendulum. Letters from Craig, tea bags, a gold chain, salvaged stamps. A chestnut, cartoons from the *New Yorker*, scribbled phone numbers, tabs of plant fertilizer. In the pigeon-hole with cassette tapes was a war medal, the blue material faded almost to white. A stone arrowhead her father must have found in the garden. A photo in an oval frame of Mr Berry as a child. He had cupid wings and a tiny bow and arrow—his legs were plump sausages—his smile was Angela's when secretly pleased. I tried to picture Dad in that costume.

Among matchbooks, keys, and cancelled cheques I found a mimeographed sheet listing Bach flower remedies and their indications. At the top she had written, 'Owen, doused June 26, eight drops four times a day.' And highlighted with yellow felt pen:

Hornbeam—integration, clearing old patterns
Honeysuckle—regrets of the past, letting go
Willow—resentment, surfacing of the dweller
Vine—inflexibility, extreme self-control
Beech—intolerance, rigidity, criticism
Rock water—self-repression, self-nurturance

In a pigeon-hole containing ribbons, business cards and a glass angel meant for a Christmas bough I discovered a clipping from the newspaper: 'U.S. Scientists Listen In On Talking Trees.' The article described experiments to discover how trees survive mass attacks by tent caterpillars and fall webworms. Ecologists had placed swarms of insects in the branches of willows and alders to see what defence mechanisms the trees might use. The trees began producing alkaloids and terpenoids —made their leaves unpalatable to the insects. The leaves began to form certain proteins in a way that made them indigestible. The insects lost vitality and became unable to resist the night cold or bacteria they would normally have warded off with ease. Nearby trees of the same species that had not been invaded began to mount the same chemical defences. The trees were too far apart for root contact—the scientists concluded that an undetected airborne chemical released by the afflicted trees warned nearby trees of the imminent invasion. On the clipping Angela had written, 'Like Debbie.'

Debbie was a teenager she had seen some years earlier. A fat, friendless girl whose sisters were mean to her and who ensured her own unhappiness by eating chocolates and failing at school. With Angela's help she began to blossom. Her sisters, robbed of the power to hurt her, treated her kindly. At the end of the year she brought her report card to Angela. The teacher had never seen such improvement over a single term. I remember how pleased Angela had been—I remember thinking how little I understood of what had happened between them ...

I folded the clipping, put it back in place—I could not go through her things. It seemed an indecency and I could only be disturbed by what I found. I had thought of her as a woman to whom things sounded right or they didn't, who relied on pitch. Someone who could not resist salesmen or grasp the bogus economies of money-saving coupons. I thought of her as a wonderful, unpremediated cook and a person who, no matter how tired or busy, conveyed warmth. Who enjoyed washing dishes, chopping vegetables, weeding the garden—any task begun and finished on the spot. Only when she told me about clients, or when Dad slighted her, or when others asked about her did my conception expand to include this part of her life.

On our twenty-first birthday I'd given her a lovely, iridescent chunk of rose quartz. It sat on the mantel above the fireplace. I'd forgotten all about it. I lifted it to feel its weight—felt a flaw on the underside—turned it over. The flaw was the inscription I had etched one painstaking letter at a time:

> I know you as I know my soul
> I love you with an ancient heart
> I pledge to share this life with you
> I vow nothing will make us part ...

Never before had I been alone in her office. I'd helped hang pictures and construct bookshelves, brought teas and flowers, dropped her off and picked her up without ever absorbing the significance of the place. She had spent six or eight hours a day in this room seeking revelation of the most delicate and intangible sort. She had shared with Craig a telephone-answering service, a waiting-room, and a commitment to an undertaking which I resented and viewed, for all my intended encouragement, as Dad would have viewed a rain dance. I had never imaginatively entered into her life. Two days after her interment I sat at her cherrywood secretary and looked out at the honey locust and felt how ignorant I'd been of the springs that had nourished her. I wondered how, after living with her for twelve years, I could have known so little about her—as I'd wondered, when we met, how I could have seemed to know her so well.

I'M NOT sure how or where—I was flying—soaring—above a coastline of complicated inlets and peninsulas. The perspective might have been gained from a light aircraft ... I wasn't in a light aircraft or anything of substance. Perhaps this is the element I found disquieting. I had no bodily presence. My perspective, my flight, the composition of my life seemed to have become at that moment an adventure of the mind ...

I remained at constant height—went lower to see if I could. I directed my flight but I'm not sure how. Far

below me the heavy woods were separated from the
water by broad sand beaches. I spotted deer and bears.
Moved closer, expecting them to run, as they do in
footage shot from aircraft, but they seemed unaware of
me.

The experience was exhilarating and yet I felt an
underlying apprehensiveness. When, in the morning, I
remembered that today was the hearing, the apprehensiveness gave way to a growing confidence. At breakfast
I ate heartily. The walk to administration had a stirring
sense of finale. The air was clear and still and beginning
to warm. I signed in with a feeling almost of poignancy.
Waiting my turn with a dozen others I felt none of the
nervousness I thought I would. I'd be freed—I'd chosen
freedom.

I was ushered into a windowless room ... sat at a
table before a three-man committee. Only the man in
the middle asked questions. His inquiries seemed cur-
sory and pragmatic. If I were put on one of the condi-
tional release programs where would I go, who would I
associate with, how would I earn an income? What had I
done to prepare myself for release? Did I consider myself
responsible for my behaviour? Capable of resuming a
productive life on the streets? If left to me, which of the
programs would I put myself on—temporary absences,
day parole, or full parole? The hearing lasted ten
minutes. The chairman asked me to step out while they
deliberated.

Too quick—my heart fell—they'd already decided.

I sat on an uncomfortable bench, reminded of truancy
and toothache and meetings with potential clients. How
many times had I been made to wait for strangers with
the capacity to affect my welfare? I felt the tenderness
around my nose and eyes—was this to be my downfall?

My instinct to help Val? I begin to see something of the grandeur and mysteriousness, and it will cost my freedom?

A hack ushered me back in. The chairman, a tidy little man with pale eyes, looked up and then nervously down—bad news. To be turned down now, after what I'd been through—I tried to prepare myself. Giles, Vernon, Boomerang, the Hound. Another year on C-Range ...

—A couple of things cause us concern. This violent incident, the fight last month—were you high on something?

I was aware of the swelling and discolouration of my face.

—No, I wasn't. A friend was being threatened.

—I wish we could be sure the same thing's not going to happen when somebody in a discotheque looks at you the wrong way.

A discotheque! How remarkable to imagine myself in a discotheque. A supermarket, a museum, a travel agency. An automobile, a bakery, an amusement park. In the presence of Jonathan or the arms of a woman. The chairman's throat-clearing suggested a need to reply.

—I intend to avoid situations that might jeopardize the terms of my release. Should you see fit to release me.

—Wasn't your common-law wife killed by the same kind of violent outburst?

—That was a long time ago.

—What about this incident in the visiting room?

—Incident? I don't ...

—Verbal abuse—profanity—physical abuse—throwing the speaker phone ...

It seemed the cruellest irony—I could have wept. My feeling for Jay, his for me ... Was I to be denied because of what had passed between us? Another year of visits, letters, snapshots of Jonathan ...

—I got upset—it cleared the air. I hope you're not going to turn me down over that. Jay and I are ... he's been extremely supportive. If I am paroled I'll live with his family ...

The chairman closed his file folder.

—Mr Wesley, you don't fall into the same categories as most applicants. You seem not to have suffered the same deprivations that are the start of many criminal lives. You have advantages of education, family cohesiveness, and financial security most residents can only envy.

—My father used to impress that on us when we were children. I never felt the truth of it until I came here.

—When you resume your old life, this may work against you. Put additional pressure on you.

—I don't intend to resume my old life as such.

—Being on the street—whatever life you lead—may be more difficult for you than some people.

—I've thought about that. Talked about it with Dr Yoshino and I'm sure we'll talk again. I hope it won't affect your decision.

—It's a word of caution, that's all. The committee has reservations, but on the basis of disciplinary reports, previous record, and the recommendations of Dr Yoshino and your classification officer, we're prepared to offer full parole, end of this month—provided you're prepared to agree to the provisions. Are you familiar with them?

—I happily agree to them.

—I hope to God we never see you back here.
—Thank you. I don't imagine you will.
The chairman opened a file folder, spoke to the hack:
—Littlefoot. Howard.

ONCE, as a child, I saw a river full of spawning salmon. The water was cold and swift-coursing—the salmon had to battle mightily. They were battered and worn but steadfast. The current was so strong that I held onto Jay when I dipped the toe of my rubber boot. The river was no more than two feet deep—it felt as though it might take me with it.

It would take me only if I wanted to go . . .

Jay and I made our way along the river bank until we came to a clearing where the water widened and lost its urgency. Rocky pools bordered the river . . . in one pool a salmon was trapped. It swam in a lethargic circle. Every so often it charged the sand-bar that stood in the way of open water. Its flesh was rotting and its luminous colour had paled almost to white. Again and again it beached itself and managed, spasmodically flapping, to get back to the pool. Jay and I decided to help. We waited until it mired itself and then picked it up. I imagined the fish would struggle but it seemed to sense our intention. We carried it gingerly ... part of its flesh came off in my hand. Dad had described to us what had happened in Hiroshima and Nagasaki—I screamed and let go—Jay tried to take the weight—the fish came apart in his hands. It landed in the river and, to our astonishment, continued on its way. It no longer had even the appearance of a salmon. A vehicle of pure will ... the embodiment of an imperative mystery for which there are no words.

Before sleep I told myself my dreaming was to have an object, and the object was to be reunited with Angela. I dreamed I was flying. I was *seeing* as if flying, moving rapidly over terrain I didn't specifically recognize but that seemed familiar. The mountains were snow-capped and majestic, the woods dense and foggy, the rivers fast and musical ...

Deep in the forest I noticed someone. I moved closer—a man, huddled in sleep. I was no longer flying, I was jumping from tree to tree, wanting to get closer without alerting him. Fitful movements, unintelligible noises—he was dreaming. I realized with a shock whom I'd stumbled on. Steathily, from behind a tree, I was watching myself dream. I'd set out to find Angela ... instead I'd found myself.

On the forest floor I stirred, about to wake. Here I understood I was in a dream and the dream was nearly over. At first I expected to wake in the forest, then I knew I was about to wake in my cell and had to return quickly. Toilets flushing—the roar didn't frighten me—the cellhouse resuming its routine. I opened my eyes. I lay on my cot, adjusting to the light—a vivid awareness came on me. I had had a choice. If I'd acted at the proper moment, if I'd known how, I could have awakened not in this cell but from the dream I saw myself having in the forest. This caused me confusion and distress. The same mind had directed both dreams and deliberately chosen to return to C-Range. How could I be sure this too was not a dream? I recalled my hearing—I'm out, I'm out! My confusion became profound. I didn't seem to be out at all. I felt the cot beneath me, the chill of the floor on my bare feet. I pulled on my issue—it had undeniable substance. The zoo smell of the tier seemed real, the sound of hawking and spitting. I was not quite awake—once I'd had chow my head would clear. For the moment, though, I felt a desperate need to reassure myself of my surroundings. I handled the objects in my cell. The solidity was comforting. I knelt, made a fist, pounded the floor hard enough to sting my wrist. Then I began to feel the wall between my cell and Vernon's. 'Solitude gives birth . . .' While I was remembering my stay in dissociation, the cell was sprung.

The trusty had five letters—Mom, Mr Berry, Val, Miriam, Rudy Briggs—the first time, in four years, I've ever got more than one.

THIS afternoon a hack fetched me from the library, a hard-eyed man whose breathing was audible. Told me I had a phone call. I thought of Mom—Wilf's death—

worried something had happened. The hack was unhelpful. He escorted me to the cellhouse gate. His ankle was sore, he didn't want to walk to administration. As a favour he let me use the gatehouse phone.

—It's the Jap. Here's the number. Dial nine first. Get cute, you're Peking Duck—I'll cook your ass six ways.

Ron himself answered, and so I had my last session by phone.

—I've got poison ivy. It's spreading all over the place. I can't stop scratching. I'm unable to keep our appointment.

—I made it.

—I'm delighted, Owen. I'm sorry I won't get a chance to see you before you go.

—Thank you for the recommendation.

—I was asked my opinion of your fitness, that's all. I don't know that they'd give my answer much weight.

We talked about what it would be like—he assured me he'd be happy to hear from me any time. He sounded irritated . . . I asked if his poison ivy was bothering him.

—I can't concentrate, can't read. I've just had an awful argument with my wife. I itch!

—Must be very uncomfortable?

—Not really . . .

—Is it the poison ivy that's bothering you, or your enforced idleness?

—Good question. I am something of a workaholic—when I'm not working I question whether my work has any value.

—I wonder if you're a bit burned out.

—Burnout. Domestic warfare. The whole catastrophe. Are you in touch with Val?

—I got a letter from him. He asked if I'd mind if he came for a visit.

—What did you say?

—That I'd rather see him the day I get out. There's a park in the city I can't wait to see again—I suggested we meet there. I got my bandages off, I tell you? I look different. My nose is broader, you can see it's been broken—but my breathing isn't impaired.

—I'd better go. Kim has just come in. I'm not in the best frame of mind to be talking.

—Ron, your doubts about what you do—how can I reassure you?—what would I have done without you?

A long silence, then a tone of voice I'd never heard from him, doubt and despondency:

—It's not me, Owen. Good luck.

TOMORROW ...

The others have taken to ignoring me. For them I have ceased to exist ... I share something of the sentiment. As if my double sits in on poker games, goes to chow, takes my place on work detail. As if I'd already been released and in the morning will be reunited with my double. My confidence is vigorous and interrupted only by jolts of wonder. I wonder if the world has changed in ways that will put me at odds with my own dated memories ... if I've adapted so thoroughly and subtly that the change in pressure will bring not only euphoria but pain, a diver with the bends. Ron has surely seen enough of us to judge ...

When I think of these years and imagine what lies ahead I'm reminded of something from a novel I found in the library: 'Fear was the medium through which he perceived his own soul, the formula through which he could confirm his own existence. I am afraid, he reasoned, therefore I am.' That line seemed to grow right out of me, but it connects to another phrase I came across recently—'an expensive way to begin living.'

Tonight I'll dream of tomorrow ...

The doors that have locked behind me will be opened before me. As I'm escorted down C corridor and out the cellhouse for the last time the others will find ways to occupy themselves. One or two will call lightly after me, as I called after Val, but it will not be a light moment. I'll cross the yard to administration ... change clothes before processing. I'll say a word of farewell and leave through the main gates.

It's five miles to the station—I'll walk briskly, without looking back. Jay said they'd pick me up ... I told him no, I'll make my own way. Said I wanted to spend some time in the park—'Maybe you and Mom and Jonathan could meet me there.' Told him where I'll be. There's a train that will have me in the city in good time. At the station I may linger—order a milkshake and a sandwich. Put a coin in the box and read the newspaper. Watch people come and go. Catch the subway and ride beneath the city. At my stop I'll climb the stairs and set off into sunshine.

Some things have changed but much is abiding. Traffic circles the park in waves, pulling away from one light and stopping at the next. The tulips, daffodils, the narcissus are over but salvia, petunias, and roses are in bloom. A cat is hiding in the flowers. Oak leaves glow with their own burnished light ... the chestnuts are starting to send out prickly spines. A lady with a plastic bag stands near the fountain, throwing crusts in the air. Pigeons are everywhere, the males puffed up and strutting, doing pirouettes and quicksteps, the timeless dance ...

Beyond them rises the music of the fountain.

All sorts of people pass through—joggers, derelicts, the elderly fellow who walks dogs for a living. Women with shopping bags, students hurrying to class, businessmen to meetings. A cop clatters past on horseback —sparrows descend on the muffins. Infirm people propped by canes ... lovers in one another's arms. I'll notice each of the faces, entranced.

I'll know you to see you, and this is how you'll know me. I'll be watching with an air of wonderment, faith, and self-possession. I'll be a man with a dented nose who wanders into the park and sits on a bench. A strong man, in new clothes, out for a walk on a summer's morning.